Applause for L.L. Raand's Midnight Hunters Series

The Midnight Hunt
RWA 2012 VCRW Laurel Wreath winner *Blood Hunt*
Night Hunt
The Lone Hunt

"Raand has built a complex world inhabited by werewolves, vampires, and other paranormal beings…Raand has given her readers a complex plot filled with wonderful characters as well as insight into the hierarchy of Sylvan's pack and vampire clans. There are many plot twists and turns, as well as erotic sex scenes in this riveting novel that keep the pages flying until its satisfying conclusion."—*Just About Write*

"Once again, I am amazed at the storytelling ability of L.L. Raand aka Radclyffe. In *Blood Hunt*, she mixes high levels of sheer eroticism that will leave you squirming in your seat with an impeccable multi-character storyline all streaming together to form one great read." —*Queer Magazine Online*

"*The Midnight Hunt* has a gripping story to tell, and while there are also some truly erotic sex scenes, the story always takes precedence. This is a great read which is not easily put down nor easily forgotten."—*Just About Write*

"Are you sick of the same old hetero vampire/werewolf story plastered in every bookstore and at every movie theater? Well, I've got the cure to your werewolf fever. *The Midnight Hunt* is first in, what I hope is, a long-running series of fantasy erotica for L.L. Raand (aka Radclyffe)."—*Queer Magazine Online*

"Any reader familiar with Radclyffe's writing will recognize the author's style within *The Midnight Hunt*, yet at the same time it is most definitely a new direction. The author delivers an excellent story here, one that is engrossing from the very beginning. Raand has pieced together an intricate w details for the reader to become e action moves quickly throughout down."—*Three Dollar Bill Reviews*

Acclaim for Radclyffe's Fiction

2013 RWA/New England Bean Pot award winner for contemporary romance *Crossroads* "will draw the reader in and make her heart ache, willing the two main characters to find love and a life together. It's a story that lingers long after coming to 'the end.'"—*Lambda Literary*

In **2012 RWA/FTHRW Lories and RWA HODRW Aspen Gold award winner** *Firestorm* "Radclyffe brings another hot lesbian romance for her readers."—*The Lesbrary*

Foreword Review Book of the Year finalist and IPPY silver medalist *Trauma Alert* "is hard to put down and it will sizzle in the reader's hands. The characters are hot, the sex scenes explicit and explosive, and the book is moved along by an interesting plot with well drawn secondary characters. The real star of this show is the attraction between the two characters, both of whom resist and then fall head over heels."—*Lambda Literary Reviews*

Lambda Literary Award Finalist *Best Lesbian Romance 2010* features "stories [that] are diverse in tone, style, and subject, making for more variety than in many, similar anthologies…well written, each containing a satisfying, surprising twist. Best Lesbian Romance series editor Radclyffe has assembled a respectable crop of 17 authors for this year's offering."—*Curve Magazine*

2010 Prism award winner and ForeWord Review Book of the Year Award finalist *Secrets in the Stone* is "so powerfully [written] that the worlds of these three women shimmer between reality and dreams…A strong, must read novel that will linger in the minds of readers long after the last page is turned."—*Just About Write*

In **Benjamin Franklin Award finalist** *Desire by Starlight* "Radclyffe writes romance with such heart and her down-to-earth characters not only come to life but leap off the page until you feel like you know them. What Jenna and Gard feel for each other is not only a spark but an inferno and, as a reader, you will be washed away in this tumultuous romance until you can do nothing but succumb to it."—*Queer Magazine Online*

Lambda Literary Award winner *Stolen Moments* "is a collection of steamy stories about women who just couldn't wait. It's sex when desire overrides reason, and it's incredibly hot!"—*On Our Backs*

Lambda Literary Award winner *Distant Shores, Silent Thunder* "weaves an intricate tapestry about passion and commitment between lovers. The story explores the fragile nature of trust and the sanctuary provided by loving relationships."—*Sapphic Reader*

Lambda Literary Award Finalist *Justice Served* delivers a "crisply written, fast-paced story with twists and turns and keeps us guessing until the final explosive ending." —*Independent Gay Writer*

Lambda Literary Award finalist *Turn Back Time* "is filled with wonderful love scenes, which are both tender and hot." —*MegaScene*

By Radclyﬀe

Romances

Innocent Hearts	Turn Back Time
Promising Hearts	When Dreams Tremble
Love's Melody Lost	The Lonely Hearts Club
Love's Tender Warriors	Night Call
Tomorrow's Promise	Secrets in the Stone
Love's Masquerade	Desire by Starlight
shadowland	Crossroads
Passion's Bright Fury	Homestead
Fated Love	Against Doctor's Orders

Honor Series

Above All, Honor
Honor Bound
Love & Honor
Honor Guards
Honor Reclaimed
Honor Under Siege
Word of Honor
Code of Honor

Justice Series

A Matter of Trust (prequel)
Shield of Justice
In Pursuit of Justice
Justice in the Shadows
Justice Served
Justice for All

The Provincetown Tales

Safe Harbor	Winds of Fortune
Beyond the Breakwater	Returning Tides
Distant Shores, Silent Thunder	Sheltering Dunes
Storms of Change	

Visit us at www.boldstrokesbooks.com

AGAINST DOCTOR'S ORDERS

by

RADCLY*f*FE

2014

AGAINST DOCTOR'S ORDERS
© 2014 BY RADCLYFFE. ALL RIGHTS RESERVED.

ISBN 13: 978-1-62639-211-3

THIS TRADE PAPERBACK ORIGINAL IS PUBLISHED BY
BOLD STROKES BOOKS, INC.
P.O. BOX 249
VALLEY FALLS, NY 12185

FIRST EDITION: NOVEMBER 2014

CREDITS
EDITORS: RUTH STERNGLANTZ AND STACIA SEAMAN
PRODUCTION DESIGN: STACIA SEAMAN
COVER DESIGN BY SHERI (GRAPHICARTIST2020@HOTMAIL.COM)

Acknowledgments

Not far from here is the Mary McClellan Hospital, a rural community hospital that sits high on a hill above the small town of Cambridge, New York. The hospital was financed entirely by a single individual, as was not unusual several centuries ago, and opened in 1919. It closed in 2003 and stands empty now, a silent testament to a bygone era. I found some pictures on the Internet that show the interior as it is now, with much of the equipment still in the rooms—old hospital beds, bent IV stands, monitors with blank faces. The halls seem eerily empty, beyond deserted, abandoned and forgotten.

For eight years of my life I was a surgery resident, and for most of that time, I spent every third night on call in the hospital. I walked the dark halls, listened to the murmurs of patients and staff, and wondered what the world was like beyond the glass where I could see the shimmering lights of the city. I can remember sitting with my fellow residents in the surgical lounge as morning approached, having spent a sleepless night taking care of in-house patients, responding to emergency calls, and finishing up the work of the day that never seemed to end, silently congratulating one another at having survived another day. Much has changed in medicine in the last decades, much for the better, but I think losing our community hospitals is not one of the benefits of progress. Now we must drive far from home to places with which we are not familiar, to be taken care of by strangers, often in surroundings where we become lost among the many.

This book did not start out as a commemorative to those lost hospitals, or lost moments in time, but as I wrote it, I felt the loss and wondered if we have not done a disservice by depersonalizing what must, after all, be one of the most human and humane experiences. This is not a book about hospitals or medicine, but a love story like all my novels are, which takes place in a singular community with the hospital near its heart. In the end, the heart of a romance novel always resides within the characters. I hope you enjoy these.

Thanks go to senior editor Sandy Lowe, who daily makes my job easier and gives me more time to write; to editor Ruth Sternglantz for understanding my work and where I'm going, sometimes before I do; to Stacia Seaman for careful reading and essential corrections; and to my first readers Connie, Eva, and Paula for constant encouragement.

Sheri found just the images I wanted for this book, and came up with a memorable cover—like always.

And thanks to Lee, who wanted to sneak up to the hospital at night with a flashlight for a glimpse of the past. *Amo te.*

For Lee, for always saying "why not?"

CHAPTER ONE

Harper Rivers ran along the shoulder of the narrow, twisting country road, the rising sun at her back and the broad Hudson lazily flowing to her left across a half mile of freshly plowed floodplain. The brisk early summer breeze cooled the sweat on the back of her neck, and the aroma of tilled earth burgeoning with life teased her senses. Her skin tingled with the pulse of blood through her veins, and the crisp air filling her lungs chased away the lingering exhaustion from a sleepless night. The rhythmic *thump-thump-thump* of her Sauconys on the cracked blacktop kept pace with her pounding heart, and her mind slowly emptied of everything except the inevitable joy that came with the resurgence of spring. She slowed as a pickup overtook her from behind and waved as the driver blew his horn before she turned down a crushed-gravel drive, wide enough for two good-sized tractors to pass, bordered on either side by apple and pear trees, their leaves a vibrant green and the first blush of blossoms glistening on the tangled boughs. A half mile ahead, a stately white country house reminiscent of a Southern plantation home with a pillared two-story front porch sat on a hill above the river. Smoke curled from one of the four stone chimneys, carrying the sweet, yeasty scent of baking bread from the kitchen hearth. She angled away from the flagstone walk leading to the formal front entrance, followed the winding rough stone path around the side of the portico to the rear of the house, and bounded up the broad wooden steps to the wide-planked rear porch. Just as she reached the screen door, a voice from inside greeted her.

"Don't come in here with those muddy shoes, Harper Lee Rivers."

"Yes, Mama," Harper said as she always did in response to the familiar order. She toed off her running shoes, left them by the door, and walked in her socks into her mother's domain. The kitchen, the informal meeting room for the entire family and most visitors, stretched almost the entire length of the rear of the home, dominated by a fifteen-foot-long timber table that had been carved from the hickory trees that once dominated the hilly profiles of upland New York farms. The rough-hewn wood had been worn down by decades of pots and dishes sliding across its surface and the vigorous polishing of generations of Rivers wives and children. The appliances had been updated, but everything else about the kitchen was as it had once been when the home was built 250 years before. The counters were of the same dark red-brown hickory as the table, the long thin grain interrupted here and there by darker knots and whorls. Hand-cut beams bearing the square scars of the axman's blade supported the white board ceiling, and gray-green flagstone formed the entrance floor adjacent to the oak floorboards. An open hearth, four feet square and just as deep, held an early morning fire to chase away the chill.

Her mother pulled a pan of biscuits from the double-stacked oven and slid it with practiced efficiency onto a stone trivet on the wood counter. Harper made a fast grab for one and just as quickly snatched her hand back when her mother swatted at her with a wooden spoon.

"You know they're best when they've cooled a little. Sit and drink your coffee."

Harper pulled out a straight-backed wood chair with a leather seat shaped to comfort by decades of occupants, plopped down at the table in her usual place, and stretched her legs toward the hearth.

"You're up early," her mother said, sliding a mug of coffee in front of her. She regarded Harper with the direct gaze guaranteed to make Harper squirm when she was keeping something secret, although she hadn't had secrets in a long time. At least none that her mother needed to know about. She tried hard not to fidget and searched her memory for a forgotten birthday or a missed family gathering. Ida Rivers was big on meeting family obligations.

"Or," her mother went on, "have you not been to bed at all?"

Relaxing now that she realized she hadn't committed a family sin, Harper sipped the strong black coffee and gave a sigh of contentment. The run and the familiar scents and sights of her mother's kitchen drained away the lingering twists of tension from the last few hours. "Mary Campbell decided to deliver a little early. Her labor took most of the night."

"First times can be like that. Everybody doing all right?" Her mother sounded interested despite having undoubtedly heard the same story in countless ways from Harper's father over the last thirty years. Maybe truly caring helped make up for all the times Harper's father hadn't been around when her mother would have liked him to be.

"Everybody's fine, including Tim. I thought for a while I'd have to get him a bed next to Mary's."

Ida laughed. "First-time fathers. Worse than the mothers by a long shot."

"You got that right." Harper grinned, leaned over, and snagged a biscuit without getting swatted this time. "I saw that Dad's SUV is gone. I thought he wasn't going to take night calls anymore."

Ida huffed. "Yes, and we won't be planting the lower forty again either."

Harper nodded as she buttered the flakey biscuit. Neither was likely to happen in her lifetime. Her father was an old-time country physician, just like she was, and if the call came, it went against the grain to tell the patient to go to the emergency room. Not when all it meant was getting out of bed, pulling on a pair of jeans and a flannel shirt, kicking into boots, and driving through the quiet country night with the company of the deer and possum and raccoons who appeared in the headlights, stared for a moment as if questioning why you were intruding on their domain, and bounded off into the underbrush with a dismissive swish of a tail. Those moments were among the most peaceful she'd ever known. Why would she pass those up while denying her patients the care of a doctor who knew them, and whom they trusted, at the same time?

"I told him I'd take his calls. I know all his patients."

"You ought to—you've been going out with him since you were ten."

"So you work on him—he's earned a full night's sleep."

Ida speared her with a glance. "You think you'll be ready to turn your patients over to someone else in another twenty-five years?"

"Okay, maybe not." Harper didn't think of medicine as a job, but as a responsibility, one she'd wanted since the first time she'd rode beside her father in the front seat of a Ford pickup with his big battered black bag between them, making house calls. She loved being greeted at the door by a friend or neighbor who opened their home to her and put their life in her hands because they trusted her. What she did mattered, and in her heart of hearts, she didn't think anyone else could do it as well. Except her father. "Maybe I can get him to cross-cover with me now and then. At least he'll get a few nights off that way."

"You suggest it, and I'll work on him." Ida wiped down the counter with a damp dish towel and asked casually, "How are things at the hospital?"

Harper went on alert. Her mother didn't do casual. She wasn't a big talker, unlike her father, who could carry on a conversation with anyone, including strangers in the market, about any topic for seemingly endless lengths of time. Her mother was direct, perceptive, and the power to be reckoned with at home.

"Fine, as far as I know," Harper said. "Is there something I don't know about that I should?"

Ida turned and rested her slender hips against the counter in front of the five-foot-long cast-iron country sink. She and Harper were built the same, tall and lanky, slender in the hips and long in the leg. Even their hair color was the same, a brown so dark it looked black in low light. Harper's hands were like hers too, long slim strong fingers. Right now Harper's fingers were clenched around the steaming white porcelain mug. Her mother's blue eyes, almost indigo like Harper's, shimmered with…worry?

Harper's shoulders tightened. Her mother was never wrong about something being wrong. Her mother had known when Harper's Kate had been ill, even when no one, including Harper's father and all his colleagues, could pin down why she suddenly wasn't eating and was losing weight. And when the leukemia had finally surfaced, there'd been no way to stop it. Harper shook off the memory of saying good-bye to Kate in the bedroom next to hers. "What?"

"Your father."

Stomach in free fall, Harper pushed the chair back and sat up straight. "What, is he sick? He hasn't said anything to me."

Ida waved a hand. "He's healthy as a horse. But something's worrying at him. He's been pacing at night, doesn't sleep even when he has the chance, and he's had a couple phone calls that have clearly upset him, but he isn't talking about it."

"Is it money?"

"Not unless he's suddenly taken up gambling."

Harper snorted. Her father had two interests in life—medicine and his family. He didn't have time for anything else and had never shown any inclination to change that. She admired him for his dedication to both and hoped that one day she would do as well, heading both the hospital, after her father retired as chief of staff, and a family, when she met the right woman to settle down with.

"Things are busy," Harper said. "ER traffic has picked up now that the weather has broken, and we're getting more tourists coming into the area. Other than that, I don't know of anything at the hospital that might be bothering him."

"Well then," her mother said as tires crunched on the gravel outside, "whatever it is, I suspect we'll know soon enough."

Harper listened to the familiar sound of her father's footsteps returning home, uneasiness settling in her middle. Her mother was never wrong about something being wrong.

Presley grabbed her roller bag off the carousel and pushed her way through the sparse pack of fellow travelers toward the airport exit. Three men in off-the-rack suits, white shirts, and dark ties held cardboard placards in front of them. One, a sandy-haired, florid-faced man in his early forties, held one with her name scrawled in black marker across it. She walked to him and he greeted her with a broad smile.

"Ms. Worth?"

"Yes." She barely managed not to snarl. There'd been no first-class cabin, and the plane had been small and cramped and the service nonexistent. She'd managed a cup of coffee that tasted like lukewarm instant and a bag of nuts for breakfast. "How far is it?"

"About forty-five minutes." He took the handle of her bag and headed for the exit. "Not much traffic out that way, so we'll make good time."

"Fine." She followed along beside him into a sunlit morning. The air was crisp and a good twenty degrees cooler than she was used to at this hour of the morning. That was a bonus, of sorts, and about the only positive thing she'd noticed thus far. The airport was ridiculously small, which explained why she'd had to take two flights to get here. Really. Could she get any farther from civilization?

He led her to a black town car. While he took care of her bag, she climbed into the back and immediately checked her phone. Hopefully he wouldn't want to chat once he saw she was busy. She scrolled through her several business email addresses and then her personal, sending instructions to her admin on several matters that had come up since the last time she'd checked. Thank God Carrie would be arriving the next day. Between the two of them, they ought to be able to wrap this up quickly.

The sooner they set the groundwork for a transition team to take over, the faster she could do what needed to be done and get out of here. The familiar anger at her brother and his maneuvering surged through her, and she tamped it down. Some battles were not worth fighting, and since he had the support of the board behind him, she'd had no ammunition with which to fight back. So here she was, pushed out of sight for the time being. The sooner she finished off the takeover, the better. Preston was mistaken, though, if he expected her to let him campaign for the CEO position while she was exiled in the ass-end of nowhere.

She glanced out the window at the city, or what there was of one, and discovered it had disappeared. Rolling hills and broad fields bordered the two-lane road. Farmhouses, white or yellow seemed to be the common color, sat along the road or back a distance on narrow dirt drives, the houses generally dwarfed by larger blood-red barns, silos, and a jumble of other buildings. No one had close neighbors. The landscape couldn't be more different than Phoenix, where the starkly beautiful desert stretched for miles to the foot of the craggy mountain faces. Here, color exploded everywhere: greens in every shade and hue, deep yellows and rich earthy browns, purple-and-white flowers—lilacs, at least she thought they were lilacs—and other plants and flowers she could not name. The dizzying riot of bold colors was annoyingly distracting, and she turned back to her iPhone.

She opened a news app and after a second realized she had no signal. She stared at her phone. Was it possible? Really? No cell service? Where in God's name was she?

Clutching her phone as if it were a lifeline to civilization, she leaned back and closed her eyes. The transition was projected to take six months. She'd give it three. Any longer than that and she was likely to lose her mind. Damn Preston and his maneuvering.

The vehicle slowed, and Presley sat up. A dented red mailbox with peeling reflective numbers perched atop a gray wooden post at the mouth of a dirt driveway. The car turned in and passed between fields of what Presley presumed was grass stretching as far as she could see on either side. Surely this was a mistake. "Are you certain this is the right address?"

"Says 246 on the mailbox, ma'am. And this is County Road 64."

"Yes, but there's nothing out here."

"Well, there's a house right up ahead past those trees. Isn't that what you were expecting?"

"I was told a house had been rented for me, but I didn't expect it to be—" She gritted her teeth. "Let's just see what we see, shall we?"

The car bumped along a lane as long as two city blocks and barely as wide as an alley. The house was a neat wood-sided square structure—yellow, of course—with a broad porch running the full length of the front, the requisite red barn—not as big as some she had seen—fifty yards away, and a clothesline strung from the rear corner of the house to a big oak tree loaded down with sheets flapping in the breeze.

"Obviously, we have the wrong place. Someone lives here," Presley said. Someone else, thank God.

The front door opened and a middle-aged woman in pale blue pants, a blue-and-white checkered shirt, and a flowered apron around her waist came down the porch and approached the car. Her graying blond hair was pulled back in a loose twist. Her smile was wide and welcoming.

Presley rolled down the window. "I'm very sorry to disturb you, I think we are in the wrong—"

"Would you be Ms. Worth?"

For a moment, Presley was almost too surprised to answer. "Yes. Who are you?"

"I'm Lila Phelps. The housekeeper."

"The housekeeper." Presley heard her voice rise at that. "I didn't know the house came with a keeper."

Lila laughed. "Well, I don't live here, but the rental agency said you'd be needing a housekeeper, and I'm right up the road. My cousin Sue works for the agent and she called me, and I can use the extra with my youngest about to go off to community college in the fall. The house needed airing out and I just finished washing all the linens. Of course, if you don't need me—"

"Do you cook by any chance?"

The woman beamed. "Does it rain in April?"

"Not where I come from," Presley muttered. She pushed open the door and stepped out. "Breakfast at six a.m., dinner at seven thirty."

"I can leave you something warming in the oven for your supper, but I'll be needing to be home come four or so to see to the family's meal."

"Fine. Just leave instructions with it."

"I can manage that. And do the wash and keep the place tidy and do the grocery shopping."

"Excellent. I'll give you a list of my preferences. I work in the morning over breakfast, so no radio."

"Don't like the noise myself."

Presley nodded briskly. "We'll get along fine, then."

"I expect we will."

Presley paid the driver, and he carried her suitcase up to the front porch. With her hands on her hips, she turned and surveyed her new home. All she could see were hills and fields and cows. There were a great many cows right up the road, and if she hadn't been able to see or hear them, she could definitely smell them. She was going to make her brother pay for this.

CHAPTER TWO

Harper's mother turned with a cup of coffee in her outstretched hand just as Edward Rivers came through the kitchen door, greeting him as she had thousands of times before upon his return from a late-night call. He smiled, kissed her cheek, and took the coffee.

"Morning, Dad," Harper said.

Edward sipped the coffee. "Mary and the baby doing all right?"

"Both fine." Harper didn't bother to ask how her father knew of Mary Campbell's nightlong labor and early morning delivery. Somehow, he always seemed to know what was happening with everyone in the community, and certainly the condition of every patient in the hospital everyone still called the Rivers Hospital, as it had been named when her great-great-great-grandfather and several local mill owners had built it 150 years before. She hadn't yet mastered his access to the local grapevine, but she was getting better every year. She'd only three years of medical practice to his thirty, so she didn't feel too bad. "I'll be heading back to check on her in an hour or so. Is there anyone you need me to see?"

He set down his cup, took off his suit coat—he always wore a suit and tie when seeing patients, in high summer or the dead of winter—and hung it on a peg inside the kitchen door. He rolled up the sleeves of his white shirt and took his usual seat at the head of the table.

"Nothing urgent. I'll be making rounds myself midmorning."

Tires crunched on the drive. Flannery's Jeep, the top already off in homage to the long-awaited warm weather, appeared outside the window above the sink and disappeared again as Flann pulled under the porte cochere. Harper glanced at her mother. "Family meeting?"

"Edward?" Ida asked.

Harper's father nodded slowly.

Ida said, "I'd better put on more coffee."

Edward rubbed his face, and for the first time Harper realized he looked far more tired than a night up seeing patients should account for. Maybe her mother was wrong. Maybe he was ill. A spear of panic, completely unlike her usual steady, calm approach to a crisis, shot through her. Her father had been her hero, the primary presence in her life, for as far back as she could remember. She was the oldest child, the first he took on rounds with him, before Flannery and then Carson, and now Margie. Kate had not lived long enough to join him. Harper couldn't imagine the family without either of her parents—her father's quiet anchor or her mother's unbending strength—or her life without them. The day would one day come. Just not now.

"Dad?"

His dark brown eyes met hers and he smiled briefly. "Wait till you hear the facts, Harper. Listen to your instincts, but never disregard the facts."

"Yes, sir," Harper said, remembering one of the first lessons she'd learned at his side.

The back door swung open and Flannery blew in, energy pouring off her as it always seemed to do. The second oldest, she'd been in motion from the time she could walk, and she'd walked earlier than them all, their mother said—always the first to climb the tallest tree, the one to ride her bike the fastest, the rebellious teen pushing every boundary she could find. Harper's father said he'd always known she'd be the surgeon, and he'd been right. Whereas Harper favored her mother in appearance, Flannery had the golden-brown hair and chocolate eyes of her father's side of the family, and the temperament of a thoroughbred born to race. She looked like the soccer player she'd been in high school, with a little less height than Harper and more breadth in the shoulders. She kissed her mother, squeezed her father's shoulder, and pulled out a chair next to Harper at the table.

"I've got an eight o'clock," she announced to the room in general.

"You'll make it," Edward said. "Routine hernia, isn't it?"

"That and an appendectomy to follow that Harper picked up in the ER last night." She nodded to Harper. "Good call, by the way. Thanks for letting me sleep."

"I was there with a delivery. No reason for both of us to be awake." Harper had called Flannery at five a.m. after seeing Bryce Daniels at three when the ER nurses had stopped her for a curbside consult. The sixteen-year-old had the classic signs of appendicitis, and she'd gotten his workup started before waking her sister.

The swinging door from the dining room pushed open and Margie, wearing a loose T-shirt and soccer shorts, came in rubbing sleep from her eyes. At fifteen she was rangy and still a little coltish, but destined to be the prettiest of them all with shoulder-length curly blond hair and vivid blue eyes. She shuffled toward the refrigerator and pulled out a bottle of milk. "How come everybody's here?"

"Your father has news," Ida said.

Margie sat on the far side of Harper as the last vehicle, Carson's Volvo, pulled in outside. Her nephew Davey's laughter carried through the open window, and a second later, Carson ambled in with the ten-month-old perched on her hip. She leaned down and kissed her father, then her mother, and took the coffee her mother held out to her before settling into her usual place on the opposite side of the table from Flannery. Slim-hipped and ivory-skinned, she looked more Margie's contemporary than ten years her senior. She kept her auburn hair short and feathered at the temples, giving her a touch of innocence that belied her core of steel. A soldier's wife, she'd been battle tested as the war in the Middle East dragged on.

"Thanks, Mama," Carson said when Ida handed her a cracker for Davey.

The room was silent save for the baby's chortling while Ida laid strips of bacon in a cast-iron pan on the stove. She turned the heat down low, poured her own coffee, and took her seat at the opposite end of the table from her husband, the four sisters ranged between them. "Well then. Edward?"

As if he'd been waiting for his wife to give him permission, he cleared his throat and looked at each of his children in turn.

"The board of trustees has sold the hospital."

For a second, Harper couldn't think above the exclamations and one pointed curse word from Flann.

"Flannery O'Connor, we'll not have that language at my table," Ida said without raising her voice.

"Sorry, Mama," Flannery muttered.

Everyone quieted.

"What do you mean," Harper said, "sold the hospital. Sold the hospital to who?"

"Can they do that?" Flannery interrupted.

"Wait," Carson said, shifting Davey in her lap as she pushed her coffee cup beyond his grasping hands. "Why haven't the staff been informed? A lot of jobs are at stake, not to mention our patients' welfare."

"It's complicated," Edward said, "but like most community hospitals that were started by a few individuals, the hospital transitioned to a for-profit institution sometime during the middle of the last century. The bank and a few major shareholders and the board of trustees control the business side of things. Apparently, the hospital's profits have been declining and the sale is the only way to pay our creditors."

"Well, decreased profits is to be expected," Harper said. "With the fall in reimbursement from insurance companies and the cost of new equipment, that's true everywhere. Our beds are always pretty full—" She glanced at Carson, who'd opted for business over medicine and now headed patient admissions. "I think?"

Carson nodded. "We run at eighty percent capacity most of the time and sometimes close to one hundred."

"So why *wasn't* the staff informed?" Flann reached for a biscuit and glanced at her mother. "How long to bacon?"

"Until I put it on the table."

Flann grinned. "Soon?"

Ida's eyes softened as she rose, stroked Flann's hair, and went to the refrigerator.

Carson started to get up. "I'll get that, Mama."

"You sit." Harper rose. "You've got the baby. I'll get it." She took a carton of eggs from her mother. "I'll do this. I can hear from here."

"Keep the heat low so the eggs don't get rubbery."

"Yes, ma'am."

As Harper cracked eggs into the skillet and listened to the questions and her father's quiet answers, a hard knot settled in her stomach. The hospital was as much the center of her life as her family. Her friends and her colleagues there were her community. She knew the halls and stairwells as well as she knew the paths and streams that ran through the land she'd grown up on. The hushed murmur of voices in the dimly lit corridors at night and the steady beep of monitors from open doorways were as familiar as birdcall in the morning and the lowing of cows outside her bedroom window at night. The hospital was an extension of her world, and she'd never wanted to be anywhere else. Her father and his father before him and his before that had been the chiefs of staff, and she had known from the time she was twelve that one day she would be too. The hospital was her destiny, and she'd never considered any other path.

She flipped the eggs and tuned out discussions of profit and shares and stockholders and other things she didn't care about. She cared about her patients, cared about the community she served, and the rest was of no matter to her. She wasn't interested in profit. She'd never been interested in money or paid much attention to it at all. She lived in what had once been the caretaker's house on four acres of land a quarter mile down the road from the big house. She had four rooms that were plenty of space until she met the right woman to start a family with, a garden where she grew her own vegetables in the summer, apple and pear trees, a dog who slept as often at her mother's as he did on her back porch, three cats who'd claimed the woodshed, and chickens who roosted in a coop beside it and gave her more eggs than she could eat. Her life was going just according to plan.

She slid the eggs and bacon onto a big white platter and put it in the middle of the table. Margie took down dishes and silverware and stacked them at the other end. Everyone automatically helped themselves.

"What does this really mean?" Harper sat back down with a fresh cup of coffee. She didn't take any food. She'd lost her appetite.

Edward shook his head. "No one really knows for sure. Maybe nothing. We've still got sick people to take care of, and that's what we need to focus on."

Flann drummed her fork on the table to a beat only she could hear. "What did you say the name of the corporation was that bought the hospital?"

"SunView Health Systems," her father said. "They're located out west somewhere."

"Strangers." Flann glanced at Harper. Fourteen months apart, they were as close as twins. They'd gone to the same medical school, had done their residencies at the same hospital, and on rare occasions had competed for the attention of the same girls.

Harper could read the warning in Flann's eyes. Change was coming, and it couldn't be good.

❖

Presley lugged her suitcase and briefcase through the front door and found herself in a central foyer facing a wide staircase against one wall. Two large rooms opened on each side, and she took a quick glance into each. On the left was a sitting room with a sofa and several oversized chairs arranged in front of a stone fireplace. An oil painting of a red barn and fields of swaying green stuff hung above the broad granite mantelpiece. She shook her head. Didn't they get enough of that view just driving down the road?

A faded Oriental rug in greens and browns covered the wood floor. The other room also had a fireplace against the far wall and walnut-stained, floor-to-ceiling wood shelves holding a haphazard assortment of hardback books, and a pair of comfortable-looking reading chairs with round, dark wood casual tables beside each one. The rooms appeared lived-in and surprisingly welcoming. She'd expected a rental house to be furnished, but this place looked as if the owner might return at any moment.

"Whose house is this?" Presley asked Lila, who waited for her at the foot of the stairs.

"It's been in the White family for a hundred years or so," Lila said. "Old Mrs. White finally gave in and went to live with her son downstate. They haven't had any buyers, so they finally decided to rent it."

"Can't imagine there are many buyers for places out here."

Lila laughed. "You'd be surprised how many city people like to try their hand at country living."

"You're right about that."

Presley followed Lila upstairs where she found three bedrooms, one with a large bathroom attached, and a second bathroom down the hall. She'd never lived with anyone—she liked to work at odd hours and didn't care to worry about someone else's schedule, but Carrie could stay here for the short time they'd be on-site. They got along well and they wouldn't actually be spending that much time in the house. Carrie had been her personal assistant now for almost three years, since Carrie had graduated from college and finished an internship at SunView. She was organized and efficient, respected personal space, and appreciated that Presley wasn't a chatterer. Exactly the kind of person Presley could tolerate having around.

She took the master bedroom with bath, dumped her bag by a broad, tall four-poster bed, and walked to the open window. Lace curtains billowed in the breeze. The room overlooked a sloping lawn to the drive and, beyond that, a broad green pasture bordered by a wooden rail fence. The air was surprisingly clean and bright. She could almost smell the green in it. The thought struck her as ridiculously whimsical, and she turned away to study the room with its tall armoire in lieu of a closet in one corner and a matching dark wood dresser topped with a huge wood-framed mirror. Another Oriental-patterned rug covered the floor, and a small chair upholstered in a floral brocade design sat by the window with a standing brass reading lamp nearby. Homey. And absolutely nothing like her condo in Phoenix, where she favored glass and steel and modern art, highly polished tile floors, and a gleaming gourmet kitchen she rarely used. Not that she really noticed her surroundings when she got home late at night and put in a few hours' work before bed.

"Talk about a fish out of water," she muttered with a shake of her head. Frowning, she scanned the wall, checked what appeared to be a thermostat, and walked out into the hallway. Leaning over the wooden banister, she called, "Lila?"

Lila appeared below and looked up. "Need something?"

"Where are the controls for the air-conditioning?"

Lila stared at her for a few seconds. "Well, there aren't any."

"Come again?"

"Most places up here don't have it. You won't need it except maybe in August, when it can get a little stuffy. Then just open the windows, and if you want a bit more air, you can put a fan in one of them. I'll see to it when the time comes."

"A fan. In August."

"Maybe."

"Wonderful." Presley added another item to her list of things she intended to torture Preston for. "Which direction is town? I thought I'd walk around and get acquainted."

"You won't be walking to town. It's about eight miles."

"Eight miles. Lovely." She couldn't wait for Carrie to arrive to see to the rest of the arrangements Preston had neglected. "All right then, I'm going to need a car. Today. Where's the nearest rental place?"

"I imagine that would be in Albany. And that's a good—"

"Yes, I know, forty-five minutes away." She considered her options. "Where would I go to buy one?"

"Well"—Lila seemed to be searching for words—"a new one or used one?"

"One that runs."

Lila smiled. "I know just the place. When you're ready, I'll drive you over."

"Let's go."

Lila's cousin's husband Clyde operated a small used-car dealership out of a garage next to his house twenty minutes away. Lila called, and a big man in baggy jeans and a faded T-shirt met them in the driveway in front of a single-story white cement building surrounded by a dozen cars and trucks.

"Good morning, ladies. You're looking for a car, I hear."

Presley surveyed the vehicles, all of which looked relatively new and surprisingly clean and in good condition. "I need something reliable with air-conditioning and GPS."

The man glanced at Lila, who gave him a nod. "Are you going to be hauling anything?"

"What would I want to haul?"

He lifted a shoulder. "Hay, sod, feed, furniture—that kind of thing?"

Presley smiled thinly. "No. No hauling."

"And I guess you won't be pulling a trailer, either."

"Not in this lifetime."

"Well then, I think I've got what you want." He showed her a relatively new Subaru hatchback with all the basic requirements and assured her it was in excellent condition. "And if you have any problems with it, just bring it back and I'll take care of it."

"Fine. Will you take a check?"

"I sure will. And I'll get the registration taken care of for you this morning as soon as motor vehicles opens up. You'll need insurance."

"I'll have my assistant call you with that information. Can you have someone deliver it to me when it's ready? My cell number is on the check. You can call me, and I'll tell you where."

"I can do that."

"Excellent." She wrote a check, handed it to him, and turned to Lila. "Might I impose upon you a little while longer? I'll need a ride to town while Clyde gets this ready for me."

"Of course. I was going to go grocery shopping and stock up the kitchen anyhow."

"Wonderful."

Lila dropped her off a little before nine.

"Thanks, Lila." Presley grabbed her briefcase. "You've been a tremendous help."

"If you need a ride back before Clyde gets the car ready, you call me. It's no bother."

"That's all right. I can always call a cab." She paused, reading Lila's expression. "Or not."

She laughed before Lila could. The absurdity of the entire situation was starting to feel normal. She waved as Lila drove away, and surveyed Argyle Community Hospital for the first time. The ivy-covered red brick building with its white colonnaded front entrance and two symmetrical wings extending out in a lazy U stood on a hillside above the village. The road up wended through what Lila had told her were apple orchards. A rolling grassy lawn studded with shrubs and flower beds bordered the circular drive in front. With its tall gracious windows and elegant portico, the place might have been a grand hotel or a private summer home. It bore no resemblance to the modern, sprawling hospitals Presley was used to. A pretty place. She started up the broad stone sidewalk, thinking of all the uses for a building like this when it wasn't a hospital any longer.

CHAPTER THREE

The hospital foyer soared two stories to a vaulted ceiling painted in swirling patterns of dusky rose, periwinkle, and pale cream. A line of brass chandeliers with candelabra bulbs lit the upper recesses, and floor-to-ceiling windows on either side of the massive entrance let sunlight in to dance across the highly polished marble floors. Presley's low heels tapped rhythmically as she crossed to a gleaming mahogany desk in the center of the expanse, behind which sat a tiny white-haired woman wearing a bright red jacket and a blazing smile. Presley glanced around and didn't see anyone resembling a security officer, and she doubted that this diminutive octogenarian could stop a flea. Hopefully the other entrances were staffed more conventionally.

"Good morning," the woman said in a surprisingly full, strong voice. "Are you here about a patient? Visiting hours aren't until one unless you're here to see someone in the ICU." She pulled over a clipboard. "I can check a room number for you."

"No, I'm not here to see a patient," Presley said, scanning the desk in vain for a computer monitor. A clipboard? Why should she be surprised? "A business matter."

"Oh, then you'll want administration." A thin bony hand pointed toward another set of polished wooden doors at the far end of the foyer. "Right through there to your left, second hallway on the right, and then follow the signs. Oh"—she held out a laminated card with a V on it— "just clip this to your jacket there."

Smothering a smile, Presley took the little laminated card and clipped it to her jacket. A visitor's badge. What next? Perhaps the plane had been caught in a time warp and she'd been transported back in time rather than simply across the country. "Thank you."

"Not at all, dear. You have a nice day."

Have a nice day. When was the last time someone had said that to her and sounded as if they really meant it? She spent her days in meetings with others just as busy and absorbed in their own projects as she was, or spearheading acquisitions that more often than not were unpopular with most of the people involved. Unused to the simple interchange, she searched for the appropriate response. "You do the same, Ms...."

"It's Mrs....Mrs. Dora Brundidge. You can call me Dora. Everyone does."

"All right, Dora. You enjoy your day."

"Why, thank you. I will."

Presley made her way from the reception area toward the main hospital entrance, slowly taking in the portraits dominating both side walls. On the left, four men, stern and serious looking in stiff, high-collared white shirts, vests, and coats, faced two men across the foyer in more modern garb. All the paintings were done in oils, the style formal, the elaborate frames gilt with engraved plaques beneath illuminated by individual brass lamps. Moving from one to the next, she perused the names. Alexander Rivers. Roger Rivers. Charles...William. Rivers all. Curious, she crossed to the right and studied the others. Andrew. Edward.

She pulled up a mental image of the report Carrie had given her on Argyle Community Hospital. Her memory was eidetic, or nearly so for practical reasons, and she sifted through the names of the board of trustees and then came to the entry she was seeking. Medical Chief of Staff: Dr. Edward William Rivers. She returned to the reception desk. Dora gave her another smile.

"Did you forget something, dear?"

"No, just curious. It looks as if the Rivers family is an institution around here."

"Oh, well I would say so," Dora said. "The first Dr. Rivers—that would have been Alexander Rivers—founded the hospital way back when the community was established, and there's always been a Dr. Rivers at the Rivers."

"The Rivers?"

"That's what the hospital was called until after the war. Then, you know, the hospital name was changed, but it will always be the Rivers to a lot of us. We were mostly all born here, and our children too." Dora laughed. "We've got some new blood over the years, of course—people moving in to try their hand at farming or raising goats and alpacas and such—but the majority of the families have been here a long time."

"Yes, of course." Presley tucked away that little bit of information. Community resistance in any kind of takeover was a possibility, although in this instance, she doubted any kind of organized or effective opposition could be mounted in time to slow the transition. She planned to be in and out as soon as possible, but it never hurt to be forewarned. "Well, thank you again."

As soon as she passed beyond the foyer into the main building, the ambience changed. The hallways were still wide and grand with paneled wainscoting and tasteful muted colors and paintings of pastoral scenes hung at intervals, but the familiar signs of hospital activity were everywhere. Small discreet signs directed patients toward radiology, the outpatient labs, admissions, and the ER. Others pointed visitors to the elevators for the intensive care unit, the surgical waiting room, and the patient floors. Hospital personnel in scrubs, lab coats, and smocks hurried through the halls, some pushing gowned patients in wheelchairs. A young blonde in a white shirt with a logo above her breast that said *Food Service* pushed a rattling cart with pots of coffee and trays of bagels. She slowed and smiled at Presley, her gaze unmistakably appreciative.

"Looking for the conference room?" the blonde asked. Her ID read *Deana*.

"Is that where the coffee is going?"

Deana laughed. She was pretty in a completely unstudied way—clear eyed, no makeup, youthful and fresh. "Yes. Grand rounds, right?"

"Afraid not."

"There's plenty more in the cafeteria, then. Need directions?"

"I can probably find it. I'll just follow the coffee."

"Good. Need any help, let me know. Always guaranteed to be fresh. The coffee, that is."

The mild flirtation was surprisingly pleasant and Presley grinned. "No doubt."

The blonde grinned back and continued off with the clattering cart. Presley followed the signs toward the outpatient area, interested to see what kind of facilities were available. More signs pointed to cardiology, pediatrics, and the walk-in clinic. A few patients waited in seating areas here or there. She backtracked and took a left turn toward the emergency room and instantly felt the controlled tension in the air.

The overhead lights were brighter, a row of wheelchairs lined one wall, and men and women in various colored scrubs hurried by. A young man in blue scrubs nodded to her as he pushed a gurney holding an old man with an oxygen cannula in his nose and a beeping portable cardiac monitor by his side. The old man's eyes were closed, his stubbled cheeks pale, and his frail body barely made a ripple in the crisp white sheet covering him. Somewhere up ahead a child wailed.

She glanced into the patient waiting area across from the closed double doors marked *Patients Only*. Rows of plastic chairs faced a cubicle where a woman in a flowered smock sat at a computer behind a sliding Plexiglas window. A frazzled brunette in low-cut jeans and a frilly white ruffled top that exposed her pale midriff rocked a red-faced, tear-streaked toddler. An old woman with thick ankles and heavy black shoes in a worn gray sweater and shapeless faded floral housedress sat against the far wall with her palms pressed against her broad thighs, staring straight ahead as if she were somewhere else. Waiting for news, perhaps about the old man. Two teenage girls with teased hair and nearly identical tight, scoop-necked tank tops huddled over their phones in another corner, thumbs flicking rapidly as they texted.

The ER swished open, and Presley caught a glimpse of a big whiteboard with names scrawled in Magic Marker next to room numbers. Charts sat in slots down the wall beside the board. Over half of the ten or so slots were filled. Busy for a weekday morning.

Presley recalled the stats for the last year. The hundred-and-twenty-bed hospital had seen over eight thousand patients come through the emergency room with an admission rate of 15 percent. The hospital ran at 85 percent capacity and the OR at 90, employed a hundred nurses, nearly that number of ancillary technicians, another twenty in the clerical ranks, and a half dozen administrators. There were no full-time physician employees—all were private practitioners with admitting privileges. The model was an old one and not particularly efficient—too many overlapping specialties and not enough centralization. The number of inpatients at any time could easily be cared for by far fewer hospital-employed physicians. However, that wasn't a problem she needed to be concerned with. The location within sixty miles of a medical center made the entire facility redundant.

As the ER doors started to close, two women walked through talking intensely in low voices. The taller, dark-haired one with a stethoscope slung around her neck was dressed casually in black pants and a neatly pressed pale blue shirt. The other, a sandy-brown-haired woman in hospital greens and a white lab coat, paused, and both scrutinized Presley.

The dark-haired one caught the door before it could swing closed and smiled. "Are you on your way in to see a patient?"

The question, or maybe it was the quick, warm smile and honey-slow voice, caught Presley off guard. A morning for surprises. "No. Thanks. Actually, I'm looking for the administrative wing."

The one in scrubs laughed, her dark brown eyes dancing. Her grin was cocky and confident. "Well, we wouldn't exactly call it a wing, but maybe a wing tip."

"That will do nicely," Presley said.

"I'm headed that way." The dark-haired one held out her hand. "Harper Rivers."

Another Rivers. Presley took her hand. It was large, warm, and strong. "Presley Worth."

"Nice to meet you."

Harper Rivers's eyes were a dramatic shade of deep blue, and Presley had a hard time looking away. She released Harper's hand. "You too."

"I'm Flannery," the sandy-haired one said, edging into Presley's field of vision. "The better-looking sib."

Presley glanced from one to the other and saw it then—the bold angle of the jaws, the firm straight noses, the full expressive lips. Eyes of a different color, but similar intelligent, confident gazes. The supply of Rivers doctors was apparently endless.

"I'll wisely reserve comment," Presley said.

Harper laughed and Flannery grinned.

"Are you new in town?" Flannery asked.

Curious, Presley nodded. "I am. How did you know that?"

The grin returned. "Because I don't know you, and I would've remembered if I'd seen you before."

"Aha," Presley said. The woman was so self-assured she didn't even pretend to be embarrassed at using such an old line, and that made her interesting. "Of course."

Harper Rivers shook her head, her expression amused. "Don't you have a case, Flann?"

"I'm going." Flannery backed up a step, her focus still on Presley. "Staying long?"

"A while."

"Excellent. If you need a tour guide or…anything, I'll be free later today. Just call the operator. She'll page me."

Harper called after her, "Let me know what you find."

Flannery tossed a salute. "Will do. Lunch?"

"Sure." As Flannery disappeared around a corner, Harper turned back to Presley Worth, who looked after Flann with amused, faintly appraising blue eyes. Harper was used to seeing interest in a woman's eyes when they considered Flann, but Presley's expression was far more contemplative, as if she was trying to decide if Flann was worth her time. An unfamiliar reversal where Flann was concerned. Harper searched for something to say that wouldn't sound like a follow-up to Flann's invitation. "Been in town long?"

"That obvious?"

Harper laughed. "Only to someone paying attention—between me and Flann, we know the families of every patient in the hospital. Plus…"

"What?"

"Never mind." Harper didn't usually strike up conversations with women out of the blue, and definitely not in the hospital. That was Flann's special skill. Flann was at ease with women anywhere and always had more dates and interested women than she could handle. Not so Harper. She preferred slow introductions and cautious explorations. She didn't date much—she liked her privacy, and dating anyone at the hospital automatically meant everyone in the community would know before the night was out. And she'd grown up with many of the women she saw outside her professional arena and thought of them as friends, not romantic possibilities.

"Oh no," Presley said. "You started it—now you have to finish."

The teasing challenge in Presley's voice caught Harper's attention. "Your tan is a few weeks too early for the local weather, and…"

Presley made a keep-going gesture.

"And you look like a city girl."

"Why do I think that might be a veiled insult?"

"Not at all," Harper said hastily. "You look terrific."

"You're forgiven, then."

Harper shook her head. "Sorry. Flann is the one with the smooth lines. I'm just a simple country doctor."

"Somehow I doubt that," Presley said. "I must be keeping you."

"I'm just making rounds. I'll walk you down—do you have a room number?"

Presley hesitated. This was neither the time nor place to discuss her purpose with anyone, and most especially not one of the hospital's dynastic family. "Actually, I'm here…about a job."

Not strictly true, but not exactly a lie either. She wondered what Harper knew of the takeover and had the odd desire not to dispel their easy exchange quite so quickly. She must be more tired than she thought.

"Come on," Harper said. "You'll want personnel."

Presley followed along. "What's your specialty?"

"Family practice."

"You work here at the clinic?"

"I staff it in rotation with about six others, but most of my practice is community based."

"And your sister's a surgeon."

"Flann's a general surgeon—she did a trauma fellowship, so she handles most anything out of the ordinary."

Presley frowned. "What's your trauma clearance?"

Harper gave her a questioning look. "Level three. Flann transfers out the complicated ones after they're stabilized."

They turned down another corridor lined with offices, the doors standing open and people visible within, working at desks.

"Are you staying in town?" Harper asked.

"Just a little ways outside."

"Family in the area?"

"No," Presley said, realizing her tone was sharper than she intended.

Harper paused in front of a partially open door. "This is personnel. You probably want to speak to someone in here if it's about a job."

"And where would the chief administrator's office be?"

"That would be the room at the end." Harper glanced at her watch. "Anyone there should be able to help you."

Presley smiled. "Thank you for the tour."

"Anytime." Harper smiled wryly as if at some private joke. "And of course, there's always Flann to continue the tour."

"Of course." Presley laughed.

"Good luck."

Presley frowned. "I'm sorry?"

"With the job application."

"Oh, yes. Thank you."

"Well, good-bye then."

"Have a good day," Presley called as Harper Rivers walked away.

Harper turned back, her expression so intense Presley caught her breath. "You too."

Presley really hoped she would, but she suspected before the day was out the Riverses and quite a few others would be less than happy to see her.

Chapter Four

Harper slid the cafeteria tray onto a table by the window and sat down facing Flannery. A lilac bush that had bloomed sometime in the last two days, its branches laden with deep purple flowers, brushed gently against the corner of the glass as if inviting her outside. Someone had opened the window, and the sweet vanilla scent of blossoms and fresh-cut grass beckoned. Down the hill, the church spire at the far end of town speared above slate rooftops, glinting in the sunlight. A twinge of spring fever and an unfamiliar restlessness toyed with her concentration. She rarely thought of escaping her schedule or her responsibilities, and the teasing urge to leave everything behind for just a day annoyed and unsettled her. She focused on Flann and the patient they shared, bringing her world back into order. "Everything go okay?"

Flannery balanced a hot dog in one hand and took a sip from the cup of steaming coffee she held in the other. "No problems. The appendix was red-hot, though. Another few hours and things could've gotten messy." She took a bite and chased it with more coffee. "It's good you jumped right on it."

"Are you sending him home tomorrow?"

Flannery nodded. "As long as he's not running a fever. I saw Tim Campbell giving out cigars in the lobby. Looks like you made his night too."

Harper laughed. "I'd say Mary did that."

"So…" Flannery polished off the rest of her hot dog in two bites and reached for a plastic plate with a huge slab of chocolate cake on it. "What's the story with the new visitor?"

Harper forked up a few pieces of salad and considered ignoring the question as if she didn't understand where Flann was headed. But she knew Flann, and she recognized the bird-dog glint in her eyes—bright and eager and relentless—when she spied quarry. No point in avoiding the inevitable. "There's probably a story there, but I don't have it."

"You can get a patient's life history in five minutes without even trying, but you spend—what—fifteen minutes with a hot-looking woman, and you don't know the story?" Flannery shook her head. "Clearly, I failed to teach you anything of importance."

"I can't remember you teaching me much of anything, seeing as how you're always trying to catch up to me."

Flannery grinned. "I'd say once I was able to walk, we were even."

"Yeah, yeah," Harper said, the game an old one and her mind only half on the familiar rivalry. Ordinarily, Flannery's unremitting competition never bothered her, and on those occasions when they bumped up against each other around a woman, Harper had been happy to concede the chase to Flannery. That idea didn't appeal to her right now. In fact, some instinctive resistance rose inside her when she thought of Flannery pursuing Presley Worth, although if she had to say why, she wasn't sure she could. She'd only spent a few minutes in Presley's company, but those few minutes had left more of an impression than had any woman she'd met in a long time. True, Presley was unlike many of the women she'd known since childhood, but her unfamiliarity wasn't what appealed the most. Presley seemed totally self-contained and just a little bit apart from everything, and that very aloofness piqued Harper's curiosity. For someone whose life was grounded in the lives of others as hers had been since birth, Harper found that very insularity intriguing. Presley was a mystery she'd like to unravel, a desire as unusual as it was disconcerting. It didn't hurt a bit that Presley had been unfazed by Flannery's teasing flirtations—unlike most women faced with Flann's megawatt attention, Presley hadn't melted, she'd teased back in a way that had put her in control. Harper spent so much time letting others lean on her, the idea of someone else in charge was appealing.

"Hey." Flannery's voice cut into her reverie.

"What? Sorry."

"I was asking for the details—where she's staying, what is she doing here, is she married, that sort of thing."

"How would I know that?" Harper rankled at Flannery's assumption that Presley was hers for the asking.

"Well, what did you talk about?"

"Nothing, really. I only spent a few minutes with her. I walked her down to the admin offices. She said she came about a job."

Flannery's brows drew down. "A job? And you didn't ask about that? Didn't it strike you as just a little odd?"

"Why would it?"

"Don't tell me you didn't notice the way she looked."

"I've got two eyes, don't I?"

Flannery grinned. "Yes, but sometimes I'm not sure you actually see anyone unless they're sitting on one of your exam tables."

"What's that supposed to mean?" Harper was feeling grumpier by the second—much the way she used to when Flann bugged her until she joined in on one of her harebrained schemes in college. Schemes that usually led to her bailing Flann out of one mess or another.

"Meaning, half the time you don't notice when a woman is sending you interested signals."

"There weren't any signals."

"Good." Flannery collected the rest of the crumbs of chocolate cake on her fork and licked them off. "Because I'm pretty sure I was getting some, so…as long as you don't mind, I thought I'd follow up on that."

The grumpiness turned to outright irritation. "Since when did you care what I thought about you chasing a woman?"

Flannery put the fork down beside her plate and cocked an eyebrow. "I can't remember any time when it really bothered you. If it had—"

"If it had, are you saying you would've done anything any differently?"

"I don't know," Flannery said, her tone curious. "I guess I'd like to think so."

"Hell, it doesn't really matter. I didn't get the sense she was sending signals to either one of us, and I think it's kind of premature for us to be sitting here discussing something that isn't even likely to happen." Harper rose and grabbed her tray. "I've got some calls to make and patients this afternoon. I'll catch up to you later sometime."

"Sure." Flannery rose, her expression pensive. "Hey, Harp?"

Harper turned. "Yeah."

"Keep your antennae tuned, just in case."

Harper laughed and left to dispose of her tray, rolling her shoulders to work out the pain that lanced between her shoulder blades. Flann was just being Flann, and neither she *nor* Flann had any reason to think Presley Worth had given them a second thought. Presley had been friendly and she'd joined in Flannery's game, but she hadn't given any indication she wanted more. Harper had no idea why that bothered her quite so much.

When her pager went off just as she reached the lobby, she was grateful for the interruption to her brooding thoughts and strode to Dora's desk. "Can I use your phone, beautiful?"

Dora laughed as she always did when Harper called her that and turned her phone to face Harper. "Of course you can, handsome."

Harper grinned. Dora was one of her favorite people. Dora had been her first-grade teacher and, like almost everyone else Dora's age in town, was still her father's patient. When Harper'd returned to begin practicing medicine at the Rivers, Dora had been one of the first to tell her how glad she was to see her back home. Harper dialed the page operator. "Harper Rivers."

"Hi, Harper," Sandy Reynolds said.

"What have you got, Sandy?"

"Your father asked me to catch you. He wants you to meet him in the medical staff office as soon as you can."

Frowning, Harper checked her watch. She had a forty-minute drive to see Charlie Carlyle, an elderly farmer with diabetes who'd called her answering service to say he was having trouble with his foot. That could be anything from an ingrown toenail to a diabetic ulcer or something worse, and she didn't want to leave him waiting too long. On the other hand, a summons from her father wasn't something she could ignore, and after what he'd told them all that morning, a call from him in his official capacity as chief of staff couldn't be anything good.

"On my way. Thanks, Sandy." She passed the phone back to Dora. "Thanks, Dora."

"Don't look so worried, Harper. Your father will take care of the Rivers. The two of you will."

Harper didn't even ask how Dora knew something was happening. Dora always seemed to know everything, as Harper'd discovered the first time she'd hidden a frog she'd picked up on the way to school in her lunchbox and Dora had discovered it within a matter of minutes, almost as if she'd had X-ray vision. She only hoped Dora was right about this too, and she and her father could handle whatever was coming.

❖

"That would be the assistant chief now," Edward Rivers said at the sharp rap on the door. "Thank you for your patience."

"Not at all." Presley, seated in a blue-upholstered club chair in front of Rivers's broad dark wood desk, turned slightly and glanced over her shoulder. Harper Rivers walked in and slowed when her gaze met Presley's.

Presley read an instant of confusion, then a spark of anger that was quickly quelled as the midnight blue of Harper's eyes turned arctic. Harper dismissed her after that first quick appraisal and focused on Edward Rivers.

"You wanted me?" Harper said.

"Harper, this is Ms. Presley Worth, Vice President of Operations at SunView Health Systems," Edward said. "Dr. Harper Rivers, Assistant Chief of Staff."

Presley rose and held out her hand to Harper. "We've met, briefly. Good to see you again, Doctor."

Harper shook her hand. "I see you got the job."

Presley smiled wryly. She deserved that slight barb. Harper Rivers might have appeared the quieter of the two Rivers siblings, but she was by no means the passive one. "Yes, it appears that I have."

"Ms. Worth," Edward said, "perhaps you could brief us on your requirements so we can see that you have everything you need."

Presley stood as Edward sat behind his desk and Harper leaned a shoulder against a bookcase with rows of hardback texts, some of which appeared as old as the building itself. Sitting put her in a subordinate position, and she needed to take command immediately in the presence of two alpha males, gender notwithstanding. Walking to one of the floor-to-ceiling windows, she put the sunlight behind her to shade her face just enough to force both doctors to concentrate on her. Smiling, she launched into her familiar pitch.

"In a transition such as this, we proceed in stages, beginning with an overall assessment of the institution, its internal operations, financial projections, et cetera. That provides us a general view of how to position the institution within the SunView system. We then move on to the second stage, which you might think of as the integration stage—where systems are streamlined, efficiency protocols are instituted, assets are reallocated—all with the aim of optimizing resources and returns. The final stage would be the placement of a permanent management team to continue the operational plan going forward."

Harper, hands in the pockets of her trousers, frowned. "What does all that mean in practical terms? Will you be bringing in your own people to run the hospital?"

Presley chose her words carefully. Harper was the scion of a medical dynasty, not a simple country doctor, and at this stage, the less actual detail the administration of the target institution was provided, the better. "SunView employs individuals who have experience in this kind of assessment and analysis, of course. At this point most of the communication will be done remotely, but I and my admin will be here on site." She glanced at Edward. "I'm afraid I'll have to impose on you to provide some office space for us."

"Of course," Edward said. "You may have this office immediately."

"Thank you," Presley said, glad that he had saved her the awkward task of informing him she was taking over in all but name. "That's very kind."

Harper sucked in a breath. Her father seemed to know a lot more about what was happening than he'd let on, and none of it made her very happy. "Wait a minute. You're not eliminating the chief of staff position—that's a medical—"

"Actually, Harper," her father cut in, "it's considered an administrative appointment, and as such, is very much part of Ms. Worth's territory now."

"You misunderstand," Presley said. "We are not removing Dr. Rivers at all. However, certain functions of the post will need to be modified, particularly those involving allocation of resources."

Harper gritted her teeth and decoded Presley's doublespeak. Her father's role as chief of the medical staff was to represent the various medical departments in budget negotiations with the board, among other things. The same board who had sold the hospital to SunView. The board who no longer held the reins, financial or otherwise, effectively giving SunView control over everything, including the medical staff. The taste of betrayal was a bitter pill, and bile soured her throat. Were the board members so shortsighted they couldn't see what they had done?

"Just how many positions do you plan on eliminating?" Harper asked.

"Naturally, streamlining operations is one of our goals." Presley smiled. "Dr. Rivers, I'm sure you can appreciate that the hospital is a business as much as it is a humanitarian institution. If the business is not viable, the hospital cannot survive."

"I haven't heard anything about patients in all of this. This isn't Silicon Valley. We aren't a biotech company."

"Indeed," Presley said. "But you are in the business of caring for people."

"Medicine is a profession. We're not selling commodities here," Harper said flatly.

Presley disagreed, but she'd heard this argument before and knew better than to engage with traditionalists like Harper at this stage. Eventually, Harper and those like her would bow to the inevitability of the circumstances. What Harper didn't yet fully comprehend was that all the power now rested with SunView and, by extension, her. Hopefully, by the time Harper did realize it, the takeover would be far enough along that the internal momentum would quell any lingering resistance.

"I can assure you, my goal here is to position this institution in a way to best benefit the community and, of course, the shareholders," Presley said with as much patience as she could muster after a sleepless night in a hotel, a cramped tedious flight, and a long morning of being greeted with polite suspicion.

As she expected, a look of distaste crossed Harper's face at the mention of shareholders. Why was it that so many doctors found the business of medicine distasteful? It wasn't as if they weren't being paid for their services, but somehow, they resented being reminded of that fact. Harper Rivers certainly qualified as one of those, but her sensibilities were not of major concern at the moment. Establishing her authority was.

"I'd like a tour of the institution, if that could be arranged," Presley said to Edward.

"Of course," Edward said. "Harper will see that you're familiarized with the hospital."

Harper glanced at her watch and made no effort to hide her displeasure. "I have patients this afternoon."

"And I wouldn't want to delay you," Presley said. "What time would be convenient for you?"

A muscle jumping in her jaw, Harper said, "Tomorrow morning should be fine. Eight a.m.?"

"I'll look forward to it."

"I'll meet you in the lobby." Harper nodded curtly, turned, and left without another word.

Presley gathered her briefcase and bag. Harper Rivers could prove to be a problem. She might do better with the other Rivers on her side, and reconsidered Flannery's invitation to show her around town.

CHAPTER FIVE

Midafternoon, Flannery stopped by the recovery room to check her two post-op patients. Mike McCormick, the laparoscopic hernia repair she'd finished right before lunch, was awake and sitting up. A husky thirty-five-year-old redhead, he'd resisted her recommendation to have the progressively enlarging mass in his scrotum repaired until he'd shown up in her office the day before with pain so severe he could barely walk. Even then, he'd browbeaten her into promising he could go home after his procedure as long as he could tolerate the postoperative pain. She reminded him what it felt like to have a good swift kick in the gonads, and he reminded her he'd had plenty of hits below the belt as captain of the football team and all the other high school sports he'd excelled in. She'd only nodded and said they'd see about him going home after he woke up.

"How are you doing, Mike?"

"It feels like somebody twisted my nuts off."

She smiled and resisted the I-told-you-so comeback. "I promise, I didn't. In fact…" She pulled the curtain around his bed and then pulled the sheet down to his midthighs. The incisions she'd made had been small ones in his groin crease and lower abdomen through which she'd introduced the scope to repair the defects in the abdominal wall from the inside. All the same, she'd had to do a fair amount of pulling and tugging on some pretty sensitive tissues, and although rare, there was always the concern there might be some compromise to the blood supply. She pulled on gloves and gently palpated his groin. "Everything is fine. There's a lot of swelling, and you're going to feel like you've got a soccer ball between your legs for four or five days, but I don't see any problems right now. I suggest you stay overnight so we can give you—"

"I best be getting home," he said, his tone firm despite his pasty-white coloring and the beads of sweat pearling on his forehead.

Flannery set humor aside. If he didn't follow her instructions to restrict his physical exercise for ten days, he'd be right back in here with something worse going on. "Mike, look. You're going to be miserable if you go home this afternoon. There's nothing you can do around the farm anyhow."

"I can give orders, can't I?"

"Sure, if you're not throwing up from the pain or the pain pills. Marianne can give orders just as well as you can. Let her take care of things until you're back on your feet."

His jaw bunched. "It's not Marianne's job to run the farm."

Flannery resisted the urge to roll her eyes. If she hadn't grown up with half her patients or their relatives, she wouldn't understand how their minds worked. "Listen, take it from me. If you let her help you once in a while, she'll know she's important to you, and women like that sort of thing."

He narrowed his eyes at her. "Is that right."

She nodded. "You can take it to the bank."

"You probably know." He sighed, his frown more for show now than anything else. "I suppose I could tell her what needs to be done."

"You could, but you might ask her how things are going and I bet you'll find out she's got things covered." She pulled the sheet up, wrote an order to increase his dose of pain medication, and clapped him on the shoulder. "I'll be by early tomorrow morning and if things look good, you can go home. Get some sleep, don't get out of bed, and let your wife take care of things for a few hours."

"Thanks, Doc."

"Don't mention it."

Her last stop was Bryce Daniels, the teenager who'd had the hot appendix. His temp was still a couple of degrees above normal, but he was awake and joking with the nurses when she pulled the curtain aside and stepped up to his bed.

"Hungry?" she asked.

"Yeah, like I haven't eaten in a week."

"You'll be getting juice and Jell-O in a while."

His face fell. "I was kind of hoping the guys could bring me a pizza. I'm really hungry, Doc."

"I believe it, but if your stomach isn't settled enough after the anesthesia and you vomit, trust me, you're going to be one unhappy dude. Let's just see how the liquids go, and if everything looks good later on this afternoon, the nurses can try you on something a little more substantial."

"Okay, but I can go home tomorrow, right?"

"As long as your temp's down in the morning."

"How big is my scar going to be?"

She held her hands up ten inches apart and his eyes widened. She laughed. "About two and a half inches. But it'll still impress the girls, don't worry."

He grinned.

"Get some sleep."

In the surgical locker room, she changed into jeans, her favorite pair of scuffed brown boots, and a plain white shirt and tossed her used scrubs into the hamper on her way out. As she was leaving the hospital, she noticed Clyde Endee talking to Presley Worth in the visitors' lot. She diverted from her planned path to her Jeep and sauntered over to them. "Afternoon, Clyde. Ms. Worth."

"Hi, Flann. I was just dropping off a new car here for Ms. Worth."

Flannery took in the shiny Subaru hatchback. Presley worked fast, it appeared. "Door-to-door service. Nice."

"You know me, service is my middle name." Clyde chuckled.

Flannery said to Presley, "All done for the day?"

"All done here. I've got some work to do at home."

"Are you the type to play hooky?"

"Not usually." Presley glanced back at the hospital and had the feeling that a dozen pairs of eyes were trained on them. As she'd walked out of the hospital, more than one individual had paused to watch her go by. Word traveled fast in a place like this, and she wondered what story was being spun about her arrival. She was used to being the outsider, the stranger who appeared on the scene to disrupt everyone's routine and, in some cases, to threaten more than one person's job. Often the only people who welcomed her were those behind the scenes who financed the enterprise or benefited from the profits. They were rarely the ones who performed the day-to-day functions of the business. Not many employees, management or otherwise, were happy to see her, but she couldn't be concerned with being liked. What mattered to her was reconfiguring the newest acquisition to position it within the superstructure of SunView in order to maximize profitability.

It wasn't her job to make anyone happy, and whether she did or didn't had nothing to do with how happy she was with the job. Her happiness was spelled out on the bottom line at the end of the day. Neither did it bother her when she made people unhappy with her recommendations and decisions. She wasn't a corporate raider—more often than not, those in control of the institutions SunView acquired *wanted* to be absorbed, hoping for a quick profit and a lot of long-term benefits. Unfortunately, many of the employees stood to lose some or all of their livelihood. If she allowed herself to feel responsible for that, she wouldn't be able to do her job, and what would be the point? She was good at what she did, and the better she was at her job, the more powerful allies she would gain at SunView, and she would need plenty if she planned to be head of the company. This hospital, like so many others, was a brief stop along her way to the top, and when she finished here, it would be forgotten as quickly as all the others.

Ignoring Flannery, who seemed to be waiting for her to say more, she turned to Clyde. "Thank you for delivering the vehicle. If I have any questions or problems, I'll let you know."

"My number's on the card there."

Presley took the keys and a booklet with paperwork. She slid the papers into her shoulder bag. "That's great. Thanks."

"Where are you staying?" Flannery asked as Clyde headed back to his truck.

"At the White place, I'm told it's called."

"Oh yeah? Pretty out there."

"If you like cows, I suppose."

Flannery grinned. "I didn't have to guess you weren't a country girl."

"Oh? And what was your first clue?"

She glanced down at her shoes. "The Manolos."

"I think I'm impressed."

"Why? That a simple country surgeon—"

"Oh, please. Between you and your sister, I've had enough of the simple country doctor routine. No, I merely don't think you look like the kind of woman to be wearing heels or to recognize their designer."

"Well, you're right about the first part," Flannery said. "But I've been known to have female friends who wear heels, and I am observant."

"That I can believe." Presley walked around to the driver's side of the car. "And you're right, I'm not a country girl."

Flannery leaned on the top of the car and folded her arms. "So why here?"

"Like I said—I'm here because of a job."

"And there wasn't anyone else…where did you come from, anyhow?"

"Phoenix."

"So no one else in Phoenix wanted to spend a few months up here in the peace and quiet, taking the country air?"

"I'm sure there was more than one person who would've loved to come." Presley smiled. "But no one who is as good as I am."

Flannery liked confident women, especially sexy, smart, slightly hard-to-get confident women. "What exactly are you doing here?"

"I take it you haven't talked to your sister yet."

Flannery straightened. "Harper? What about her?"

"Nothing serious," Presley said, surprised by Flannery's instant protectiveness laced with suspicion. Seeing the two of them together earlier, she'd sensed they were competitive, but that wasn't what she was reading now. Flannery looked ready to do battle. Presley tried to remember the last time Preston had ever been protective of her, and decided that would've been exactly never. Even as children they were adversaries, competing for their parents' attention—when they were around—and jockeying for positions of favor with others. They'd never been friends, let alone allies.

"Her version of events may be slightly different than mine, but as I'm sure almost anyone in the hospital will be able to tell you within the next few hours, I'm here to spearhead the transition of the hospital into SunView Health Systems."

"Something tells me Harper wasn't happy to hear that."

"Your sister impresses me as someone who doesn't care for change."

"Harper cares about this community, and especially this hospital, more than she cares about anything except family. If the change is a good one, she'll be open to exploring it."

"Well, I'm delighted to hear that. What about you? Are you flexible as well?"

"I like to think so."

"Good. Then perhaps, if you are serious about showing me around, we can get together when you're free. I don't know much about the area and I'd like to."

"How about dinner tonight?"

Presley hesitated. Dinner was a little more personal than she wanted to get with Flannery Rivers. She had more than enough experience to recognize interest from another woman, and she didn't need the complication. "I've got a number of things to finish this evening. I'll have to take a rain check."

"Some other time, then."

"Yes."

"How about tomorrow afternoon, say three?"

"You can call me tomorrow in the medical staff office. I'll let you know."

Flannery stepped back as Presley slid into her car. "I'll do that."

❖

Harper pulled in behind her father's battered fifteen-year-old Ford Bronco and climbed up onto the back porch. Her father, still in his white shirt and dress trousers, sat in one of the trio of rocking chairs with a glass of iced tea in his hand. Behind him the door was open and the top twenty music countdown floated out through the screen from Margie's bedroom. Harper sat next to him and for a moment said nothing as they rocked in time, watching the sunset spill over the mountains.

"How long did you know this was coming?" Harper finally asked.

"There've been hints of something in the works since the end-of-year financials came out." Edward sipped his tea and continued to slowly rock, one foot flat on the wood porch, flexing and relaxing, propelling the chair back and forth. "Since I didn't get a vote, I wasn't kept up to date. I didn't expect them to move quite so quickly."

"And there's nothing to be done about it?"

"Once the ink is dry, the deal is done, I imagine."

"What do you think is coming?"

Edward looked at her solemnly. "I honestly don't know, Harper."

Harper clenched her jaw. Helplessness wasn't a feeling she welcomed or was used to. Headlights flashed, and Flann's Jeep pulled down the drive. A minute later, Flann dropped into the third chair.

"That roast beef I smell?" Flannery asked.

Their father glanced over at her. "It's Thursday, isn't it?"

Flannery grinned. "Roast beef or short ribs. Either one works for me."

"I have to run by the Rivers later," Harper said. "Do your post-ops need anything?"

Flannery shook her head. "They should both be fine. What do you have going?"

"I had to admit Charlie Carlyle. He's got a rip-roaring cellulitis in his foot and I want to make sure he's gotten his first dose of antibiotics tonight."

"Uh-oh," Flannery said. "I told you those toes were going to go."

"If we can get ahead of it, he'll keep his foot for a while longer," Harper said.

"Good. Let me know if you want me to look at it."

"I will."

"I ran into the lady of the hour this afternoon," Flannery said casually.

Harper tightened her grip on the arms of her chair. She wasn't sure what bothered her the most, that Flann and Presley had connected again or just the reminder of what Presley's presence here meant. "Oh?"

"Mmm-hmm. She mentioned she'd talked with you earlier and that she was in charge of the transition. Whatever that means."

Edward said, "That appears to be the question of the hour."

Flann's grin flickered out. "Is there some kind of problem already?"

Edward shrugged. "It's hard to say. From what little we know, it would appear that Ms. Worth can do just about anything she wants, and until we know what that is, we don't have any say at all."

"It's just not the right way to do things," Harper said. "This is our hospital, our patients who will be affected. If they'd let us know what was happening, we could have prepared for it. We could have apprised them of the community needs and shown them how vital the hospital is—not just for healthcare itself, but for jobs."

"We don't know that we won't have an opportunity to do that," her father said.

"Keeping us in the dark is just another form of showing us who's the boss," Harper said.

Flannery got up and poured herself an iced tea from the pitcher that sat on a table nearby. She poured a second glass and handed it to Harper. "I might be showing her around town tomorrow afternoon. Maybe I can work on her a little bit."

Harper carefully balanced the glass on the flat wooden arm of her rocking chair. "Showing her around? So she took you up on your offer to be a tour guide?"

"Seems so." Flannery grinned.

"You might be wise to remember she's not here on a friendly mission."

Flannery's eyes darkened. "You don't know that, Harp."

"And you don't know otherwise." Harper rose, pulled open the screen door, and headed for the sanctuary of the kitchen before she took another poke at Flann. She had no reason to be angry with Flann and didn't care to ask herself why she was.

CHAPTER SIX

By the time Harper helped her mother and Margie wash up and stow the dishes, it was close to nine. She folded the dish towel, laid it over the towel rack, and opened the cabinet for the broom.

"Go on out to the porch and have a drink with your father and Flannery," Ida said, taking the broom from her. "You've done enough cleaning for one night."

"I've got to head back to the hospital in a few minutes," Harper said. She'd carefully avoided talking about Presley Worth with Flann during dinner, but the subject was bound to come up again if they all started talking hospital business, which they surely would over drinks on the porch. She wasn't even sure what was bothering her about Flann showing Presley around town. Flann might have a tendency to rush into situations without much thought to the consequences, but somehow things usually ended up all right in the end, mostly because Flann was too good-natured to hold grudges and always knew when to step away before things got too complicated. The trouble was, everything about Presley spelled complicated, right from the beginning. She wore power easily and was clearly used to being in control. No matter how attractive and intriguing she might be, she was someone whose interests might not be in line with theirs. Harper drew up short. Attractive and intriguing? Maybe Flann wasn't the only one whose judgment was skewed.

"You and Flannery bashing heads over something?" Ida said.

"No," Harper said too quickly, earning a raised brow from Ida. Harper grinned. "We're good. Just different speeds, as usual."

"How are things at the hospital?"

"I'm not sure yet. The new manager has arrived—a woman named Presley Worth."

"What does she intend to manage?"

Harper braced her arms on the counter behind her and shook her head. "That's the question I'd like answered."

Ida patted her cheek. "You're smart. You'll figure it out."

"I hope I do before it's too late."

Flann rounded the corner and headed for the refrigerator. "Too late for what?"

"Me to have a drink." Harper pushed away from the counter and grabbed her jacket off the peg. "I'm headed to the Rivers."

"Get some sleep," Flann called after her.

Harper waved a hand and jumped into her Chevy pickup and five minutes later was headed up the hill to another place she thought of as home. The Rivers stood like a guardian above the town, its windows glowing golden against the night sky. The reception desk was empty, and only the echo of her footsteps kept her company as she walked through the deserted halls. She nodded to the night nurse on four as she checked on Charlie first. He was snoring softly, his ailing foot propped on a pillow. She flashed her penlight on the chart hanging at the foot of the bed. His temp was still elevated but hadn't spiked. Good enough. She left quietly and took the stairs down to the surgical floor. Glenn Archer, a PA who often assisted Flann in the OR and covered the surgical floor at night, was at the desk.

"How's it going?" Harper asked. She and Glenn, a rangy blue-eyed, sandy-haired ex-high school basketball star, had been in the same graduating class, but Glenn had opted for the Army right out of high school. After her enlistment was over, she'd come back to the village to live, having been trained as a medic.

"All quiet. Flann's two are doing fine." Glenn pushed out a rolling chair and Harper sat. "I hear we're due for a shake-up."

Harper rubbed her face. "Seems like it."

"Any details?"

"Not yet."

Glenn scanned the telemetry monitors as she spoke. "Doesn't feel right, somehow. Who are these folks?"

"Not sure yet." She pictured Presley and a myriad of impressions flashed into her mind. Presley's face—elegant, composed, remote; a quick flash of sharp wit when jousting with Flann; a hard glint of steel when discussing business. Attractive and intriguing. Harper sighed. "We'll know soon, I think."

She talked with Glenn a few more moments. Everyone was resting comfortably. No one needed her attention. Finally she gave in and went home. At eleven, she was still restless and wide-awake. Too many things running through her head—change was on the horizon, and change almost always meant losing something. She sat in the rocker on her front porch trying to pick out the constellations in the clear, star-filled night sky. She'd never been very good at it. Kate had been the one to see shapes in the clouds and stars. Harper usually had to be content with finding the Big Dipper and the North Star. There were so many stars up there, scattered it seemed in random, endless patterns, dwarfing the world below. Tonight, though, a face kept forming as her lids lowered and her vision drifted. Presley Worth. Who was she?

The question wouldn't give her peace. Eventually, she retrieved her laptop and settled back on the porch to search for answers.

❖

Presley woke to unnatural quiet, a faint breeze cooling the bare skin of her shoulders. Sunlight slanted through the open window across from her bed. Absent were the rumble of traffic, the humming of mechanicals within the walls and beneath the floors, the distant wail of sirens, the shouts of trash collectors and all-night revelers. Life in the city was all about noise. Now she was surrounded by silence. Not absolute, she realized as she lay thinking about the day to come. The wind made its own humming tune. Birds trilled and chirped and cooed. Beyond that, though, the world was terrifyingly still. Ordinarily when she woke, her first sensation was of energy charging through her—the challenge of a new day, the opportunity to test herself—a fire in her blood. The calm peacefulness of this morning felt as unnatural as if she had suddenly been required to breathe underwater. She was out of sync with this place. Off balance and feeling more alone than she had in a long time.

She'd always been solitary, despite being a twin. She and Preston were not like those stories of twins Hollywood liked to make movies about. They had never been close. Their parents, internationally renowned financiers, had barely enough time in their busy schedule for one child, let alone two at once, and the needs of their offspring had been left to a series of nannies and tutors. Presley had quickly learned that the only way to gain a little bit of notice was to excel at the things her parents valued—academics, athletics, business—all while traveling in the proper social circles. Her greatest competitor for their attention was Preston. Now that her father was divesting himself of the responsibility of the day-to-day running of the corporation, she was in the biggest battle of her life. Sometimes it seemed she had been fighting forever for something just out of reach.

She threw back the covers and swung her legs to the floor. Self-analysis was a waste of time. She was in charge of her life, her future. What mattered was what she did. Actions produced results, and results were all that counted at the end of the day. With a wave of anticipation, she reminded herself that at the end of this day, Carrie would be here, they'd have the beginnings of their team in place, and she could get started on wrapping up this assignment. Preston was very wrong if he thought he could bury her somewhere while he moved a step closer to taking their father's seat at the table.

She took a quick shower and, since she wasn't due to meet Harper Rivers until eight and it was barely five thirty, pulled on loose workout pants and a T-shirt and shuffled down to the kitchen. Lila had left the coffeepot plugged in ready to go and, according to the thoughtful note next to the coffeemaker, all she had to do was push the button. Even more thoughtful was the small wicker basket with three fat blueberry corn muffins nestled under a hand-embroidered cotton napkin in the middle of the table. She chose a golden muffin and put it on a ceramic saucer she found in the glass-fronted cabinet above the sink. Within a matter of minutes she had a cup of coffee and the muffin and, after grabbing her iPad, was headed out to the back porch to have breakfast in the astonishingly cool morning air. Sitting down on the top step, she balanced her iPad on her knees, sipped her coffee, and absently broke off pieces of the muffin and popped them into her mouth as she scanned the morning news.

After a few minutes, she felt the prickly sensation on the back of her neck she often got when someone was watching her. She checked the time on her tablet—Lila was due soon but she hadn't heard a car drive in. Who in the world would be walking around out here at this time of day? Slowly, she searched the expanse of the backyard down to where the drive curved around to the barn and saw no one. Of course she saw no one. There was no one there. She went back to reading and then she heard it. An ear-splitting screech that ended abruptly on a choking rattle. Gripping her tablet, she raised her eyes, prepared to jump up and run for the house.

It was standing about ten feet in front of her, one foot held up in the air, its head cocked to the left, blinking slowly. Its tail feathers were ragged but brilliantly colored: red and blue and golden brown. Its wings looked just as scruffy as its tail, with a few short feathers poking out at odd angles and looking as if they were about to fall out. It made another sound, a crowing croak, and bobbed its head.

"Go away." Presley waved a hand. "Shoo."

It put its foot down gingerly and hobbled a step closer.

"No, not this way." She pointed in the general direction of the driveway. "Go that way. Go back to…wherever." It hop-walked several more steps closer.

She drew her legs up onto the stair below where she sat. She didn't think chickens—or whatever it was, exactly—attacked people, but she wasn't leaving her bare feet exposed as an enticement. "No, no, no. Go back wherever you came from."

"Could be that's one of old Mrs. White's brood," Lila said from inside the kitchen door. "I bet they couldn't catch him, and they just left him behind."

"Well, he needs to go back to wherever he's been staying. He's getting poop all over the lawn."

Lila chuckled. "Good fertilizer."

"Not when it's on the bottom of my shoe."

"Hmm. Looks like he's got a bum leg. If you want, I'll have one of my sons come out and take care of him for you."

"Good," Presley said, returning to the news. The crowing resumed, the short caws rising at the end as if he was asking a question. She ignored it and he stopped. After another minute or two of silence, she peeked up. He was three feet in front of her, studying her with a disconcerting stare.

"You're not very smart, are you?"

"Caw?"

"Lila? What is this thing?"

"A rooster, last time I looked."

"What's it good for?"

"Not much, not without the hens. Roosters are handy for protecting the chickens—keeping the predators away. And of course, if you want baby chicks—"

"God forbid."

"Well then, he doesn't really have much to do now."

Presley hesitated. "What do you mean, your son will take care of him?"

"He's lame. Probably no one's been feeding him, and he doesn't have a flock to look after. He doesn't look too old to make a decent stew, though."

"Oh." Presley looked back down at the news and couldn't find her place. Out of the corner of her eye she saw the rooster peck at the bare ground as if searching for some morsel. She broke off a corner of her muffin and tossed it toward him. His head bobbed as he studied it.

"Go ahead. It's better than the dirt you've been picking up."

The feathers on his neck gleamed in the sunlight, flashes of iridescent purple and blue as subtle as jewels. The sounds he made changed, the pitch rising as he pecked apart the small bit of corn muffin with obvious enthusiasm.

"Lila."

Lila peered out the screen door again. "Yes?"

"Don't bother your sons with him. He'll probably just go on back to wherever he came from."

"All right, if you're sure."

She wasn't. "I'm sure."

She went back to the news with the soft clucks of the busy rooster keeping her company. When she rose to get ready for work, he was still scratching about in the yard. "Lila," she called as she walked inside, "what do these things like to eat?"

CHAPTER SEVEN

Harper parked in the staff lot behind the hospital and let herself in through the employee entrance with her ID card. She hadn't slept much and had decided to start rounds early. At six thirty, a half hour before shift change, the halls were still quiet. She'd always loved the hospital at night, when a hushed stillness fell over the dimly lit halls, a serene quiet that seemed to promise hope for those who saw the new day and peace for those who did not.

Walking to the stairwell, she ran the list of patients in her head. Plenty of time to see them all before meeting Presley. She'd learned a few things about Presley Worth the night before. At least what Presley Worth chose to show the world. Thirty years old, only daughter of Yolanda and Martin Worth, twin of Preston. MBA from Wharton at twenty-three. VP of Operations at SunView at twenty-six. Brother Preston's title was loftier—Chief Financial Officer—but organizationally apparently equivalent to Presley's. Twins, still. Father was CEO, mother COO. High-powered, influential family. Presley had never married, supported humanitarian causes, and appeared to have no personal life beyond attending the obligatory charitable and business functions. What she did have was a record of successfully spearheading much of the expansion of SunView Health Systems from a regional Southwest healthcare network into a transcontinental consortium of hospitals, short- and long-term-care facilities, and allied enterprises. Harper hadn't been able to find out much more than that, but she wasn't done digging yet. If SunView was to be her new employer, she wanted to know who—or, more accurately, what—it was all about.

On impulse, she bypassed the stairs and turned down the east corridor toward admin, wondering if her father might be in the staff office catching up on paperwork as he often did early in the morning.

His door was partly open and the light on, and she started in, expecting to hear his voice as he dictated reports or discharge summaries. She drew up short, remembering too late the office wasn't his any longer.

"If you're sure you can find it, call me when you get settled," Presley said. "I'll show you around and get you started on the staff assessments...About what you might expect. An abundance of dinosaurs."

Harper halted, unable not to hear the conversation.

Presley laughed. "Around here, putting out to pasture is more than a metaphor...See you soon."

Harper knocked on the door, refusing to skulk away as if she'd intentionally been eavesdropping. She wasn't surprised by Presley's view of the Rivers as provincial and old-fashioned, considering the circles she usually moved in, but the snap judgment irked all the same. Traditional didn't mean outdated.

"Come in," Presley called.

Harper pushed the door wide and Presley rose behind her desk. She glanced at her watch when she saw Harper.

"I'm sorry, am I late? I thought you said—"

"No, I just happened to be here."

Presley wore another understatedly elegant suit, a pale green shirt over rich chocolate trousers. The jacket hung over the back of what had been Harper's father's chair. Her golden-blond hair was held back with a paler gold tie. She looked crisp and efficient and commanding. She should have looked out of place, but somehow she didn't. She wore authority well, and that confidence was compelling. Harper slid her hands into the pockets of her slightly rumpled khakis. Presley was studying her in turn. Her gaze, acute and unapologetic, traveled over Harper's face. Harper wondered what she was looking for, and what she saw.

"Do you do this often?" Harper asked.

Presley leaned forward, her fingertips resting on the surface of the desk, her gaze holding Harper's. "What, exactly?"

"Take over hospitals?"

"We acquire new facilities several times a year," Presley said.

"And then what do you do with them?"

"I plan to provide a prospectus of SunView's activities that I think will give you a better understanding of who we are." She frowned slightly. "I'm afraid the lines of communication haven't been handled as well as they should have been regarding this acquisition. I wasn't in charge of the initial negotiations. So I apologize for the lack of information. I plan to rectify that as soon as possible."

"If you weren't in charge, who was?"

"Another department," Presley said coolly.

"So why apologize?"

"Because I'm here now, and I am in charge."

Harper appreciated Presley's refusal to pass the buck, whether out of loyalty or sense of responsibility. Both counted in her book. "I understand. It's sort of like here."

"I'm sorry?"

Harper grinned wryly. "The board kept this quiet until the deal was done."

"I can assure you, Dr. Rivers—"

"Harper."

Presley nodded. "Harper. None of this was undertaken with the intention of secrecy. SunView dealt with those who controlled the financial—"

"So I was told. But there's more to us than facts and figures, you know."

"I know," Presley said.

"Do you?"

"I will."

Harper knew the heart of the Rivers wasn't going to be found in the ledgers and balance sheets, and she wanted this woman, this stranger who seemed to hold the fate of a big part of the community in her hands, to know that too. "Let's postpone the tour. Make rounds with me this morning instead. Get a look at what the hospital is really like out from behind that desk."

Presley's first instinct was to refuse. She had just started delving into the financials and had the entire day planned out. Carrie was on her way to the house from the airport and ought to be at the hospital by midmorning. She didn't really have time for anything other than a quick survey of the physical layout. And what could she possibly learn from trailing after Harper while she visited patients?

"Don't you think the patients would find that an intrusion?"

"If there's anything sensitive, we'll ask their permission. But I doubt it."

"I really don't have—"

"How can you run a healthcare system and not know what it is that we really do?"

Presley stifled her irritation. The question just underscored how little she and Harper had in common. One didn't need to know how an airplane engine worked to run Boeing, or understand nanomaterials to manage IBM. That was what the technical departments were for. "Running a hospital profitably occurs on a different plane than dispensing care. I wouldn't be surprised if you were happy accepting chickens in payment for your services, but most of us have moved beyond that now."

"Right. Because I'm one of the dinosaurs."

"Ah." Presley glanced at the open door. No one had been around when she'd arrived before dawn, and she'd been careless. She wouldn't let that happen again. There was no point apologizing, not that she was inclined to. Her assessment of the staff, no matter how flip, was also accurate. The physicians with admitting privileges were an aging group with the exception of a handful like Harper and Flannery. Most were well beyond retirement age and, she was willing to bet when she looked at their statistics, probably had a preponderance of elderly patients with few resources who overstayed the recommended average, putting a strain on the hospital's resources and lowering the reimbursement quotient.

"I wasn't actually thinking of you with that remark."

Harper shrugged. "I have been known to take a dozen eggs now and then."

Presley laughed. "I completely believe that."

"You can be pretty sure I mean what I say."

"I suspect that's a family trait."

"Among others."

Presley put her laptop to sleep. Transitions always went more smoothly when the hospital's power brokers were cooperative. Harper Rivers—the whole Rivers family—was enmeshed with the hospital and the community. Antagonizing any of them was not prudent. If spending an hour tagging along with Harper would help, she'd make room in her schedule.

She slipped into her jacket and slid her cell phone into her pocket. "All right, Dr. Rivers. Educate me."

❖

Harper hadn't expected Presley to agree. She'd seen the indecision in her eyes and could almost read the dismissal in her mind. Hiding her surprise when Presley joined her, she led the way back to the main hospital building, pointing out the administrative offices as they passed.

"The head of admissions is over here," Harper said, pointing to the door to her sister's office. "Carson should be in around eight. She can tell you just about anything you need to know about hospital visits, admission stats, placement, that sort of thing. She deals with social services pretty regularly as well."

"That would be"—Presley scanned her mental files—"Carson Rivers."

"That's right."

"Let me guess." Presley paused. "Sister?"

"Third oldest, right."

"Wait a minute." Presley smiled, warmth softening the usually cool planes of her face. "Harper, Flannery, Carson. Who in the family is the Southern-author fan?"

"They're some of my mother's favorites," Harper said. "She and my father met when he was doing his residency in Charlotte. She said if she had to move north into Yankee territory, her children would be reminded of their Southern roots."

"Harper," Presley turned the word over musingly. "It's Harper Lee, isn't it? Harper Lee Rivers?"

Harper nodded.

"Flannery O'Connor Rivers?"

Harper grinned. "That's right."

"Carson McCullers Rivers?"

"Right again."

Presley laughed, and her laughter transformed her. She was still elegant, but softer, more approachable, the light dancing in her blue eyes hinting at hidden humor. "Tell me, is there a Kate Chopin Rivers too?"

The punch to the heart was no less powerful for being familiar. Harper kept her smile in place. "Kate was the fourth."

Presley's laughter disappeared and gentle sympathy filled her gaze. "I'm sorry."

"Yeah. Me too."

"Are there others?"

"Margaret Mitchell, the youngest. Margie is fifteen."

"No boys?"

"I guess my mother wasn't as fond of the Southern male authors."

"Hmm. Is Margie bound for medicine too?"

Harper laughed. "She swears she's forgoing medicine for professional soccer."

"Breaking the family mold."

"We'll see. I went through a period when I was planning on being an organic farmer."

"You, a farmer?" Presley shook her head. "I can't see it."

"I grew up on a farm, although I didn't do a whole lot of hands-on farming. I was too busy following my dad around. But we've got some cows, chickens, a few pigs, and plenty of fertile pastureland. One of our neighbors farms that for us."

"Never thought about leaving?"

"I left for medical school and residency." Harper pushed open the stairwell door and held it for Presley. "And I was ready to come back. Not enough time to think. Too much noise."

"Noise?"

"In the city. Always something moving, always something changing. Always something making noise."

"Most people think of that as progress. And exciting."

"I don't see why progress has to be noisy." Harper opened another door. "This is the fifth floor—the top floor. A mixed population of med-surg patients who no longer require acute nursing supervision. Most of the patients up here will be ready for discharge in a few days."

"How many beds?"

"Eight rooms a side, two beds each on this floor. We're about half-full up here right now."

While Harper went to the supply room to get what she needed for rounds, Presley looked over the physical facilities, taking note of the number of nurses, aides, clerks, and other personnel. The staffing seemed adequate, but not excessive. The hospital was obviously old, but in good repair. The walls were freshly painted a neutral eggshell, the floors practical industrial tiles in a complementary tan. When she glanced into one of the patient rooms, she saw two large windows overlooking a grassy lawn. Pleasant. Peaceful.

Harper guided her down the hall. "The patient we're about to see is ready to go home. Euella Andrews. She had a stroke about a year ago and has been managing at home with her daughter's help. Unfortunately, she fell several weeks ago and suffered a hairline fracture to her femur. Flann decided not to operate and put her in traction. She started—"

"Your sister's a general surgeon, isn't she?"

"That's right, with a trauma certification. She's qualified to handle straightforward orthopedic problems, and the consulting orthopedists are just as happy for her to do it. Saves them getting out of bed at night to put on casts or review X-rays."

"What happens if you have a complicated orthopedic problem—open fractures, joint replacements, that sort of thing?"

"Then we'll refer or transfer."

"Orthopedic procedures reimburse well, but the rehab can be costly," Presley said. "Not a bad compromise."

"Our thinking was it made sense to treat what we could—keeps the patients closer to home and our staff busy."

"There, you see? We can find common ground."

"Good to know."

From there, they worked their way down through the wards, checking patients, ordering tests, charting progress. The patients greeted Harper as if Harper held the key to all the mysteries of life. She was relaxed and conversant with the patients, good-naturedly answering their questions and reviewing the treatment plan when they were ready to go home, chiding some of them to follow instructions. She introduced Presley as one of the hospital managers, and that seemed to be all that was necessary for her to be accepted. If the same thing had happened in Phoenix, the risk management team would probably have had people sign consent forms before they even let her into a room. Here, all it took was Harper's introduction. She could see how that kind of freedom would appeal, especially to someone like Harper for whom the hospital was like a second home. Unfortunately, the days of medical fiefdoms were long over. Everyone from the state to the insurance companies wanted a say, and part of her job was seeing that the hospital and everyone in it stayed on the right side of the line. Breaches in regulations were costly.

As Harper was finishing a note, the phone rang at the nurses' station. A male clerk who looked all of fifteen answered, listened, and held the phone out to Harper. "Page operator for you, Harp."

"How do they know where you are?" Presley asked.

Harper laughed. "They always know." She took the phone. "Harper. Okay, tell them I'll be down in fifteen." She passed the phone back, racked the chart, and motioned to Presley. "ER consult. Let's grab a cup of coffee on the way."

Presley snuck a peek at her watch, surprised to see how much time had passed. Usually when she was forced into social situations, she was bored senseless before the hors d'oeuvres were finished. This had been unexpectedly engaging. Harper was warm and compassionate while being thoroughly professional and effortlessly in command. The patients obviously loved her. "I suppose I can spare a few more minutes. Coffee sounds delightful. I'm buying."

"You're on."

They took the stairs to the first floor, since Harper apparently did not believe in using the elevators. After pouring a large cup of dark coffee from a stainless steel urn, Presley grabbed a doughnut on the way to the checkout counter. Harper introduced her to Luanne, the cashier, who gave her a long inquiring stare. Luanne looked to be in her early twenties, full-bodied, with bottle-blond hair and sharp, appraising eyes. She turned slightly, a subtle redirection of her attention to Harper.

"Haven't seen you out to Elmer's the Hilltop lately, Harper."

"Been pretty busy."

"A little relaxing will do you good, don't forget."

Harper took Presley's change and picked up their tray. "I'll keep that in mind."

Presley slid into a seat at the dining table next to Harper and reached for her powdered-sugar doughnut. "I imagine you know everyone here."

Harper sipped her coffee. "Pretty much. One way or the other."

"Ah, yes."

Harper laughed. "Not that way."

"I can see where that might be problematic. Hospitals aren't known for privacy."

"That might be the first understatement you've made."

"Still, I imagine after a while no one has any secrets." The idea disturbed her. She much preferred the seclusion of her offices, where she knew what to expect and could decide how much to reveal.

"You might be surprised by the place."

"You might be right." Already, Presley's normal routine had been upended. After all, she was sitting in the cafeteria in the middle of the morning with a woman she had nothing in common with, enjoying herself.

CHAPTER EIGHT

S o tell me," Harper said, leaning back in her chair at the cafeteria table, "what do you need to know from the medical staff?"

Presley hesitated. She rarely interfaced personally with the staff at institutions SunView acquired, her decisions being several levels removed from the employees. Somehow she'd already broken her pattern at ACH and wanted to extricate herself diplomatically. She would far prefer the occasional smile from Harper than the barely disguised suspicion. "Well, I've just started and—"

Dr. Rivers, STAT, ER. Harper Rivers, STAT, ER.

"Come on." Harper shoved her chair back and took off at a jog.

Presley automatically followed, whispering a silent thanks she'd worn low heels she could actually manage to run in that morning. Dimly aware of people hurriedly stepping aside, she focused on Harper as they sprinted through doorways, down hallways crowded with staff and patients, and around corners. Finally she recognized the entrance to the emergency room. Harper slapped an oversized red button on the wall and the big metal doors swung inward. Harper, steadying the stethoscope draped around her neck down against her chest with one hand, raced through without breaking stride. Presley ducked in as the doors closed, vowing to take up jogging as she struggled to catch her breath.

"What have you got?" Harper called to no one in particular.

A woman wearing a Snoopy smock pushed aside a curtain and leaned out into the hall. "Down here."

Presley stopped at the edge of the curtain as Harper hurried into the cubicle, taking in the eight-by-eight space in one quick glance. Her stomach plummeted. She didn't belong here in this harshly lit place where the air crackled with foreign energy and fear. She belonged in the quiet, orderly realm of benchmarks, options, and margins. She didn't look away, having agreed to see Harper's world.

A toddler, naked except for plastic training pants covered with multicolored polka dots, lay in the middle of a stretcher far too large for the tiny form, surrounded by towering adults who dwarfed the small body even more. Only the face was visible, haloed by blond ringlets, the features covered by a breathing mask that a grim-faced woman of fifty inflated with rhythmic squeezes to a gray football-shaped bag filled with air. A young woman, not more than twenty, stood staring with terrified eyes behind the people gathered around the stretcher, arms wrapped around her midsection, a keening sound rising from her throat.

Presley tugged her lower lip between her teeth. Leaving was akin to surrender, and she would not do that while the struggle continued.

The woman wearing the Snoopy smock, her name tag indicating she was Rose Aello, RN, said, "She came in with a URI. Her O2 sat was a little low. That's why we called you. Then she just stopped breathing."

The older woman squeezing the bag, Paula Jones by her ID badge, said, "I'm getting a lot of resistance. We're not aerating very well."

Harper pushed her way to the head of the stretcher and Paula made room for her. After a quick listen to both sides of the child's chest, Harper slid both hands under the child's shoulders and pulled her upward until her head was at the very edge of the stretcher. "Where's the laryngoscope?"

"Here." Rose handed Harper an impossibly large-looking instrument with a fat silver handle and a curved extension with a light at the end. Somehow Harper got that enormous thing into the toddler's mouth and peered inside. "I'm going to need a tube. Let's try a number four pedi."

Rose rummaged in the cabinet and pulled out an assortment of long plastic tubes, individually wrapped in clear cellophane. She tore one package open and pulled out a tube. "Ready."

Everything was probably happening quickly, but to Presley time seemed to stand still. *Breathe, breathe, breathe* kept running through her mind, eclipsing all else.

Someone pushed in beside her and Presley glanced away from the bed. Flannery Rivers, in scrubs, a paper mask hanging around her neck, her sandy hair tousled.

"You need me, Harper?" Flannery said in a strong, steady voice.

"Not yet." Harper didn't look up. She held out her hand and Rose handed her the tube.

"Thanks," Harper muttered.

"Paula, honey," Flannery said casually, "want to get a cut-down tray in here, just in case?"

"Got one right over here," Paula replied.

"Good enough." Flannery leaned back against the wall and crossed her arms, looking as relaxed as if she was waiting for a bus. Presley caught her eye and Flannery winked.

Presley understood then that Flannery had total confidence in Harper and was content, despite her obvious instinct to take charge, to wait until Harper needed her. What an interesting and foreign dynamic that was. To trust and be trusted so completely. Presley turned back to Harper, a disconcerting ache in her chest.

"Flann," Harper said, peering into the child's throat, "can you give me some cricoid pressure? I can't see around the epiglottis it's so swollen."

"Sure thing." Flannery pushed away from the wall and pinched her thumb and forefinger in the center of the baby's throat. "That help?"

"Better," Harper said, her focus absolute.

The frightened young woman—the baby's mother, Presley assumed—started to sway, all the color drained from her face. "Oh my God." Her voice echoed with hollow horror.

"Here," Presley said, sliding an arm around the young woman's waist. "There's a chair right behind you. Sit down and let the doctors and nurses work. Everything will be all right." The words came so automatically she couldn't take them back and hoped she hadn't lied. And yet, watching Harper and Flannery, she couldn't believe anything else.

Alarms rang, jagged green lines jumped across a monitor on a high shelf above the bed, and the child lay so still. Never had stillness been so terrifying.

"I think I'm in." Harper hooked a line connected to an oxygen tank up to the tube she'd inserted in the child's throat. "Somebody listen."

Flannery tugged the stethoscope from around Harper's neck and placed the end on the toddler's chest, the instrument looking far too large against the miniature rib cage. She moved it quickly over both sides of the tiny torso. "Sounds good."

"Color's coming back," Rose said.

Flannery glanced up the monitor. "O2 looks good too. Nice job."

Harper looked up at her sister and flashed a quick grin. "Thanks. Appreciate the backup."

"No problem. Need anything else?"

"We've got it."

Flann nodded and stepped over to Presley. "I see you're getting a firsthand, up-close-and-personal introduction to the place."

"Yes." Presley took a deep breath. The room jumped into stark relief, as if a curtain had been swept aside. Harper's hands moved with quick certainty as she secured the tube to the child's cheek with strips of tape. Her fingers were long and tapered, elegant as an artist's at work. "A bit more dramatic than I'd expected."

"Harper has always been the showy one," Flannery murmured.

Presley laughed softly at the obvious lie. "I noticed."

"I'm still free later."

"I'll have to see how my schedule is running." Presley wasn't certain she could take any more of the Rivers clan in one day. There was something so raw about them, as if they'd somehow escaped the veneer of civilization that created an invisible shield around everyone else she knew. Their intensity scraped against her nerve endings and stirred feelings both uncomfortable and intriguing.

"I'll look forward to hearing from you when you're free."

Flannery disappeared and Presley knelt by the young mother. "Everything is going very well. Do you need anything?"

The young woman, a girl really, turned eyes dilated and nearly blank with shock to Presley. "She was fine last night. Just a little runny nose. Then this morning she had a cough, and I didn't like the way it sounded. All raspy, like. My husband said I should bring her in. Maybe I waited too long."

Presley searched for the right words. God, this was awful.

Harper squatted down and took the mother's hand. Her shoulder touched Presley's and for an instant, Presley absorbed the hard strength of her. The unexpected comfort shocked her into pulling away.

"You didn't wait too long," Harper said. "She developed swelling at the back of her tongue, and it blocked her airway. Kids get this sometimes and it happens really quickly. You brought her in and that's what matters."

The mother clenched Harper's hand so hard her knuckles turned white. "She's going to be all right?"

"We're going to put her in the intensive care unit and watch her really closely. She'll be getting antibiotics. You should go to the cafeteria and have something to eat. One of the nurses will come down and find you when it's time to see her."

"You're sure?"

"I'm sure."

Rose came over and took her by the arm. "Come on, sweetie, I'll walk you down."

Presley waited at the nurse's station while Harper wrote notes and orders and called the intensive care unit to tell them about the little girl. Finally, Harper pushed back her chair and stretched her shoulders. She seemed completely calm, as if she hadn't just saved a child's life. Her disheveled hair was the only sign she'd just been in the middle of an emergency, and on anyone else the look would probably have been a studied effect. On Harper the result was rakishly appealing.

"What was that?" Presley asked, squelching the flicker of unsettling allure.

"Acute epiglottitis—it's uncommon, but not really rare. Kids decompensate really quickly. If she hadn't been here when the episode started…" She raised her shoulder.

Presley got the message. Harper was conditioned by generations of tradition to believe the hospital was essential to dispensing care, but in twenty-first century America, there were other more cost-effective models. "What about urgent care centers? According to our geographic searches, there are quite a few within reasonable driving distance."

A muscle in Harper's jaw jumped. "Urgent care centers have their place. They're great for routine problems, but they're not designed for emergency care. They transfer out anything of a serious nature. And this?" She shook her head. "I had trouble getting that tube in."

"And if you hadn't been able to? Couldn't she have been transported to a medical center with pediatric intensivists?"

"Not safely. Flann would've had to do an emergency tracheostomy. In the emergency room, on a child? Not many people could do it."

"I see," Presley said. "And what if you and your sister hadn't been immediately available? I'm guessing no one else here could have done what you did."

"We're always available."

"Unusual, and admirable. All the same, let's say the mother hadn't had the option of coming here. Then she would have driven to a tertiary care center to begin with."

"Why would I want to assume that?"

"Just hypothesizing, Dr. Rivers," Presley said carefully. "We consider such things when determining risk management, for one thing."

Harper rose, her expression shuttered. "Peggy. That's the little girl's name. Peggy Giles is going to be fine. Her mother brought her to the right place."

"Of course." Presley couldn't argue, at least not now. She'd seen the truth of Harper's statement. "You—all of you—were impressive."

Harper's gaze captured hers. "Will you take the time to know who we are? What we do?"

"That's why I'm here."

"Is it?"

Presley searched for a truthful answer. "We work on different sides of the same street, Harper."

"Then walk on mine awhile. A month—spend a month with me in my practice."

Presley laughed. "I can't do that—I've got a schedule to keep. I…" *I need to wrap this up before Preston shuts me out.*

"Afraid to see the faces of the people behind the numbers?"

"That's not fair," Presley shot back. "You don't know me or what I do."

Harper raked a hand through her hair, her jaw clenching. "You're right. So educate me."

"Fine. I will."

Harper grinned and Presley glowered. What had she just agreed to?

❖

Presley left the ER and, halfway back to her office, abruptly changed her mind. She followed the exit signs to the side entrance and walked around to where she'd parked her car. She had too much nervous energy to sit behind her desk. The restlessness was a totally alien sensation. Work was her touchstone, her office the place she escaped to when the emotional ups and downs of dealing with her parents and the mental stress of jousting with Preston wore her down. But right now, her body refused to settle, and she climbed into her car and drove down the winding road away from the hospital with the windows open and the wind whipping through her hair. The image of Peggy Giles, so limp and lifeless, and the primal keening of her mother pursued her.

She pulled into the long dirt drive leading to the Whites' and sat gripping the steering wheel, the faint mechanical ticking of the cooling engine loud in her ears. She hadn't really let Harper goad her into wasting hours trailing after her, had she? She'd have to find a plausible excuse to withdraw. The more time she spent with Harper, the more she'd have to defend a position Harper could never appreciate or accept. Harper was an idealist, the worst kind of person to involve in business decisions. God. She needed to draw a firm line in the sand before a simple job got out of hand.

When she finally looked up and saw the rental car parked by the barn, she almost cheered. A little bit of normality at last. Carrie was here, solid, reliable, dependable Carrie, who understood the way she thought and didn't take issue with her simply for being realistic. She hurried up the walk into the house. "Carrie?"

"Out here," Carrie's lilting voice announced.

Presley left her briefcase by the stairs and strode to the kitchen. The room was empty, a covered plate of what she hoped were more of Lila's muffins on the table, and the screen door open. Outside, Carrie leaned against the back-porch post. "Hi! You found the place, I see."

Carrie turned, her deep green eyes shining. Wisps of her shoulder-length red hair clung to her milky cheeks. "This place is amazing."

"That's certainly one word for it." Presley scanned the yard. It was empty except for patches of deep yellow daffodils that seemed to have cropped up in the last few hours. The temperature had climbed but was still absurdly cool for June.

"Really! Everything is so green. And trees everywhere. It smells wonderful."

Presley studied Carrie suspiciously. What could she say to that? Everything *was* amazingly green and golden and brilliant blue and ridiculously idyllic. And clearly, Carrie had already breathed too much of the intoxicating air. Hoping to bring her back to earth, she asked, "Have you been upstairs? Either one of the open rooms is yours."

"I have. I took the one looking out the front. It's an awesome view. Have you been exploring?"

"Ah, I haven't actually walked around the place yet, but it seems like all the necessities are here."

"What's the hospital like?"

"About what you'd expect—better maintained than most places that aren't even half as old, with a fairly steady census."

Carrie pursed her lips. "I got the feeling Preston saw this as a quick turnover, maybe transitioning to long-term care or some kind of outpatient imaging center. Depending on the reimbursement profiles."

That was SOP for small outlying places like this, but simply hearing that it had been part of Preston's plan made Presley resistant. She doubted he'd done more than look at the financials for the last several years. He wouldn't have had the patience to do a geographic or demographic analysis of the area. "Yes, well, we'll know more when we've had a breakdown of resources and usage."

"Yes, we ought to be sure we head in the right direction." Carrie rose. "What about the staff? Any issues?"

Presley immediately thought of Harper. She could handle Harper—she just needed to remain firmly in charge and remember why she'd come. "Not so far."

"Good. I'm ready to dig in, then."

"Are you sure?" Presley wanted to return to the hospital, but strangely, her first thought wasn't of work. She wondered if she might run into Harper again. She quickly pushed the thought aside.

"Totally. Can you give me fifteen to take a quick shower?"

"Don't hurry."

After Carrie disappeared inside, Presley sat on the stairs to wait. While she checked her mail, she half expected the rooster to appear to annoy her. After a few minutes he was a no-show. Maybe he slept in the barn during the day. She supposed she could go check while she waited.

The big barn door slid back surprisingly easily as she pushed it to one side. The interior was huge, with a row of empty stalls along one side under a loft still piled high with bales of hay. Light filtered through the metal-mesh-covered windows in the stalls and slanted through the cracks in the board walls. The hot, steamy air smelled sweet.

"Rooster?" Presley walked down the wide aisle and caught a flicker of motion out of the corner of her eye. Her pulse jumped. Empty barns didn't have rats, did they? "Rooster?"

The answering cry was distinctly un-Rooster-like. Stepping forward cautiously, she peered into a dim corner and shiny eyes stared back.

"Oh!" She jerked back as her brain deciphered the shapes. Little heads, little faces. Kittens. Four—no, five.

"Caw?"

Presley spun around. Rooster hopped up. "Oh no. This is not good."

"What isn't?" Carrie said from the doorway.

"Livestock everywhere," Presley said.

Carrie joined her. "Look how cute! Where's the mother?"

"Not too close, I hope." Presley flapped a hand at Rooster. "Shoo. Go. Cats. Birds. Bad. Go."

He cocked his head and didn't move.

"Should we feed them?" Carrie said.

"No! Maybe they'll go away."

Carrie's face fell.

"Fine. Why not!" Presley stalked toward the door and Rooster obligingly followed. "Why don't we just give up business altogether and become farmers."

"Ah," Carrie said, unable to hide a smile, "we can probably manage both. Multitasking is our specialty."

"Right." Presley slid into her car and started the engine. Carrie jumped in beside her. Rooster watched as she U-turned around and roared away. Simply perfect.

CHAPTER NINE

Harper dictated Peggy Giles's admission H&P and a procedure note, and headed for the ICU to make sure the baby was stable. She had no reason to go down the east corridor, although she wondered if Presley had gone back to her office and had to force herself not to wander over to check. What would be the point—they'd come to an impasse and they'd probably only argue. She wasn't sure how things had unraveled quite so quickly. Presley had actually seemed interested and relaxed while they'd been making rounds, and Harper had enjoyed introducing her to patients and describing their care. Sharing her work came naturally, given that everyone in the family was part of it and always had been, but she'd rarely discussed it with anyone outside the family, not even the women she'd dated. There'd never seemed to be any need, when Flann or Carson or her parents were always around to bounce things off or share an exciting story with. Today had been different—showing Presley what the Rivers meant to her, to everyone within its walls, mattered on more than a professional level. Sharing her world with Presley had been satisfying in a way she hadn't expected, at least until Presley had retreated into the alien landscape of budgets and cost-benefit analysis and other things that didn't belong anywhere in the province of caring for patients. The thread of connection they'd been weaving had abruptly snapped, and that bothered Harper more than she wanted to admit. Fortunately, she had more important things to occupy her mind.

She walked through the ICU to the room at the end where they put the pediatric patients. Peggy was the only child in the unit. She lay in the center of the bed, her arms and legs outstretched and connected to IVs, EKG leads, a blood-pressure cuff, and a urinometer. The breathing tube ran to the ventilator beside the bed. She looked like a pale blond doll amongst all the equipment. The nurse who was charting vital signs smiled when she walked in.

"How's she doing?" Harper asked.

"She's been fine. We just sent a blood gas."

"Great." Harper listened to her chest. The breath sounds were clear and evenly distributed on both sides. She'd had to sedate her so she would tolerate the breathing tube and would need to keep her that way as long as the tube was needed. Hopefully, the steroids would kick in quickly, the swelling would go down, and the antibiotics would knock out the infection. As quickly as kids went bad, they bounced back too. "Did someone go to get her mother?"

"As soon as I get her cleaned up a little more, I'll send Nancy down for her."

"Thanks. Call me if anything changes." Satisfied that everything was stable, Harper charted a few notes. She was done at the hospital and had no more reason to stay. She especially had no reason to drop by admin, but the urge to see if Presley had remained was still there, an annoying presence in the back of her mind like the throb of a sore tooth. Pushing the impulse aside, she left the ICU.

Flann, still in scrubs, sauntered down the hall in Harper's direction. "I was just going to check on her."

"She's stable."

"Good." Flannery fell in beside Harper as she headed for the stairwell. "So how did our Ms. Worth come to be down in the ER during all of that?"

"When did she become our Ms. Worth?" Harper heard the crankiness in her voice. Every time the subject of Presley came up her hackles rose for no good reason. Of course, the woman herself was irritating enough to be the explanation. Flann's obstinate refusal to recognize anything about her other than the fact that she was attractive and intelligent just added to her annoyance.

Flann grinned. "Well, I figured since we were sharing—"

"Knock it off, Flann."

"Oh, sensitive. Is there something I should know?"

Harper stopped walking and jammed her hands on her hips. "It seems like you should already know without being told. Presley is not a member of your fan club. She's here to take over the hospital, and we don't even know what the plans are."

"I didn't know I had a fan club. Is there a website?"

Harper blew out a breath. "You know, sometimes you are a real pain in the ass."

"Really?" Flannery raised her brows. "I never knew you thought that."

Harper laughed. Flann could always make her laugh, even when she'd broken one of Harper's toys, or gotten them both in trouble with one of her harebrained schemes, or drawn the attention of one of the girls Harper had given a thought to. She couldn't stay mad at her. "Would you just think about something besides your hormones? Just this once."

"I was," Flann protested, the devil-may-care glint in her eyes at odds with her innocent tone. "I was thinking I'd go undercover, and when Presley falls victim to my charms, she'll tell me everything, and I could report back."

"Your charms notwithstanding," Harper said, "I don't think she's going to fall victim to anything at all. If we're not careful, we'll be the ones picking ourselves up off our asses."

"You're really worried, aren't you," Flann said.

"Aren't you?"

"I sort of thought I'd wait to see what was actually proposed before I got all doom and gloom about it."

"Spend some time with her," Harper said, and immediately regretted the suggestion. Why the idea of Flann and Presley together bothered her so much was just another irritation. Why should she care? "Listen to the questions she asks. I'm not getting the sense that she thinks the hospital's all that necessary."

"Come on, Harper. Why would they buy it if they didn't want it?"

"I've been looking into SunView. There are more things in the SunView Health System than hospitals, and a lot don't involve direct patient care."

"Yeah, but this is a functioning hospital."

"Do you really think that matters?"

Flann grimaced. "Yeah, I do."

"I hope you're right," Harper said, but she had a bad feeling that Flannery's legendary intuition was off this time. Presley might not be the cold, mechanical number cruncher she'd first taken her to be. That was evident from the way she'd reacted in the ER a little while ago. She'd comforted Jenny Giles instinctively, and that sort of kindness came from genuine caring. Those flashes of warmth disappeared pretty quickly when she started talking about the reason she was here, though. Then she was all hard facts and cold figures, and the questions she asked seemed to be leading to the conclusion that the hospital was superfluous. Nothing could be further from the truth. The hospital was the heartbeat of the community. Or, Harper had to admit, at least the center of her life. She couldn't help thinking Presley meant to destroy it.

❖

Flannery glanced at the big clock on the OR wall: 3:05. An hour and nine minutes. Excellent time. She checked the incisions again and cauterized the last few small bleeders.

"Happy up there?" she asked Ray Wilcox, the anesthesiologist.

"Smooth as can be," Ray said. "What do you figure, fifteen minutes?"

"That sounds about right." Flannery looked across the table to Glenn, who had assisted her on the laparoscopic cholecystectomy. Glenn had good hands and would have made an excellent surgeon, but she said she liked being a PA, liked the direct patient care without the hassle of running a practice. Flann counted herself lucky to have Glenn as backup at night and a first assistant in the OR. "You want to finish closing for me?"

"Sure." Glenn held out her hand and the scrub nurse passed her the needle holder and suture.

"Page me when she's extubated."

"Will do."

Flann stepped back from the table and waited for the circulating nurse to untie her gown. She pulled it off and tossed the gown into the hamper and the gloves into the trash. "Thanks, everybody."

She grabbed her white coat from a hook inside the locker room and stopped in the family waiting area to talk to Margaret Hancock's husband. Earl Hancock wore faded work pants, worn boots, and a pressed white shirt frayed at the collar. His hands were chapped and scarred, the knuckles swollen from decades of hard physical labor in all kinds of weather. He'd shaved close that day, and a couple of nicks marred his weathered cheeks. His deep-set blue eyes were clouded with worry. Margaret and Earl were high-school sweethearts and had been married going on forty years. Like Flann's mother and father, they were lifelong friends and lovers and partners. She'd seen it work, knew it could, but her parents' example was a lot to live up to. The idea of trying and failing kept her from getting too involved with anyone. She'd leave that particular legacy to Harper. That was one area in which she had no desire to compete.

"She's fine," Flann said. That was likely all he'd hear, but she'd repeat it all later if need be. "She'll be in the recovery room in about fifteen minutes."

"Can I see her?"

"Not in there. She'll be asleep yet anyhow. The gallbladder came out without any problems. She had a few stones, and I suspect that's what was causing all the pain every time she ate."

"So she's going to be better now?"

"I think she's going to be a lot better. She'll need to take it easy for a week or so at home, but we were able to do everything through the small incisions I told you about, with the laparoscope, so she won't have too much pain and the healing will be a lot faster."

He rubbed his jaw. From his expression, he didn't really understand everything she was talking about, but he took her at her word and his eyes cleared. "That's good then."

"Better than good. That's excellent." She clapped him on the shoulder. "The nurses will let you know when she goes upstairs and her room number."

"Okay. Thanks, Doc."

"You bet."

Flannery made a quick stop in the OR control room to check on her room. Two rows of four monitors showed the interiors of the eight operating rooms. She'd been in OR six. Glenn had finished sewing and was cleaning the abdomen before putting on the dressings. Flannery reached through the window, nodding to the ward clerk, and flipped the toggle on the intercom. "Is the tube out, Glenn?"

Glenn looked up. "Yes."

"Everything good?"

"Yep."

"Thanks." She flipped the toggle back. "How you doing, Darlene?"

"Can't complain," the thin redhead with tired eyes said. She'd married her high-school sweetheart right after graduation and at twenty-five had four kids already. Flannery didn't think much of her husband, who had trouble keeping a job, but Darlene seemed happy enough with him, which was probably what really mattered.

"You look terrific," Flann said. "I like your new haircut."

Darlene's eyes lit up, and she patted her hair self-consciously. "Thanks."

"You're welcome." Flannery waved and took off down the hall. So far, the day was looking good. Her surgeries had gone like clockwork and all her patients were doing fine. She had nothing scheduled for the rest of the afternoon except possibly a few hours with a very attractive woman who challenged her on most every level. She strolled by the admin offices and ducked into the alcove by the staff office, expecting to see her father's secretary ensconced at the desk. She drew up short.

She'd known Alice Cunningham her entire life and enjoyed flirting with the cheerful sixty-year-old. The woman behind the desk, however, was not Alice. Not by a long shot. She looked about twenty-five and like she ought to be doing commercials for natural health products, she appeared so completely untarnished. Creamy complexion, red-gold eyebrows over spring-grass-green eyes, and shimmering hair the color of polished copper. Loose waves fell to her shoulders and framed her oval face. Except for the lace-topped figure-hugging plum-colored top she wore, she might have stepped down from a horse-drawn carriage a century ago. As Flann watched, pleasantly entranced, those green eyes widened and the full rose-tinged lips parted.

Flann said, "I'm staring, aren't I."

"Yes, you are."

"Forgive me." Flann pressed a hand to her chest. "I couldn't help myself. You are truly beautiful."

"Ah." Pink colored the ivory cheeks. "Thank you."

"I should be thanking you."

"Is there something I can help you with?" She spoke slowly, as if to a dangerous animal she wasn't quite certain was safe, or to a madman.

Flann laughed. "Let's start again. I'm Flannery Rivers. And who are you?"

"Carrie Longmire. Administrative assistant to Presley Worth."

"Aha. The boss's right hand."

Carrie laughed. "Well—"

"Actually," Presley said from the doorway of her office, "she's occasionally both my hands and my brain. And she's busy."

"I am," Carrie said quickly, pulling her keyboard closer.

Flann spun around. "Hello. Are you ready for your tour of the local wildlife?"

"I'm afraid my schedule—"

Carrie coughed delicately, and Presley shot her a look. Flann watched the silent exchange and noted that the beautiful Carrie Longmire held considerable sway with the formidable new hospital exec. Interesting.

Presley sighed. "We did work through lunch, and I suppose it would be a good idea for both of us to get a introduction to the area."

"Excellent." Flann looked from Presley to Carrie. The day just kept getting better. "I would be delighted to escort you both."

Carrie popped up from behind her desk and grabbed an oversized leather bag.

"I'll just be a minute," Presley said and disappeared into her office.

"Does she bite?" Flann whispered.

Carrie smiled sweetly. "Only when necessary."

CHAPTER TEN

Flannery drove them into the village and parked on the main street, a two-lane road running through six or seven blocks of the village proper. The area would have been called quaint except that on close inspection many of the buildings showed unmistakable signs of deterioration and at least a third of the storefront businesses were closed. The village itself was an odd mixture of residences and businesses mingled together, as if houses had been built with an eye toward the proximity to the essentials of community life—work, school, and church. Several old brick factories stood along the river, their windows broken out and, in some cases, the roofs collapsed or damaged by fire.

"What was the industry here?" Presley asked.

"The Hudson River Valley has always been agricultural, but in the early settlements the river also provided power for mills, primarily flax, and transportation routes for textile and paper production. Once those goods started shipping by rail and manufacturing eventually moved out of the country altogether, the factories died away. Now tourism and agriculture are the primary sources of income in this area."

Carrie said, "I read somewhere recently that a big electronics factory is locating near here. That will bring in new money, won't it?"

Presley was impressed. Carrie had always been a self-starter, which was one of the many reasons she would do well. Her amiable, outgoing manner put clients at ease, and she had a keen business mind coupled with an aggressive determination to succeed. That little tidbit about a major new industry in the area was news, and something she'd have to factor in to her projections.

"That's true, at least the factory is being built not far from here," Flannery said. "But in general, people don't like to commute, so I'm not sure how much housing spillover we'll get. Still, the hospital draws from a large catchment area throughout the rural counties and provides jobs for a lot of the local community."

"How far are we from the major highway? The Northway, isn't it?" Presley said.

"Not far—at least not by rural standards. Probably twenty minutes, but then it's another fifteen or twenty to the next regional hospital and a good forty-five to anything larger than that."

Presley made a mental note to include that data in her assessment. She pointed to a feed store across the street. "That place—would they have rooster food?"

Flannery stopped, a grin spreading across her face. She'd changed into jeans and a polo shirt before they'd left the hospital, and she looked more like one of the tourists ambling along the streets than the urban surgeons Presley was used to dealing with. "No, 'fraid not."

Presley frowned. "Mail-order then?"

"I don't think so."

"Well then, where—"

"You could probably get *chicken* food, if you're talking about, you know"—she made flapping movements with her arms—"cluck, cluck."

"I see. Thank you for being so very helpful." Presley tried to hide her smile with a glare. Flannery was charming enough to pull off the teasing, a friendly bantering Presley had never shared with anyone. Her family was not big on humor, and people she worked with wouldn't assume the familiarity. When Flannery laughed, her brown eyes alight, Presley relented and joined in.

"How about people food?" Carrie asked. "Any place in town good for takeout or eat in?"

"There's a diner, opens at three and closes about two."

"Wait," Carrie said. "Three in the afternoon until two in the morning?"

"Other way around—a.m. to p.m. No supper. Most everybody's inside and in bed soon after the sun goes down. No late-night business."

"You're not really serious," Presley said.

"Actually, I'm not exaggerating by much. The farmers are all up and out before sunrise, and once the sun goes down there's not much to do around here. So supper is an early affair and then everyone turns in."

Presley sent up a prayer to the gods of the Internet that she'd at least be able to contact the outside world somehow at night while the rest of the community slumbered.

"Where's the supermarket?" Carrie asked.

Flannery pointed in the opposite direction from which they'd arrived in town. "There's a small grocery on the far end of town with local produce in season and just about anything you'd need in terms of essentials. Good pizza and sandwiches too. There's a big organic full-service place about twenty-five minutes south of here."

Carrie looked aghast. "Twenty-five minutes. For groceries."

"That and most big department stores, for clothes and that sort of thing."

"Oh my God." Carrie looked at Presley. "You knew and you didn't warn me."

"I didn't want to ruin your flight."

"Come on," Flannery said. "I'll buy you an ice cream while you recover from the culture shock."

"This makes up for the grocery a little," Carrie said as they sat on a wooden bench in front of the ice cream shop with enormous cones of homemade ice cream.

When they'd finished, Flannery took them through the rest of the town and pointed out the post office, the small, still-family-run pharmacy, the pizza place, the diner, and the bar that served food until ten at night. All in all it took them forty minutes of leisurely walking.

Presley couldn't argue the village had its charms, with its quiet, almost genteel sensibility, but she suspected she would soon chafe at the absence of readily accessible conveniences. She glanced at her watch. "I think Carrie and I should probably make a quick run to that supermarket you mentioned. Our housekeeper is going to help with the food shopping, but we don't have much of anything else in the house."

"You said you hadn't had lunch and it's almost suppertime," Flannery said. "Come to my house for dinner."

"No," Presley said quickly. Too quickly to be polite, probably, but the idea of socializing further with Flannery was out of the question. Flannery was for all intents and purposes her employee. "Thank you, but you've already been far too kind."

"Oh, sorry," Flannery said, "I gave you the wrong idea. I'm not cooking. That would be my mother. Everyone has dinner at the big house on Friday night."

"Well, we certainly can't intrude." Presley backed up a few steps and glanced at Carrie for support. A family dinner. That meant Harper would be there. While Flannery had been entertaining her and Carrie, she'd managed not to think about the way she'd left things with Harper earlier. She couldn't recall the last time anyone had seen her lose control like that. Seeing Harper at dinner would require a truce if not an apology for losing her temper, and that would just be—awkward. "I'm sure your mother wouldn't appreciate surprise gue—"

"My mother is used to us bringing friends home. We've been doing it all our lives."

"Yes, but we're not dressed and—"

Flannery raised her brows. "You don't look naked to me."

Presley shot Carrie another look.

"You know," Carrie said, "dinner would be great if it really wouldn't be a huge imposition on your mother. Maybe we could help? I'm pretty good in the kitchen."

Flannery laughed. "Not unless you'd like to lose some of your appendages. My mother might put you to work, but you'll have to wait until she deems you worthy. Let's go, we're not that far away."

"I really don't thi—" Presley's protest died as Carrie grabbed her arm.

"I think meeting the *Rivers* family would be a wonderful idea," Carrie said.

Outmaneuvered again. Bowing gracefully to the inevitable, Presley said, "For a short while, yes. Thank you so much."

"Like I said," Flannery said, leading the way back to her Jeep, "entirely my pleasure."

❖

The house at the end of the long drive was different than anything Presley had seen in town or the surrounding farmland they'd passed through in the last ten minutes. The stately mansion, sprawling along the water's edge, was surrounded by copses of trees and fields of corn just breaking through the earth that swept like soft green wings along the riverfront. From the drive, the front of the house had a formal appearance with tall symmetrical windows set in brick, and heavy white colonnades framing the entrance. A Volvo sat under a porte cochere on the left, and Flannery pulled up behind it.

"Good, Carson's here. Have you met her yet?"

"Not yet." Presley had wanted to have a little more information before she talked to the third Rivers sister about hospital census, admission patterns, medical records, and other demographic data, but now her plans had been preempted. An all-too-familiar occurrence lately and not one she welcomed.

Carrie leaned forward from the backseat. "This is amazing. How much land is there?"

Flannery cut the engine and opened her door to admit a breeze smelling of earth and water and green things. "The original parcel was fifteen hundred acres. Over the centuries, some was portioned off to the offspring of the original owners so the children could homestead near their parents and grandparents. Currently, we have a little over five hundred acres."

"Do you live here, then?" Presley asked, secretly horrified at the thought of living anywhere near—let alone with—her parents. Obligatory dinners and social events always turned into critiques of her and Preston's latest accomplishments, or lack thereof.

"Not me, no." Flannery's expression closed for an instant before her usual smile returned. "Harper has the old caretaker's place just back up the road a quarter mile, and Carson and her husband Bill have ten acres round the next bend."

Of course Harper would be the one closest to home, Presley thought. She was the heir apparent not just at the hospital, but here too.

"Five hundred acres." Carrie stepped out and looked around. "It's magnificent. And I think I smell dinner."

Presley walked between Flannery and Carrie on the way to the house, preparing for a less-than-warm welcome. She doubted anyone in the Rivers family was happy about the transition. But Carrie was right, meeting the family was a good way to judge what she might be up against in the next few weeks. She refused to consider it might be the next few months.

Another porch stretched the length of the back of the house, facing a long grassy slope down to the river. Across the river, which looked to be a quarter of a mile wide, were at least four more huge fields and a white farmhouse beyond those. Otherwise there were no neighbors in sight.

"Here we are." Flannery held open the screen door and gestured them inside.

Steeling herself, Presley walked into an enormous kitchen redolent of something wonderful. A younger woman who had to be Carson, since she looked like a red-haired copy of Harper, sat at the table with a child in her lap. A gold wedding band glinted on her left hand. An older woman with dark hair streaked with gray at the temples and striking blue eyes the same shade as Harper's, wearing a red-and-white checked apron around her neck and a plain blue cotton dress, chopped carrots at a cutting board by the sink. She glanced over and took in Presley and Carrie in one swift glance.

"Hello. I'm Ida Rivers."

"Presley Worth," Presley said. "Please forgive us for intruding, but Flannery—"

Flannery strode by and kissed her mother on the cheek. "I told them there was plenty of room at the table and the best food in the county right here."

"Well, you weren't lying about the first part."

"Hello," Presley said, shaking Ida's offered hand and turning to the woman at the table. "You must be Carson."

"Guilty." Carson reached around the baby, who was waving a cookie in the air with vigorous delight, and took Presley's hand. "Good to meet you."

"I'm Carrie," Carrie said, shaking hands all around. "I'm Presley's admin."

"Welcome to town." Ida went back to her preparations. "Flannery, get our guests something to drink."

"Wine? Beer? Something soft?"

"Would iced tea be a possibility?" Presley asked.

Carson laughed. "In Mama's house? Always."

Flannery edged around her mother and took glasses down from a glass-fronted wooden cabinet hanging above the counter. She set them on the table and filled them with tea. Presley took a glass and sat at the plank table as a vehicle rumbled outside, followed a moment later by footsteps. The screen door swung open and Harper strode in.

Harper stopped abruptly, taking in the group. For just an instant, Presley thought she saw pleasure sweep across Harper's face before Harper glanced at Flann and something else moved into her eyes. A question. Or displeasure. She had probably been looking forward to a pleasant family dinner only to discover, instead, the enemy in her camp. Her gaze settled on Presley.

"Hi, Presley."

"Harper. Good to see you again." And despite the way they'd parted, it was. Harper radiated a deep, intense energy that caught one up like the slowly building pleasure of a fine wine, heady and strong.

"Hello," Harper said to Carrie, holding out her hand. "I'm Harper Rivers."

"Carrie, Presley's admin."

"Nice to meet you."

"Have you heard from your father?" Ida asked.

"A few minutes ago. He's on his way." Harper leaned against the counter and stared at Presley. "How was your afternoon?"

"Educational," Presley said, her throat dry despite the iced tea. Harper had changed as well and wore faded black jeans, an open-collared white short-sleeved shirt, and black boots. She must have just showered. Her hair was still damp and a few thick strands clung to her neck. She looked lean and taut and darkly forbidden. As with the finest chocolate, one bite would never be enough. Presley gave herself a mental shake. She'd never really cared for chocolate. "Flannery is an excellent guide."

"No doubt."

The glint in Harper's eyes brought heat to Presley's face. She pulled her gaze away when the swinging doors on the far end of the room opened and a teenager barreled in. The last Rivers sibling. Tall and coltish and destined to be a blue-eyed beauty.

"I'm starving." The girl glanced around, took in Carrie and Presley. "Hi, everybody. Dinner soon?"

"Soon enough," Ida said.

"Awesome." With the remarkable self-assuredness of a teenager, she passed through the kitchen and out to the back porch, a book under her arm. As she passed, Presley caught a glimpse of the title. *Money in the Twenty-first Century*.

"We'll have dinner when your father gets home," Ida announced to the room in general. "Let's say half an hour, if I know what on his way means to him."

"Is there anything we can do—" Presley began.

"Yes, you can relax and enjoy yourselves. Flannery, Harper, show your guests around."

"Oh, that's really not nec—"

Carrie jumped up. "If it's all right, I would love to see the house. I adore old historic homes."

"You're in the right place," Flannery said. "I'll give you a tour. Presley?"

"If you don't mind, I think I'll just enjoy the view." Presley escaped to the back porch and out of range of Harper's brooding gaze. The teenager was sitting on the top stair, her back against the carved white post. "Do you mind company?"

"Nope. I'm Margie."

"Presley. How's the book?"

"Not bad, but I think it's already a little outdated. They're recommending bonds, for one thing."

Presley nodded. "That's a problem with books—by the time they're published, some of the data is already outdated, especially in fast-moving areas like the economy."

"Are you here about the hospital?"

"Yes."

"Independent institutions like the Rivers have trouble running in the black."

"Sometimes."

Margie set the book aside and wrapped her arms around her knees, studying Presley with unwavering scrutiny. "Can you turn it around or are you going to liquidate?"

Presley wondered if the girl was a plant. Maybe she was just a very young-looking twenty-something. She tried to remember what Harper had told her about the order of the siblings. She could have sworn there were only four. She hedged. "I just got here. No decisions without data, right?"

"True, but someone must've done it before the acquisition, though, right?"

Presley narrowed her eyes. Definitely a plant.

From behind them, Harper said, "Margie, subjecting a visitor to an inquisition would be considered impolite even by Yankee standards."

Margie grinned at Presley. "Sorry."

"Not at all," Presley said. "If you like, I can give you a couple of titles you might enjoy better than that one."

"Great, thanks."

Harper said, "Dad just called and he's going to be just a few minutes later than he thought."

Presley stood and dusted off her trousers. "I'll leave you two—"

Harper stepped closer, her intense gaze all Presley could see. "Would you like to take a walk down to the river?"

The words came out before she could stop them. "I would. Yes."

Chapter Eleven

Harper guided Presley on a winding stepping-stone path across the grassy lawn and down toward the river where clusters of maples and evergreens leaned out above the water, their branches swaying gently in the breeze. As they walked, she slipped her hand beneath Presley's elbow. "It's a little uneven on these stones. I'm sorry."

"That's all right. I think I'll have to give up wearing any kind of heels."

Harper laughed. "You'll probably be fine inside the hospital. Besides, you look good in them."

"Ah…thanks."

Presley seemed surprised and maybe a little embarrassed by Harper's comment. Harper felt much the same. She rarely—okay, possibly never—commented on a woman's appearance, at least not one she wasn't dating. Presley somehow had her acting unlike herself in all sorts of ways.

They stopped on the riverbank where craggy boulders edged the water. An occasional powerboat sped by, its engine an unnatural growl in the otherwise still air. Strands of Presley's hair floated around her face, and Harper had the urge to catch one in her hand and tame it back into place—or loose all the rest.

Presley turned and caught her staring. For a long moment neither spoke. Finally Presley broke the silence. "I didn't realize the river was so large this far north. I've seen it in New York City, of course."

"It doesn't really narrow until a little farther upriver from here, although there are falls intermittently along the way."

"Do you have a boat?"

"Not anymore. We did when we were kids, but none of us have

much time, and truthfully, there's too much traffic on the river now. I prefer to canoe or kayak on some of the smaller lakes around here."

Presley threaded an errant lock back into place with a swift, economical gesture, as she seemed to do everything. That motion decided Harper—she definitely wanted to tug free the clasp at Presley's nape and watch the wind run through her thick hair like subtle fingers. Presley was a woman who needed rumpling.

"I suppose after a week in the hospital, getting away to someplace quiet is what you're looking for," Presley said.

"Most of the time." Harper slid her hands into her pockets to avoid embarrassing them both again and watched the waves ripple by on the river. "Although I've always liked quiet places."

"Oh? And where did you go to find that in a house with four sibs?"

Harper considered how to answer. The question was personal, and she didn't do personal easily. She found herself wanting to answer, which made her pause. Parts of Presley came out when she was away from work that Harper very much enjoyed. Presley's question indicated she'd remembered Harper had once had four sisters, even though she had only mentioned Kate once. Presley listened and took note of things. There was power in listening, and Harper already was at a disadvantage. Presley had the ultimate authority at the hospital, and now she was here at the farm, the one place Harper always believed to be unassailable. This was where she came when she was disappointed or uncertain or disillusioned. When she'd walked into the kitchen and seen Presley at the table, her first reaction had been pleasure, followed quickly by disquiet. Presley had looked right sitting there, and there was no reason she should. Harper had intended to limit her socializing with Presley to the simple courtesies extended to any guest in her home until her mother came up beside her as she leaned on the counter by the open window, listening to Presley and Margie talking on the back porch.

"Took you by surprise, didn't it," Ida said. "Them being here."

"Yeah."

Ida rubbed Harper's shoulder. "You're not one for liking surprises."

"You think I would be after all these years with Flann."

"True enough." Ida laughed. "Sometimes, Harper, you have to look beyond what you know to find what you want."

Harper glanced at her mother. "Could you speak plain on that?"

"I think I just did." Ida gave her a little shove. "Go entertain our guest. I raised you with better manners than this."

Harper had done as her mother asked, and when Presley had agreed to the walk, she'd been surprised again at the pleasure the prospect of a walk gave her. Now she was enjoying their lazy conversation that ambled like the breeze through the grass, shifting direction with careless ease, and enjoying looking at her too. She puzzled over the inexplicable urge to share something even more personal than the time they'd spent together in the hospital. Practicing medicine was personal, but this, this place was a private passion and secret pleasure. Presley watched her, waiting, as if knowing she was trying to come to a decision. That was enough to make her decide.

"Come on," Harper said, "I'll show you."

"All right."

Harper took Presley's elbow again and led her away from the river onto a cool, shadowy path through the trees. Twenty yards in she stopped, and Presley glanced around before giving her a questioning look.

"Do you think you can climb in those shoes?" Harper asked.

"Climb? As in a tree?" Presley's voice rose as if Harper had suddenly lost her mind.

Harper grinned. "Sort of. More like a ladder. But if you don't think you can handle it…"

Presley's eyes sparked. Clearly turning down a challenge was not in her nature. "Can I do it without shoes?"

"I guess it depends on how tough you are."

Presley immediately kicked off her shoes and stood barefoot on the soft mossy ground, her hands planted on her hips. "Ha. Show me this ladder of yours, Dr. Rivers."

Chuckling, Harper guided her around the trunk of a huge oak tree that had to be hundreds of years old, given the width of the trunk. On the far side, wide thick boards had been nailed to the trunk, forming a ladder climbing into the thick branches overhead. Presley tilted her head back.

"All right," she said slowly. "I think I should go first. If I fall, I'll expect you to catch me."

"I promise."

Presley stepped onto the bottom rung and reached up for the one above her head. When she wavered, Harper grasped her waist. Presley looked over her shoulder, one eyebrow quirked.

"Where exactly am I going?"

"You'll know when you get there. Grab the next one and step up." Harper tried not to stare at the very shapely ass directly in her line of sight.

"I don't generally set out on a journey without knowing exactly what my destination will be."

"I think my mother just said the same thing about me. Maybe we should take an adventure."

Presley stared down at her for a moment longer. "Perhaps we should."

She turned back to the tree and started to climb. Harper waited until she'd gone up several rungs and then started after her. "Doing all right?"

"It's not as hard as I thought it would be."

"I'm right behind you."

"And if I fall, we're both going down."

"You won't fall."

"I suppose at least I'll have someone qualified to remove the splinters."

Harper smiled to herself.

"Wait, there's something up here. Oh!"

Harper scrambled up as Presley disappeared. She reached the hatch in the floor of the tree house and levered herself inside. Presley was already looking out the window toward the river. "Worth the splinters?"

"This is incredible!" Presley spun around, amazed by this hidden treasure in the trees. Harper grinned at her, her pleasure so obvious it was contagious. Presley's stomach fluttered in the oddest way. Now she understood why Harper had hesitated to reveal it. This place was special. "You built this?"

"Flann and I started it as a lark when we were kids," Harper said quietly. "But I've been working on it all my life."

"Can I…" Presley gestured, wanting to explore.

"Sure. It's totally safe."

Presley slowly circled the room. More than a room. The tree house was really a cabin nestled in the branches of the huge oak that rose through the center of the room and out through the roof. The plank floor circled the trunk for ten feet on all sides, with windows on each of the four walls. A sofa with soft plum cushions took up part of one wall, bookshelves another, and a wood-burning stove the corner between the other two. The walls themselves were plain unfinished wood, gnarled and grained and obviously very old. The screened windows and a trap door over the hatch enclosed the space entirely.

She studied the books on the handmade shelves, expecting medical tomes or historical fiction with local settings. Instead she saw rows of numbered Tom Swifts and the Hardy Boys and Nancy Drew—originals, from the look of them.

"Let me guess—Tom Swift for Flannery, the Hardy Boys and Nancy Drew for you?"

Harper rocked on her heels, studying her with that intense probing gaze. "How do you conclude that, Sherlock?"

Presley laughed. "Well, my dear Watson, Swift is an adventurer, first and foremost, and that would appeal to the surgeon in Flannery. The others are detectives, who study clues and ferret out hidden secrets. Much more in keeping with a medical specialist."

"You know a lot more about medicine than you let on," Harper said.

"Thanks." Unexpectedly pleased again, Presley settled on a window seat beneath an open window, stretched out her legs, and propped her elbow on the narrow sill. From this height she could see patches of water framed by sun-dappled leaves and bits of blue sky peeking through the branches overhead. The isolation appealed to her. But more than that, the peace was a refreshing breeze cleansing her soul.

"It's sort of like a cocoon, isn't it," she murmured.

Harper came to stand beside her. "I always thought of it like a cave."

Presley looked up at her. Her skin shone golden in the slanting late-afternoon light. They might have been anywhere, in any age, and the timeless moment called to Presley in some primal way. "Either way, it's a place to rest, maybe hide, and perhaps emerge changed."

"I always thought of it as a place to keep things from changing." Harper's smile was crooked, whimsical.

"And there is our difference."

"One of them."

"We don't need to be on opposite sides of this, you know, Harper."

"Maybe we aren't. I guess time will tell."

"Yes."

"Where do *you* go?" Harper asked. "To hide?"

Presley didn't have an answer Harper would understand. "There's nothing I want to escape from."

"You're lucky, then."

"Not really." Presley sighed. "I just let go of some of the things I wanted a long time ago."

"What kind of things?" Harper stepped back and leaned against the tree. In her faded denim, plain shirt, and scuffed boots, she looked completely at home in the rough, hand-built room. She could have been a frontiersman from two hundred years before. Perhaps she would have been happier then too—living simply where honest work received honest reward and a chicken sufficed as well as a silver coin in payment.

She was also waiting for Presley to say more, but she'd already said far too much. "I bet you're good at getting your patients to reveal their secrets. You have a way of looking at someone that makes it seem like you're really interested."

"I am. But most of them want to tell."

"I don't."

"I know."

"Besides, there's nothing much to tell. I enjoy my work." Presley knew she sounded defensive. "So there's nowhere else I'd rather be."

"I enjoy my work too. But sometimes we have to step away from it in order to come back stronger."

"You can't step away until the battle is won."

"What battle are you fighting?"

Presley felt heat rise to her face and waved her hand. "Figure of speech."

Harper looked as if she didn't believe her, but this time she didn't press. "Okay."

"What do you do when you don't want to be alone?" Presley wanted to know as much as she wanted the conversation on safer ground.

"I play softball."

"Of course you do." Presley laughed and shook her head. "The all-American pastime."

Harper grinned. "There's a hospital team. We're part of the local league. We could use another player or two. How about you and Carrie?"

"Me? No," Presley said emphatically. "I have no idea if Carrie knows anything about softball. And we're probably not going to be here long enough to really contribute."

Harper stiffened. "Really? How long do you plan on staying?"

"I expect the initial phases will be done well before the summer is over."

"And then you leave."

"Yes. We'll put a transition team in place and—"

"And you'll move on to your next conquest."

"No, I will go back to the head office in Phoenix."

"And do what there?"

"Nothing that would interest you, I'm sure." Presley didn't know how Harper had suddenly turned the conversation around to her again, but she wanted to put an end to that right now.

"Try me."

"I'm sorry?"

"You don't know I won't be interested unless you tell me."

Harper's tone held both challenge and invitation. How did she manage that? Presley said, "Just some business challenges that need my attention."

"Is Preston your only sibling?"

"How do you know about Preston?"

Harper lifted a shoulder. "The Internet."

"The Internet. You've been investigating us."

"Wouldn't you?"

"Absolutely," Presley said quickly. "And yes, Preston is my only sibling. We're twins, actually."

"Like me and Flann."

Presley frowned. "I didn't realize you were twins."

"We're not really, not biologically, but we're close to that in some ways. When we were growing up, Flann was actually much more verbal than me even though she's the younger. Once she got started, people worried I was never going to talk. She did that for both of us."

"I am not at all surprised." Presley laughed. "I'm sure you were the quiet, thoughtful one and she was the adventurer, always the first one to try something new. You would've been much more cautious."

Harper grimaced. "You make me sound boring."

"Not at all. Simply careful."

"Careful." She nodded. "Maybe."

"I'm glad you showed me this tree house. I think I can almost understand the pleasure of escaping."

Harper smiled. "You really should try it sometime."

"I think maybe it takes a tree house."

"Then you should build one."

"If I ever decide to, I'll have you design it for me."

"My pleasure."

Mine too, Presley almost said, and caught herself just in time. The air was still and warm inside the tree house, the scent of leaves and bark a sweet backdrop. The sun at her back painted the floor in swatches of gold. Harper stood half in shadow and half in sunlight, the contrast a reflection of her hidden depths. She was far more complex than the simple country doctor she liked to project—she had a secret life, secret pleasures she obviously didn't share easily. Presley discovered she wanted to open those hidden doors to Harper's secret self. That desire was not without risk. Harper's gaze was the most direct Presley had ever known, unwavering, searching, making her feel as if all of her secrets were on display, making her feel vulnerable in a way both frightening and exhilarating. Despite feeling exposed, she wouldn't look away, wouldn't yield to the faint tremor growing in her depths. Her heart hammered in her throat.

"Harper," Margie called up from below. "You up there?"

Harper's gaze never left Presley's. "Yeah."

"Mama says dinner. Dad just drove in."

"All right, we're coming." Harper smiled ruefully. "Sorry. Family calls."

"Yes," Presley said, although the concept was foreign to her. Her family commanded.

Harper reached down to open the hatch and held out her hand. "You should go first. I'll help you get started down."

Presley slid her hand into Harper's. Her fingers were warm and strong and sure. Like her. The trembling spread into Presley's core, but she didn't let go.

CHAPTER TWELVE

Presley judged she had five minutes at most on the walk up to the house to prepare to meet Edward Rivers again. She had no doubt he would be polite, but she regretted the distrust she was going to see in his eyes. Not that she could do anything to change that. She had not created the circumstances, and even if she had been in charge of the acquisition and not Preston, she would very likely have done exactly the same thing. Business was business. She was not responsible for ACH running in the red. That situation had been years in the making. The hospital management couldn't be faulted for anything other than wishful thinking and having failed to keep up with the times, while physicians like Edward Rivers were notoriously bad businessmen and likely hadn't noticed the changing landscape. Harper's generation tended to be savvier about financial realities, although if Harper was any example those lessons hadn't penetrated into this area. The economy of medicine had been changing rapidly for the past decade, and those institutions and physicians who couldn't adapt would eventually be displaced. None of that was her doing, and now she was in no position to reverse it. She was not here to save ACH. She was here to give the greatest return possible to SunView and its investors. Still, she wished she was not the instrument destined to bring about events that would surely alienate the Rivers family.

Harper slowed when they were halfway up the hill to the house. "I meant to mention—you can change your mind about coming with me on calls. I understand you have a job to do, and you're busy."

Presley's relief was instantaneous. There was the opening she'd wanted and had been wondering how to bring about since she'd let her emotions rather than her brain speak for her. Now she could step back, out of the Rivers family's circle of influence, and return to anonymity.

She would always be accountable and would always be willing to take responsibility for her decisions, but she was most effective working behind the scenes, not out in the open where she would have to see the confusion and anger and pain in Harper's eyes or the sad resignation in her father's. She wouldn't have to see Harper at all, and considering how effortlessly Harper distracted her from her goal, that was for the best. Logically she should jump at the offer.

"Trying to get rid of me?" she said instead.

"Not at all. I…" Harper shrugged and looked mildly bewildered. "I enjoyed taking you around this morning."

"I enjoyed it too. So let's stick to the plan."

"It's not always enjoyable. Sometimes it's boring, sometimes painful, sometimes aggravating." Harper laughed. "Especially in the middle of the night."

"It's very quiet around here at night," Presley said. "Flannery tells me everything closes at sundown."

"Flann exaggerates," Harper said. "Actually, a little bit earlier than that."

"Wonderful," Presley muttered, and Harper laughed again. She liked Harper's understated humor, the playful tone an invitation— subtler and somehow more personal than Flannery's—for her to join in. She might not be a joiner, but Harper was hard to resist. "So really you'll be doing me a favor and saving me from the dangers of *Dancing with the Stars*."

"That I'd like to see."

Harper's smile sent heat shimmering across Presley's face. "I'm afraid it's a well-guarded secret."

"Safe with me, then." Harper pressed a hand to her heart.

Presley believed her. "So we have a date?"

Harper's gaze intensified. "I'll need your number."

"Let me have your cell," Presley said.

Harper immediately slid her phone from her front pocket, tapped in a password, and handed it over. Presley selected contacts, entered her name and cell phone number, and handed it back. Over Harper's shoulder, she saw Margie standing on the back porch watching them. "Your little sister is very bright."

"My little sister is exceptional, and she is also prone to inquisitiveness." Harper glanced back and raised her voice. "Somehow, she never grasped the concept of private space. A habit likely to get her hung upside down by her ankles out her bedroom window."

"You wish you were strong enough," Margie called back, a taunting grin on her face.

"Don't forget the last time," Harper said. "I seem to remember screams for mercy."

Margie looked outraged. "I was nine!"

Harper chuckled.

Presley felt a moment of envy. Margaret Mitchell Rivers was an intelligent, bright, self-confident young woman whose family told her she could do and be anything, because she was special. All Presley could remember was never having been quite good enough. "You have a wonderful family."

"We're not always so wonderful," Harper said. "Flannery's a wiseass, Margie is a nosy nudge. Carson—" Harper paused. "Actually, Carson is pretty much always perfect. Cheerleader, prom queen, married the captain of the football team, graduated summa from college."

"Where is her husband?"

"Afghanistan."

"Ah. That's really hard."

Harper's jaw tightened. "He hasn't seen his son except on the Internet. We taped the delivery for him."

Presley touched Harper's hand. "Hopefully he'll be home soon."

"Yeah."

The screen door banged and Flannery called down from the porch. "Stop lollygagging. Mama won't serve until everyone is here."

"Sorry," Presley said. "I'm keeping you from your family."

"That's all right. No one will starve."

Presley smiled. "Come on. Let's go join them."

Everyone was seated when they walked in. Two empty chairs sat on either side of the center of the table. Presley sat between Margie and Carson, and Harper took the one opposite her between Flannery and Carrie. Edward Rivers sat at one end and Ida at the other. The table was laden with platters of chicken and potatoes and vegetables and hot rolls and sweet corn and salad. It was all she could do not to moan out loud. She hadn't had a decent meal in—she couldn't remember when.

"Well, go ahead," Ida said from the head of the table and a bevy of hands instantly reached to the center of the table. For the next few minutes no one spoke as platters were passed and silverware rattled.

Finally, Carrie said, "I don't think I've ever seen food like this all in one place in my life."

"Neither have I," Presley said. "It all looks wonderful."

Ida laughed.

"Don't take too long admiring," Flannery said, "or else it will all be gone."

The talk flowed easily, with Edward asking after Carson's husband Bill and Margie telling everyone about her soccer team's current standing in the upcoming schedule and the baby occasionally punctuating the conversation with happy babble. Presley was content to listen and answer whatever polite inquiry was directed at her with vague references to her home and family.

At one point Flannery said, "Thunderbirds' first practice is tomorrow, don't forget. You're playing, right, Harp?"

"'Course."

Flannery leaned around Harper and said to Carrie, "Can you play softball?"

Carrie gave Flannery a lofty look. "Can eagles fly?"

Suddenly conversation stopped and Carson, Harper, and Flannery stared at her.

Carrie colored. "What?"

"Slow pitch or fast pitch?" Carson asked.

"Fast pitch."

"What position do you play?" Harper asked.

"It's been a while—I played some in college."

Harper straightened. "You played college ball?"

"Some. I was a reliever."

"Reliever? Reliever!" Flannery's eyes sparkled. "Pitcher?"

"That's right."

"We practice tomorrow afternoon at three. I'll pick you up," Flannery said.

"Oh, but I—I just got here and I've work—"

"You should, Carrie," Presley said. The excitement in Carrie's voice was hard to miss, and if she didn't find some social outlet, she'd just end up working all the time for what might turn out to be several months. While that might be all right for Presley, it wasn't fair to expect Carrie to keep her hours.

Carrie's eyes gleamed. "Are you sure?"

"Yes. Positive."

"All right," Carrie told Flannery. "I'm in."

When the meal ended, everyone carried their plates to the long counter next to the big deep sink. Ida said, "Carson, Margie, I think it's your turn tonight."

"Yes, Mama," they both said and rose to begin loading the dishwasher and doing the larger dishes by hand.

Edward said to Presley, "Would you care for a short whiskey, Ms. Worth? We usually have a little drink on the porch after dinner."

Harper and Flannery took down glasses.

"Mama?" Harper said.

"Not just yet, sweet. The rest of you go on ahead."

Presley rarely drank and when she did it was always wine, but she understood she was being invited to a Rivers ritual that had less to do with the alcohol and more to do with time spent together. Her family tended to operate in reverse—social interactions were often the excuse for consumption.

"Carrie?" Flannery asked. "Something for you?"

Carrie, ever sensitive to politics and subtle signs of power, shook her head. "I'm not much of a whiskey drinker, so I think I'll stay here and lend a hand." She grinned at Margie. "Maybe get some more local gossip."

A minute later, Presley followed Harper, Flannery, and Edward outside where a trio of rockers sat on one end of the long porch looking down toward the river. Flannery hoisted herself onto the railing and leaned back against the post, whiskey glass in hand. Presley took the rocker between Edward and Harper, and they all sat in silence for a few moments as the sun set beyond the river. As twilight crept onto the porch and a chorus of night sounds filled the air, Presley waited for the interrogation to begin, expecting Edward Rivers to bring up the issue of the hospital transition. But the conversation, slow and easy, turned to the things most country people probably talked about—the weather, the local economy, the look of the early crops. Edward asked a few questions about patients, none of whom he referred to by name, but it was obvious he knew everyone Harper and Flannery cared for. Listening, Presley closed her eyes and drifted in the warm evening air, the burn of the whiskey spreading through her and the sonorous voices of the Rivers doctors blending with the distant rush of water and wind.

❖

Harper crouched in front of the rocking chair and gently touched Presley's knee. "Presley?"

Presley's eyes jerked open and she gripped the arms of the chair as she glanced around. Her gaze fell on Harper. "Oh my God. I am so completely embarrassed."

Harper grinned. She'd yet to see Presley off guard, and her consternation was appealing. She looked younger and just a little unsure. "No need to be. You weren't snoring."

"Well, that's a small blessing. I do apologize. I'm afraid it was just so," she lifted a shoulder, "relaxing."

The sound of her voice held surprise, as if relaxing was not something she was used to doing. Harper was vaguely pleased that Presley had been able to do that there, on the porch, in the still, peaceful evening. As long as she could recall, these moments with her father had been among her most favorite. Sometimes that was the only time she saw him, as he was so often away from home on calls. She'd been surprised when he'd invited Presley and wondered what he had hoped for her to know about them. Her father never did anything without a reason. She'd been secretly glad when he hadn't brought up the question of Presley's plans for the hospital. This was neutral ground. This was family. She realized her hand was still resting on Presley's knee, and she drew back.

"It's actually only been a few minutes. Flann just got a call, so she's leaving. When you're ready to go home, I'll drive you and Carrie back."

"It's late," Presley said. "We should go."

Presley rose at the same time as Harper. Presley was only inches away in the semi-darkness with only moonlight silvering the planes of her face. Her scent mingled with the flowers that Harper's mother had planted along the porch, a hint of spice amidst the sweetness. Their eyes were almost level, and Presley's searched hers. Harper's heart beat faster, her fingertips tingled.

"It's been a wonderful evening," Presley said, her voice husky.

"Yes," Harper said, meaning it. From the instant she'd walked into the kitchen and seen Presley at the table, she'd thought of nothing except her. She was a captivating puzzle, one thing on the surface—cool, refined, commanding—and another in her hidden reaches—warm, engaged, and attentive, as she'd been when talking with Margie. As she'd been in the tree house—embracing the things that mattered to Harper with genuine delight. At the family table, Presley had studied each of them, her eyes probing and discerning. Presley looked and listened and saw what mattered, even as she kept her own secrets close.

Secrets Harper wanted to unlock. Seeing her here in the gathering night, her shields and barriers falling away as she slid into the vulnerability of sleep, Harper saw only a beautiful woman, and she would've been happy just to sit by her side in the deepening night. But Flann had been quietly watching too, and Harper didn't know what she might see.

"Thank you for the tree house too," Presley said.

"You're reading my mind."

"Am I," Presley said softly in the near dark.

"Yes." Harper almost took her hand. Even a touch might say too much and she held back. "Whenever you feel the need to hide, the door's open."

"Next time, I'll dress for it."

Harper wanted to say she looked beautiful just as she was. The urge to touch her was still so strong and unexpected she stepped away before she could. "You did just fine as you were."

"Well," Presley said, a note of reluctance in her voice, "I'll find Carrie."

"I'll meet you at the car."

Harper hurried from the porch, as if the distance might keep her safe from feelings she didn't want to face. She started the car and a minute later Presley and Carrie emerged. She got out, walked around, and opened the doors for them. Presley got in front with her. Carrie leaned over from the backseat between them. The roads were empty, and the drive only took a few minutes.

"It's so dark out here," Carrie said when Harper turned down the drive to the White place.

"No streetlights. No city glow," Harper said.

"That's what it is," Presley said. "I never realized the stars and moon could be so bright."

"You should leave your porch light on when you go out at night," Harper said.

"You're right," Presley said. "I can barely see the porch."

As Harper pulled up in front of the house, her headlights illuminated the side yard.

"Wait, stop," Presley said sharply.

Harper braked. "What is it?"

"Rooster."

Harper glanced around and saw nothing in the road. She hoped she hadn't run over it. "Where?"

Presley pointed through the windshield. "There. In the tree. What is he doing?"

Harper followed where she gestured and laughed. "He's roosting."

The rooster hunched on a lower branch of the oak, his head tucked down and his body close to the branch.

"Why is he out here?"

"He needs a perch. The chicken coop has probably collapsed," Harper said.

"Is that safe?" Presley asked.

"Probably."

Presley shifted to face Harper. "Probably?"

"There are predators that might bother him, but he's likely safe this close to the house and in the tree."

"I suppose he's used to it," Presley said softly, gazing back at the tree. "Being the only one."

Harper studied her, her elegant suit, her sophisticated style, her polished beauty. For all of that, she radiated loneliness. Harper gripped the wheel. "I can take a look at the coop for you, see if it needs repairing."

Presley shook her head. "I'm sure he's fine, and you're much too busy to waste your time on that."

Carrie leaned forward from the backseat again. "Yes, like playing softball. Will you be at practice, Harper?"

"Planning on it."

"Great." She glanced at Presley. "Sure we can't talk you into it?"

"Ah, no." Presley smiled, her face soft in the glow of the dash lights.

Oddly disappointed, Harper pulled all the way into the turnaround so her headlights illuminated the walk up to the porch. "I'll see you there then, Carrie. If Flann can't make it, I'll stop by and give you a ride."

"Thanks. See you soon." Carrie jumped out and closed the door, waiting beside the car for Presley.

"Have a good weekend," Presley said.

"Yes. Good night."

Harper waited until Presley and Carrie entered the house, then turned around and started down the drive. She expected the weekend to be busy—they always were, and time usually passed quickly. Tonight, though, Monday had never seemed so far away.

Chapter Thirteen

The sun came up without the accompanying blast of heat that quickly followed at home. Instead, the breeze on Presley's skin was cool and invigorating. She'd been reading in bed since four when she'd finally given up trying to sleep. She hadn't fallen asleep easily, either. She'd still been replaying the events of the last few days, particularly the afternoon and evening with Harper. From the moment they'd met, Harper had occupied far more of her attention than any woman had managed previously. She wasn't a nun and she enjoyed female company, socially or sexually, but she rarely thought about the women after the evening had passed. She just hadn't found any of those interactions memorable enough to interrupt her concentration or distract her from her busy schedule. Harper had somehow changed all of that.

Harper was constantly disrupting her plans and her equilibrium. That odd effect was, of course, purely situational and perfectly understandable. Harper and her family were focal players in the new acquisition, and she needed to find a way to work around them because she doubted working with them would be possible. And working around Harper was a little bit like trying to drive around the Rockies rather than taking a pass over the crest. Harper was as immovable and impenetrable as an ancient rock formation.

Tired of thinking about things she couldn't control, she pulled on sweats and a T-shirt and went to see what culinary miracles Lila had left in the kitchen. Not only could she get used to the weather, she could definitely get used to the food. Plain and simple and rich in flavor and substance, a lot like the people. She poured coffee, took it outside, and reminded herself to keep on point and not to be seduced by the rural charms—or the rural charmers.

A few minutes later, Carrie said from the doorway behind her, "I woke up to the most amazing smell."

Presley looked back. "Today it's cinnamon rolls."

Carrie came out carrying a steaming cup of coffee and a roll on a paper napkin. She sat down on the top step opposite Presley and stretched her legs down the stairs. Presley broke off another piece of the still-warm, soft bun and tossed it onto the ground, where Rooster promptly pecked it into tiny bits. When he'd devoured them he clucked and regarded Presley with bright black eyes.

"He seems to like it," Carrie said.

"I think he likes almost anything, but I doubt a steady diet of breakfast muffins and cinnamon rolls is very good for him."

"He does look a little raggedy."

"I know," Presley said broodingly. "I don't think he likes being an only rooster."

"At least he's getting fed," Carrie said between bites. "Speaking of which, where is the magician who made these things? If you tell me it's you, I'm going to cry that I didn't know about it before this."

Presley laughed. "Not hardly. That would be Lila. She's already been and gone."

"She must have been here before the sun came up because it's not even six."

"I think that's late for these parts."

"Huh," Carrie said. "I'm used to getting up early, but everything here seems on a different timetable. Time passes differently. At least it felt that way last night."

"I think that's because everyone here still functions as if it were 1920," Presley muttered.

"That bad?" Carrie tossed Rooster some roll. "The Rivers doctors seemed pretty sharp."

Presley sighed and sipped her coffee. "Their medicine, technically, can't be faulted. It's their practice models that haven't changed in God knows how long. No, wait"—she held up a hand—"check that. I think I do know how long. Since at least Edward Rivers's father began his practice, and I'll wager his father before him. They still make house calls."

Carrie nodded. "I realized that when Flannery left to go see a boy who'd apparently fallen off the roof of a barn and fractured his arm. That's the kind of thing that would go to urgent care at home."

"I agree," Presley said.

"Although Flannery said by the time she got to the boy's house and took care of his arm, it would take less time than if the family took him to the emergency room, someone else saw him first, then called her, and then everyone waited for her to show up."

"That's true, I'm sure," Presley said. "Convenient for the family, but tough on the doctors. They're saving the patients a few hours at the expense of their own time."

"In this case, the doctors don't really seem to mind. Strange, isn't it?" Carrie said musingly. "Everyone just seems to take it as normal."

"I guess for them it is. But they ought to at least be charging more for the convenience it affords the patients."

Carrie pursed her lips. "Is there an inventive way to code for it, do you think? So the reimbursement would better fit the level of care?"

Presley smiled. Carrie wasn't going to be her admin for long. "That's what you're going to look into. Find out who the major insurers are in this area. Review their scales and payment levels and see if you can find any holes."

"I thought we were going to turn this around fast," Carrie said cautiously.

"The Rivers doctors are not going to let go easily."

"That would be the understatement of the century, but they're only a small part of the hospital."

"Do you think that means they have only a little power?"

Carrie shook her head. "Edward Rivers seems quiet and easygoing, but I had the feeling he was taking our measure over dinner."

Presley smiled. "You mean, like we were taking his?"

"Exactly."

"I don't think any of them can be taken for granted."

"They're all sort of interesting, though, don't you think?"

"Interesting. Yes," Presley said, "that would be one word."

"Hot might be another."

"I don't think I want to go there." Even as she said it, Presley realized it was definitely true. The last thing she wanted to do was think about the appeal of the Rivers sisters or the fact that Carrie might feel the same way.

"Harper—" Carrie began.

"Harper is the heir apparent. She's as important in the greater scheme of things as her father."

"I was going to say Harper seems like the quiet one, compared to Flannery, but I think Flannery's flip attitude is just a smokescreen. She's not nearly as uninvolved as she might want us to believe."

Presley nodded. "I couldn't agree more."

"So," Carrie said, blotting up the crumbs with a fingertip. "Just pretending you were going to taste the local menu, what's your flavor? Dark chocolate like the quiet, intense family doc or something with a little more zing—mint chocolate chip surgeon, perhaps."

"I would prefer not to think of the Rivers sisters in terms of edibles." Presley definitely did not want to imagine taking a taste of Harper. She was afraid if she did, anything less might leave her hungry.

Carrie laughed. "Probably safer. I could see that becoming a craving."

"I was planning on going into the hospital for a while." Presley rose and dusted off the back of her sweats. She scattered the rest of her cinnamon roll on the ground for Rooster. What she needed was work to get her back on track.

"I'll come with you."

"No. Really. Get settled. You'll have plenty to do come Monday."

"Are you sure? I've got my laptop. I can get started on the insurance—"

"I mean it. Get unpacked, maybe drive around the neighborhood if you want."

"Should I start apartment hunting? I don't want to be an imposition."

Presley waved a hand at the house. "Look at this place. It's huge. You might as well stay here." She hesitated. "Besides, the company will be nice."

Carrie gave her a surprised smile. "Great. I'd love to stay."

"Then it's settled." Presley went back inside to pour herself another cup of coffee. She wished everything was settled as easily. She planned to spend the rest of the weekend looking at the numbers, but she didn't expect them to tell her anything different than what she already knew. The hospital was dying.

❖

Harper heard the sound of tires crunching on gravel, got up from the kitchen table, poured another cup of coffee, and carried it out to her back porch. Flann, in the rumpled blue shirt and jeans she'd worn to dinner, climbed out of her Jeep and trudged across the yard. Her eyes were bloodshot, and dark circles made her deep-set brown eyes appear even deeper. Harper held up the coffee, Flann took it, sipped deeply, and slumped against the porch post.

"Long night," Harper said. "I thought it was supposed to be a quick callout."

Flann rubbed her face. "The arm wasn't the problem. I splinted him and set him up for X-rays in a couple of days when the swelling goes down. But then a pickup and a Mini Cooper played chicken out on 46. They're still picking up the pieces."

"Jesus," Harper said. "Why didn't you call me? I would've come and lent a hand."

"Glenn was on call, so I had plenty of help in the OR. The driver of the Cooper, a nineteen-year-old girl visiting from out of state, never even made it to the hospital. The young guy in the pickup—wife, and two kids in diapers—was coming home from a bachelor party for his cousin. They think maybe he fell asleep. Ruptured his spleen, perforated his colon, broke his femur all to hell. He'll be rehabbing for six months."

"Anybody we know?"

"Distant relative to the Durkees, I think. I didn't know him, though."

"You get any sleep at all?"

"Couple minutes while they got the OR set up and then for a little bit while I waited to see how he was gonna do in post-op."

"He going to make it?"

"He ought to, barring unforeseens. His leg's a mess. The ortho guys will have to take care of that. I got it stabilized, so they have a few days to fool around with it."

"You know, if you hadn't been there, that guy would've died."

"Maybe. But you know the argument. He would have gotten a fast ambulance ride to the nearest level one or two, or maybe even a medevac hop. Statistically, if it didn't take too long, his chances ought to be about the same."

"Yeah, except look at where we are. How long do you think it would've taken to get all that organized, even if it only meant a forty-five-minute ride in the bus? Tell me he wouldn't have tanked en route."

"Sure, he probably would have the way his spleen was gushing. But EMTs and paramedics are as good as us most times handling that kind of crisis."

"True enough. But they're not going to open up a belly if he crashes."

"Can't argue. I do have the God factor going for me." Flann drank some more coffee and stared at her, a bit of life sparking back into her eyes. "What are you getting at, Harp?"

Harper flushed. "Not getting at anything. I'm just saying—"

"You sound like you're trying to put together a case. You think we've got a fight coming, don't you."

Harper leaned against the opposite post, shoving her hands into her back pockets. The muscles in her jaw throbbed and she consciously unclenched her teeth. She'd lain awake half the night thinking about what might be coming, and what—if anything—she could do about it. Presley hadn't revealed anything she could really sink her teeth into, but the trustees wouldn't have wanted to unload the hospital if they hadn't thought it was a losing proposition. Presley was a businesswoman, through and through, and everything about her said she was good at it. "I don't think SunView is in the business of charity."

"I'm sure you're right," Flann said. "But they are in the business of business—and they want to make money. If the hospital can make money again, then what would be the point of not making that happen?"

"I don't know—a bigger profit margin? I don't know what drives people like..." She almost said Presley, but she couldn't lump Presley into the faceless mass of people she didn't know and couldn't understand. Presley was not a faceless name. She'd already become more than that. She was a flash of humor, a sudden brilliant smile, an unexpected gasp of wonder. She was a surprise and an enigma. Fascinating and frustrating.

"She's interesting, all right," Flann said, as if reading Harper's thoughts.

Harper's shoulders stiffened and her jaw tightened up again. Heat rose up the back of her neck. "I gathered you think so."

"Margie says you took her down to the tree house."

Harper focused on a doe and two fawns grazing at the edge of the cornfield. "Margie has a big mouth."

"Granted. So did you?"

"Yeah. Mama ordered me to show some manners."

"I know, she said the same to me. I took Carrie on a tour of the house."

Harper flicked her a look. "You making some kind of point?"

Flann didn't grin, and that was a sure sign she was dead serious. "I might be. You could be headed for trouble there, Harp."

"I'm not headed anywhere."

"Maybe. What did she think of the tree house?"

"She liked it. What's not to like?" Remembering Presley's delight, a quick stirring of pleasure raced through Harper's belly. "She pegged you for the Tom Swift."

"She reads people. You got that, right?"

"Yeah." Of course Flann would see what she had seen in Presley. The two of them, for all their outward differences, had always thought alike. They competed because they loved the same things, and what was better than beating someone you respected and admired? She'd never been bothered by the competition before.

"Did you try out the couch?" Flann asked casually.

Harper shot her a look. "That's your style, not mine."

"Now there's something I've never noticed before." Flann grinned. "One of these days that halo is going to slip, Saint Harper."

"You trying to piss me off?"

"Did you at least make some kind of move?"

"I just met her."

Flann pointed a finger at her. "So you thought about it."

"My heart's beating, isn't it?"

"Sometimes I wonder."

"Yeah, yeah," Harper muttered, going back to studying the deer.

"I got no problem with you entertaining a beautiful woman while she's in town," Flannery said lightly. "But she's not going to be here very long, and if things go the way we think they might at the hospital, the two of you are going to end up on opposite teams."

"I know that. And that's why nothing's going to happen."

"You sure about that?"

"Unlike you, I don't get led around by my gonads."

Flann's grin, weary but irrepressible, widened. "You should try it sometime. Hell of a rush."

"Hear me on this. I don't plan on pursuing a personal relationship with Presley Worth."

"Well then, you wouldn't mind if I—"

"Don't test me," Harper said softly, "because I can still beat your ass."

"Yeah, that's what I thought," Flann said. "And you haven't been able to beat my ass since we were in middle school."

"Oh yeah? And what about that time—"

"I'm not going there with her, Harper," Flannery said, serious again. "I don't think you should, either."

"Seeing how we both agree, we've got nothing to worry about." Harper tossed the dregs of her coffee onto the ground. "Come on in. I'll make you breakfast."

CHAPTER FOURTEEN

All the office doors in the admin wing were closed and the halls deserted at eight on Saturday morning. Relishing the privacy, Presley unlocked the door to her new office and set up her laptop on the desk. After scanning her mail and deleting messages that required no follow-up, she keyed in the security information needed to give Carrie access to business accounts, insurance contracts, and admission statistics. Then she pulled up the summary Preston's team had provided and confirmed what she'd suspected—the acquisition had been pushed through quickly due to ACH's trustees' panic over mounting debt, with only a superficial accounting of net profit. Preston had been in a hurry too, probably so he could get her out of the way while he wooed supporters. If she could find evidence that the buyout was financially risky and ill-advised, she could call Preston's judgment into question. She pulled up the last five years' financials and started to break down the data. When her cell phone rang, she checked the time. She'd been working for three hours.

"Good morning, Jeff," she said, leaning back in her chair and stretching the cramped muscles in her back. She swiveled around to the window and was startled once again by the view. She half expected the glare of glinting steel and shimmering heat waves she was used to out the broad sheet-glass windows of her high-rise office in downtown Phoenix. Instead she found rolling hills a dozen shades of green, a crystal blue sky, and white clouds as fluffy as cotton candy. She turned back around.

"How are things in the Appalachians?" Jeff Cohen asked.

"The Adirondacks, not the Appalachians," Presley said, smiling. Jeff was her counterpart in marketing, a vice president who had worked his way up from sales with amazing speed, and he'd done it without connections. He'd gotten the job because he was the son of one of her father's college fraternity brothers, but unlike so many of the nepotistic appointments that littered the landscape at SunView, Jeff actually deserved the job and proved it. He was also one of her few friends in or out of the office, and she trusted him as she might have trusted a brother, had her brother been anyone but Preston. She'd known him most of her life, even though he was several years younger. Their families socialized, and while in college, she'd even dated him for a short period of time. When she'd realized she was never going to have more than friendly feelings for him, she'd broken it off. He hadn't seemed heartbroken, and five years later he'd come out to her, although not to his family. Currently, he was dating the daughter of another well-placed family and would probably marry, produce heirs, and find his private pleasures elsewhere.

"What's the situation up there?" Jeff asked.

Presley filled him in on what she knew and what she suspected in terms of the hospital's financial status. "There are decades of loans, investments, debt, and collections to sort out. It will take me a while to untangle it all."

"I thought it was supposed to be a straightforward reappropriation of assets," Jeff said. "The place sounds ripe for a long-term care facility."

"Possibly." Presley would have agreed with him a few days before, but now she wasn't so comfortable with a hasty decision. "There's a lot more going on up here than we realized."

"There's a lot more going on down here too," Jeff said, "and I think you need to be here."

Jeff was the kind of person who somehow managed to be friends with everyone and never appeared to be choosing sides. Consequently, everyone talked to him, and he was always a font of information that was timely and accurate. If he said something was going on, then she needed to take him seriously. "What exactly?"

"Word is Preston's courting management heads nonstop. Since you've been gone, his schedule is packed with luncheons, dinners, and meetings with power players."

"I'm not surprised. With my father set to retire at the end of the year, he's lining up supporters."

"The vote might be a ways off, but you'll be starting from behind if this goes on for long. Can you get back here?"

Her first inclination was to say absolutely. She could manage the dissolution of ACH from Phoenix once Carrie was up to speed, but she still had to decide what to do with the physical facility and draft plans for construction and restructuring the management team. She'd get Carrie started on investigating local contractors that week. "I don't think it'll take very long to get a handle on what needs to be done here. I'll get back as soon as I can."

"Sooner will be much better than later."

"I appreciate you calling me."

"I'll let you know if anything else develops. Be careful of the locals, I hear they might bite."

Presley laughed. "Everyone here is perfectly charming." She'd been about to add *perfectly safe*, but when she thought of Harper and the way her pulse kicked up when she did, safe was the last word she would use to describe her.

❖

Harper moved her stethoscope over John Prince's broad, sun-speckled back, listening to the wheezes and crackles that filled both lung fields. Stepping back from the stretcher, she hung her stethoscope around her neck. "How long have you been short of breath?"

John's weather-beaten face twisted. He was forty-three but could have been a decade older. His chest and arms were ropy with muscles, his abdomen starting to soften with the effects of a few too many beers and burgers. "Not so long. Few days, maybe. The damn cough is making it hard for me to sleep is all."

She leaned back against the wall. "A few days?"

He lifted a shoulder and didn't meet her eyes. "Maybe a week."

"Have you been having chest pain?"

"Sore muscles now and then, nothing unusual."

She was used to her patients, especially the men, downplaying their symptoms. Almost everyone in her practice were farmers, small business owners, and working poor. Their common denominator was they needed to work to survive, and very few of them had any kind of nest egg to tide them over if they didn't have a steady income. Many of them went without medical insurance to pay for heat during the winter or seed during the spring or shoes and clothes for their children. And many of them ignored physical problems until they became so severe they were forced to seek medical attention. John was one of those. If he was here in the ER on a Saturday morning, something had happened to scare the hell out of him. She suspected it was more than a cough that had brought him in.

"Coughing woke you, did it?"

He nodded. "The wife's been nagging me about it. Says she can't sleep for the noise."

And his wife was frightened too. "We'll get an EKG and a couple of blood tests. Then we'll talk."

"Can't you just give me some medicine for the cold?"

"If it's a cold, I might be able to," Harper said. "But let's see first."

"How much is it going to cost?"

"We'll work something out when the time comes. You need the tests, John."

He blew out a breath and gripped the paper-covered examination table with both hands. "All right, Doc. Whatever you say."

A few minutes later the nurse brought her the EKG strip. As she had suspected from the history and physical signs, the abnormalities suggested cardiac damage, possibly chronic. Silent MIs were not rare, and even those producing symptoms were often ignored by patients or written off as muscle strains or indigestion. John was lucky he wasn't one of the high percentage of men whose first heart attack was fatal. When she went in to talk to him, his eyes were frightened. In her experience, people always knew when their condition was more serious than they wanted to believe until the moment when they were forced to accept they had a problem.

"There's some abnormalities on your EKG, John. What it tells us is that there have been some problems with your heart that you might not even have been aware of. We need to find out exactly what the trouble is. That means a few more tests."

He swallowed audibly. "Is it bad?"

"The fact that you're here means it's not as bad as it could be, but we won't know for sure until we can study the blood flow to your heart. I want you in the hospital while we do that so we can monitor you."

"I can't stay now," he exclaimed. "I've got new crops in the ground and more work than I can handle with the herd. I don't have time to be away from the farm—who's gonna look after things?"

"I can't let you go home. Right now there's fluid in your lungs and that tells me your heart isn't working as well as it should. We can take some of the load off that with medication, but we need to find out what the underlying cause is." She'd heard a variation of this argument from the time she'd started following her father on rounds and had had it herself at least a few hundred times. She'd learned a long time ago, men like John Prince would not be persuaded out of fear for themselves. "You've got, what—three kids, all of them still in school? You need to take care of yourself so you can take care of them and Sally Lynn."

"Jesus, Doc." He rubbed his face. "What am I gonna tell Sally Lynn."

"I can talk to her first if you want me to."

"Yeah, that would be good." He stared at the floor. "I don't want her worrying."

"She won't if you let me take care of you." She squeezed his arm. "We'll get this sorted out and we'll get you back to work. All right?"

He lifted his eyes and searched hers. She held his gaze. He needed to see that she was confident. He needed to believe in her.

"Okay."

"Good. I'll go get Sally Lynn, and we'll go over things together."

By the time she finished admitting him, it was almost eleven thirty. She hadn't had anything to eat since she'd made pancakes and eggs for Flann at six in the morning. Flann had gone home to go to sleep, and her big plans for the day had been to plant a half dozen tomato seedlings in the back garden. That had been put on hold when she'd gotten the call from the PA in the ER who thought John Prince was on the verge of heart failure. After seeing John into the elevator to the ICU, she stopped in the cafeteria to grab lunch. As she carried her tray to a table by the window, she saw Presley sitting alone with a cup of coffee, a half-eaten sandwich, and her iPad. She hesitated, then headed for her.

"Do you mind some company?"

Presley looked up and smiled. "Not at all. Please." She put her iPad aside. "Just finishing rounds?"

"No, had a patient in the ER to see. You?"

"Just finished up."

"I guess I can't talk you into softball?" Harper asked, biting into her turkey club sandwich.

"You're nothing if not persistent. But no."

Harper grinned, twisted the top off her bottle of water, and took a swallow, studying Presley. She was dressed for work again—soft pale green shirt with a cream-colored jacket and black trousers. Her makeup was subtle, her hair loose and pushed back behind her ears. She wore a single ring on the ring finger of her right hand, a square-cut dark red stone in a gold band. Simple, elegant. Exactly like her. "Persistence is often rewarded."

"Not this time, I'm afraid," Presley said. Charming was an understatement where the Rivers sisters were concerned, but now she was forewarned—and armed. "I do need to know where to get rooster—*chicken* food, though."

"For the rooster in the tree?"

"Yes. Well, he's not in the tree right now. He's digging around in the yard."

"It's summer," Harper said. "With all the grass and hay around, he's probably doing pretty well."

"I was just reading that he should have grit and some corn and high-quality food as well. I have a list already of what I need."

"You looked that up on the Internet, huh?"

Presley regarded her guardedly. "Yes, why?"

"You realize you could have asked just about anyone here and they would've been able to tell you."

"Number one, I don't know anyone here except you and your family, and number two…" She shook her head. Harper was far too good at getting her to discuss things she had no intention of discussing. "Never mind."

"And number two," Harper said with maddening self-assurance, "you're used to doing things for yourself."

Harper was right, and her perceptiveness left Presley feeling uncomfortably exposed. "I suppose, yes, that's true. Aren't you?"

"Sure—unless someone knows more than I do and I can save myself time and a headache by asking."

"That means you have to trust them," Presley pointed out.

Harper gave her a long look. "It does."

"Seeing as you weren't around, I was forced to turn to other sources of information."

"Does that mean you trust me?"

Presley flushed. Damn it, Harper was doing it again. "Where chickens are concerned."

Harper laughed. "If you're done with lunch, I'll take you to the feed store and we can see about outfitting your rooster."

"That's not necessary. If you just tell me—"

"I'd like to," Harper said.

"If you're sure, I'd appreciate it." Presley paused. "In fact, I'd like that too. For Rooster's sake, of course."

"Of course." Harper's slow-lidded smile sent a shiver down Presley's spine that she resolutely ignored.

Chapter Fifteen

Presley wandered around a store creatively called Tractor Supply consulting the list on her iPhone of things she needed for Rooster. While she shopped, Harper chatted with one of the clerks at the checkout counter. She paused in one section containing racks of shirts and pants and boots. Who knew you could shop for clothes at the tractor store? She plucked a green-and-white checked shirt from a hanger and held it out. The simple style and bright colors had a certain charm. She laughed to herself, thinking how that would go over in the boardroom matched with a pair of jeans and boots. The memory of Harper looking totally at ease in a plain white shirt and faded jeans reminded her that actions, not the outward trappings of success, were the true measure of ability.

"Looking to expand your wardrobe?" Harper said from behind her.

Presley put the shirt back. "Just…curious."

"That navy would look good on you." Harper held up a cotton top with a scooped neck.

She was right. The blue would complement her eyes. Looking at clothes with Harper seemed too familiar, too personal, somehow—as if Harper were mentally dressing or undressing her. The intimacy was unnerving. Growing up, Presley had shopped with her mother and had quickly learned to accept her mother's choices over her own desires. She'd occasionally shopped with friends in high school until one of the girls was caught shoplifting, and Presley's parents threatened to freeze her credit cards if she continued with unauthorized purchases. As an adult, she had a regular personal shopper at one of the upscale department stores who would choose an assortment of pieces for her when she called and have them ready for her to try on when she arrived.

She held up the top and had no trouble imagining Harper in a big sunny bedroom, a backdrop of brilliant blue sky outside the window, slowly easing the simple cotton shirt over her head. Of her breasts falling free and Harper's hands—

"I guess it makes sense to shop here while you're getting the rest of your supplies." Presley put the shirt back and quickly walked on with no destination in mind.

"The clothes tend to be better made for hard work," Harper said when she caught up to her. "And in a lot of cases less expensive than similar things at regular department stores."

Presley grabbed a pair of women's work boots. Thankfully, they didn't conjure the slightest erotic thought in her head. "I'm trying to figure out what I would be doing to need these."

Harper laughed. "If you had chickens, you might want to wear them while you're cleaning out the coop."

"Give me a little time to get my mind around that," Presley murmured and set the boots down.

"City girl."

Harper's tone was teasing and Presley decided she liked it.

"Come on," Harper said, "there's something I want to show you."

"I'm breathless with anticipation."

"Then just hold that thought."

Harper reached out, and for a second Presley thought she was going to take her hand. A flush of pleasure raced through her as she lifted her own, automatically ready to take Harper's. Harper stilled, that dark unfathomable look back in her eyes. The breath inexplicably stilled in Presley's chest.

"This way," Harper said quietly, her hand slowly falling back to her side.

Presley nodded, knowing she should feel foolish, but she didn't. For just a few minutes, she wanted to let go of everything she'd been trained to do and want, and just follow her instincts. And her instinct was to follow Harper.

She pushed her oversized cart down rows stacked with big bags of animal and bird feed, through aisles filled with fence posts and stakes and all manner of tools, large and small, watering troughs, and other equipment. Toward the back of the warehouse, waist-high barriers screened off four sections about eight feet square. Harper stopped and pointed into one of them. Presley looked down and caught her breath.

"Oh." A frightening melting sensation filled her chest.

A dozen fluffy yellow balls, about four inches high with feet, scurried around, pecking at the straw and the crushed feed in a little tin tray with miniature beaks so fragile they didn't even appear real. Little feathers, coarser and darker, displaced some of the fuzz covering their wings.

"Chicks." Presley stated the obvious and hoped she sounded less girlish than she felt.

"Yep. They're the last of the bunch. It's a little late in the season and these are bigger than they usually are when they go home, but that's a good thing because you don't have to be as careful about the temperature as you would if they were hatchlings."

"They're really cute."

Harper cradled one in her hands and passed it to Presley. "Here."

Having no choice, Presley took it. The feathers were incredibly soft, and its bright black eyes reminded her of Rooster's, inquisitive and lively. It pecked at her finger and she laughed. "They never stop that, do they?"

"Pretty much never. Chad says if you take half a dozen, they're yours for five dollars."

Presley stared at her. "What in the world would I do with half a dozen chickens?"

Harper grinned. "That rooster will know what to do."

Presley raised a brow. "I imagine that he would. But aside from the obvious, I don't think we can trust him to take care of all the other matters."

"Chickens pretty much look after themselves, once they're a little bigger. I'll take a look at the coop and get it back into shape for you. Nature will do the rest."

Reluctantly, Presley put the chick back into the pen. "I can't. I have no idea how to look after them, and what about when I'm gone?"

"You'll find someone to take them. Or eat them."

Presley gasped. "Certainly not."

"If you change your mind, they'll be here a few more days."

"Rooster is quite enough of a responsibility," Presley said and backed away so she wouldn't see the milling chicks and could quash the impulse to take them home. "Besides, we have cats in the barn. They might eat them."

"Barn cats know about chickens. They'd probably be friends."

For an insane moment, Presley considered it. They were cute and, from her reading, not very much trouble at all. And she'd get eggs…

Reason mercifully prevailed. She'd be long gone before these little ones were ready to lay eggs. "No."

"Okay," Harper said, her tone suggesting she wasn't convinced Presley was convinced.

To prove her certainty, Presley pushed her cart hurriedly to the checkout counter.

Once outside, Harper piled the supplies in the back of her pickup truck. "I'll drive you back to the hospital so you can get your car."

Presley checked her watch. "Don't you have softball practice this afternoon?"

Harper nodded.

"Where?"

"Out past my place a bit." Harper opened Presley's door for her.

"Thanks." Presley was used to people opening doors for her, but when Harper did it, she felt special. Harper treated her as if she was all that mattered—as if time had no meaning when they were together. She climbed into the truck and Harper started the engine. "That took longer than I expected. If you drive me back to the hospital, you're going to be late."

"That's okay. I'm having fun."

So am I. So much fun, she'd lost track of time, something she never did. "Flannery will object, I expect. Just take me home—I'm on your way. I'll have Lila drive me to get my car when she leaves today."

"How about I stop home and change, and you come with me to practice. I'll take you home after and carry this stuff in for you."

Presley frowned. "Wait. What are you talking about? Why would I go to practice?"

Harper grinned and pointed at the sky. "Saturday afternoon. Blue sky, warm sunshine. It's a beautiful day. Carrie will be there too. What are you going to do at home?"

"Well, I—" Presley folded her arms, aggravated at being put on the spot, and thought about her usual weekend activities. An hour at the gym in the mornings, an espresso on the way back to her condo, and then catching up on the week's news on her iPad. By the afternoon, she'd be bored and end up working until the obligatory business or family gathering on Saturday evening. She hadn't considered what she'd do here on the weekend. The gym was out, since she hadn't seen anything resembling one in town. She had no plans for the evening and had already worked half a day. She had several books on her iPad she was planning on reading—but that sounded like an excuse, which it wasn't. Not exactly. "I have quite a few things already planned."

"Three hours," Harper said, "counting the trip to your house and mine. If you're not enjoying yourself, I'll take you home."

The idea of relaxing in the sun was oddly appealing. There was nothing waiting for her at the White place except Rooster, and he'd be there later in the day. And spending a few hours watching Harper would be no hardship. "All right, but I want your word that you won't badger me about playing."

"I swear." Harper swung left out of town. "What's your sport, then?"

"Golf." Her parents had signed her and Preston up for golf lessons when they were eight, explaining golf was the sport of the business world and that many a deal was brokered on the greens. She didn't particularly enjoy the game, but she was competitive, and that was enough to make her a good golfer, and her parents were right. She often spent a weekend morning on the greens at her club discussing business with financiers, real estate developers, politicians, and CEOs. "Do you play?"

"No." Harper rolled down her window and the smell of country wafted in. Hot tar, green fields, livestock. "There's a public course about ten miles from here. A lot of people around here play. If you miss playing—"

"I don't."

Harper glanced at her. "Why do you play, then?"

"It's good for business."

"I see." Harper didn't sound as if she thought that was much of a reason to do anything.

"I thought all doctors played golf," Presley said testily.

"A lot do, for the same reasons. But if I'm going to spend time doing something, I'd rather it be for pleasure."

"Like today."

Harper glanced over at her. "Yes."

❖

Harper pulled down the drive and stopped in front of her house. Originally the farm manager's house, the plain two-story wood building was set back a hundred yards from the road with a cornfield beginning another hundred yards beyond her back porch. The barn was out back to the right, her garden to the left, and the chicken coop in between. Chickens roamed across the grass in front of the house. She cut the engine and swung around the front of the cab to hold open Presley's door just as Presley was climbing down. Harper held out her hand and Presley took it, leaning into Harper as she steadied herself.

Presley looked around, her fingers tightening around Harper's. "They're so pretty. And they're all different."

Harper pointed out the various chicken species one by one. "Which is your favorite?"

"Oh," Presley said, laughing. "A chicken aficionado I'm not. I like the white ones with the speckles, though."

"Mmm, good choice. They're nice and tender. Roast one up on a Sunday afternoon—" She ducked when Presley swatted at her shoulder. "Seriously, sometimes we do have to eat the livestock. Kids learn that pretty early in life."

Presley glanced down. She was still holding Harper's hand. No one else was around, and suddenly, the intimacy was overwhelming. She had no idea what she was doing. Worse, when she was with Harper, she forgot why she'd come to this place where she had no place, where her job put her at odds with everyone, especially this woman who seemed able to make her forget herself with alarming ease. She released Harper's hand. "It must be very difficult for children, for anyone, to grow fond of an animal and then…"

"Farm kids have to learn that animals, like crops, are part of what keeps a farm going. The smart parents teach their children not to name the animals that will eventually be culled for food or other reasons. The 4-H clubs give the kids a place to bond with their animals and bring their pets to show off. No good parent would sacrifice one of those."

Presley had wanted a dog. Her parents had said no—they traveled too much, and then there would be prep school. "It's so different than what I'm used to."

"What is that?" Harper didn't care if she was late for softball. She'd been playing all her life and practice was more social outing than anything else. Flannery would give her a hard time, but it wouldn't risk her position at shortstop. She was still quick and had one of the strongest arms on the team. Flann was a better batter, but then Flann was always the flashier of the two of them.

Right now, she couldn't think of anything she'd rather be doing than standing in her front yard, surrounded by a bunch of clucking chickens, talking to Presley Worth. Presley didn't know her, but she seemed to want to, and that mattered more than anything else at that moment.

All her life, Harper had been known by everyone. When she started going on rounds with her father, everyone knew her father and her mother and her, even though they'd never met. Her story was known before she'd even lived it. Most of the time she didn't mind, but sometimes the familiarity left her feeling invisible. With Presley, she felt completely new, and when Presley looked at her, she felt solid and seen. She wanted to tell her everything, from the silliest stories of her childhood to what it meant to her to have the faith of her patients and her community. She wanted to tell her what mattered, what lived inside her.

"It's a long story," Presley said, "and you're going to be late."

"I don't care," Harper murmured and moved a step closer. Presley's hand came to rest on her chest and her eyes widened, full of questions. Her fingers curled into Harper's shirt.

"Harper, this isn't—"

Harper kissed her, there in the hot summer sun under a blue, blue sky with the sounds and scents of life all around them. She gently stroked Presley's forearm, reveling in the soft, silky texture of her skin. Presley's lips were even softer, satin against her own, tempting her senses. Presley's mouth slid softly over hers until their lips fit perfectly. The breeze was cool and fresh against the back of her neck, and every sensation was magnified a thousand times. She didn't need to breathe. She was more alive than she'd ever been, never having known until this moment she'd been sleepwalking, waiting for the woman whose kiss would taste like eternity. Hunger exploded, sending fiery need raging through her. She slid her arm around Presley's waist, pulled her closer, and pressed her mouth harder to Presley's, wanting more. Presley's palm pushed back against her chest, pushing her away. The kiss dissolved, leaving Harper with only the sound of her own breathing harsh in her ears.

"Harper, no," Presley said softly.

Harper let her go, stepped back, searched for words in her addled mind. "I…seem to have forgotten myself."

Presley drew a deep breath and waited a second for the swirling in her head to dissipate. She hadn't moved, at least she didn't think she had, but she had no memory of how she'd ended up in Harper's arms. She remembered exactly how that had felt. Her body still tingled with the memory. Harper's body had been hard, hot, powerful and for an instant, Presley surrendered. Surrendered, something she never, ever did. In a heartbeat, every instinct spurred her to fight back. To fight the wanting and the longing and the insanity of that kiss. When she was sure her voice was steady, she said, "You are an excellent kisser, Harper."

Harper's mouth twisted into an ironic smile. "Even if uninvited?"

"Invitation was not required, and to say I didn't enjoy it would be a lie." She made herself smile, made her voice lighten. "Let's chalk it up to"—she gazed around, pointed to the sky as Harper had before—"the effect of this incredibly beautiful day."

"All right," Harper said, her voice husky. "We can try that."

"I'll wait out here while you change your clothes."

"Are you afraid to be alone with me?"

Presley bristled. "Of course not. A kiss is not an assault. It's flattering. And enjoyable. And you, you are a gentleman."

Harper laughed but her face was strained. "Thank you."

"You're welcome." Presley would not allow Harper to accept blame where there was none. She wasn't even sure she hadn't somehow invited that kiss, although she would be sure not to again. "And I'm willing to bet there's iced tea in your refrigerator."

"Am I my mother's daughter?"

"Yes," Presley said, "and your father's."

"We can't forget that, can we?"

"I'm afraid not, Dr. Rivers."

CHAPTER SIXTEEN

Presley sat on Harper's back porch with a glass of iced tea while the chickens that had followed her around the corner waddled back and forth across the yard. She'd sat on more porches the last few days than she ever had in her life and was beginning to see the value of letting one's mind drift in the sunlight or the twilight. Today, though, nothing was going to settle her mind, or her body for that matter. Harper was inside changing, and Presley was grateful for the few minutes alone to try to collect herself. The kiss had taken her off guard. She'd been kissed before, but never in her recollection when she wasn't expecting it. Kisses were not something that happened unless she decided they would. Maybe it was only the element of surprise that had made the kiss so incendiary, so overpowering. Maybe she was only shaken because she hadn't prepared herself the way she usually did, hadn't weighed and considered what would naturally follow, hadn't already decided that more, for an evening at least, would be pleasant. She hadn't chosen to be kissed.

There had been nothing pleasant about Harper's kiss. Pleasant was a far too inadequate word for what had happened when their lips touched. The heat, the force of it, had surged through her, knocking barriers aside like floodwaters careening over parched land, deluging everything in its path. She'd been helpless to stop and desperate for more, opening like the crevices in a thirsty earth, aching to be filled until she overflowed. She'd known desire she hadn't imagined possible. She was no blushing virgin, but thinking about the way she'd responded to just a simple kiss brought heat to her cheeks and everywhere else. She pressed the cool, sweating glass to her forehead and closed her eyes.

What a monumental misstep. Of all the people in this town, Harper Rivers was probably the worst person she could have become involved with. She'd practically compromised herself professionally, something that had never happened, not once in her life. Not that anything between them, friendship or more, would make a difference to her decision-making, but it was simply bad form. And worse than that, she'd let things get out of hand with someone she genuinely liked. Harper was funny, warm, attentive, and mesmerizing in her intensity. She was honest and strong. And damnably sexy.

When she could think a little more clearly, she'd need to find a way to extricate herself gracefully from a relationship that was moving too fast, without alienating Harper. If only the spinning sensation in her head and the hungry churning in her middle would go away.

The door behind her opened, and Harper emerged. Presley took in the long length of bare legs, tight black athletic shorts, and a sleeveless T-shirt that molded to Harper's lean body. Her breasts were subtle curves beneath the cotton, an invitation Presley refused to acknowledge despite the dryness in her throat and tightness in her depths. Harper's eyes were dark and brooding again. Her hair was tousled, and Presley had an inexplicable urge to run her fingers through it, to tousle it even more. She rose and held out the empty tea glass. "As good as your mother's."

Harper smiled for an instant. "That's because it is."

"You like living so close to them, don't you."

"Far enough for privacy, close enough to stay in touch."

Presley nodded as if she understood, although she didn't. "I see my family regularly. The times are in my appointment book."

Harper's gaze softened, her mouth gentled. "No one ever had to tell me family came first. It's just always been."

"I'm not sure I'd be good with anyone so close, so inside."

"I can't imagine being without it."

"Is that what you want? For your life."

"Yes." The shadows fled Harper's eyes. "A wife, a big house, at least four kids, a few dogs, a couple of cats, chickens—"

Presley laughed and held out her hand. "Yes, I see. You are your father's daughter."

"And my mother's."

"Yes." Presley felt a little better. A little more grounded. They were so wrong for each other. She was right in stopping things at a kiss. "We should go so you aren't any later."

The drive to the baseball field took less than ten minutes, and they didn't make conversation on the drive. Presley spent the time divided between looking out the window at the endless stretch of green, a color she still couldn't quite get used to in so many varieties and abundance, and watching Harper's hands as she drove. Her hands were sure and strong, her fingers long and slender. As Harper's hand cupped the head of the gearshift, Presley remembered the press of Harper's palm against the center of her back, the hold possessive and unquestionable. She rarely let herself be possessed, even during sex. She didn't mind aggressive lovers, as long as no one thought to dominate her. Yet she'd welcomed the subtle control in Harper's hand drawing her closer, gone willingly into the inferno of Harper's embrace. She'd thrilled to Harper's power.

"Do you still want to stay?" Harper asked quietly as they approached the field.

"Of course." Presley smiled. To leave now would be to admit the kiss had unsettled her, and confessing weakness was not in her makeup.

"Good." Harper pulled in at the end of a long line of vehicles, mostly pickup trucks and SUVs of one kind or another. She turned on the seat to face Presley. "There's sunscreen in the glove box in front of you. If you weren't planning on being outside today, you might need it."

"You're right, I will. Thanks." She smeared some of the lotion on her face and bare arms, aware that Harper was watching her as she did. She liked it when Harper looked at her. She hurriedly finished and put the lotion away.

Harper came around to open her door, and she climbed down. Harper guided her with a hand on her arm but moved away as soon as they started for the field. Harper carried her glove and had pulled on a worn blue baseball cap that sat low on her forehead and shaded her eyes. All Presley could see was her mouth, and that was the last place she wanted to look. She studied the ball field instead. A big mesh backstop stood behind home plate. Two sets of bleachers faced the field on opposite corners and, surprisingly, were half-full of people, some with coolers, babies in strollers, or umbrellas for shade. Obviously, watching practice was a form of entertainment for more than those who were actually playing. The team was mixed men and women, about fifty-fifty as far as she could tell.

Harper stopped by one set of bleachers. "If you want to leave, just give me a wave. I'll take you home."

"I'll be fine. Enjoy the practice."

"I'll see you in a while." Harper ran over to where Flann and

Carrie were tossing a softball back and forth. Flann said something, and Harper waved her off and kept walking. Carrie looked over to the bleachers and waved, a big smile on her face. She, at least, was having a good day.

Presley waved back and climbed to the top row of the bleachers and looked for Harper. She spied her at shortstop. A tall, thin African American man was hitting balls to her from home plate. Harper moved with lithe grace, fielding the ground balls and whipping them to first base. She was quick and fast and strong. After a few minutes, Flann selected a bat from a stack against the fence and strolled to home plate. Carrie took the mound and pitched to a small blonde crouched behind Flann. The first ball whizzed past Flann.

"Lucky pitch," Flann shouted.

Carrie only smiled. Flann swung at the second pitch but missed. A few hoots of laughter and catcalls rose from the players on the field. She hit the third ball, a grounder that skidded past Carrie. Harper scooped it up from behind her, tossing it to first base. The rest of the players rotated at bat and Carrie pitched, alternating with several other pitchers who, from what Presley could tell, were not as fast or accurate as Carrie.

"She's gonna kill the other teams," Margie announced, dropping onto the bench beside Presley. She wore a ball cap similar to Harper's, a sleeveless navy T-shirt with *Thunderbolts* emblazoned above a cloud slashed through with a jagged lightning bolt, and baggy shorts. Sipping a soda from a tall cardboard cup, she stretched her legs out in front of her and propped her elbows on her knees.

"She seems to be good," Presley said.

"She's really good."

"Do you play?"

"I do, but I like soccer better. It's faster. How about you?"

"How about me what?"

"Do you play?"

"No. A little tennis. Golf mostly."

Margie drained her cup and set it aside. "Do you like your job?"

"Yes," Presley answered automatically, even as a small part of her hesitated.

"Which parts?"

Somehow she didn't have to ask what Margie meant. The girl was incredibly intuitive. That, combined with her inquisitive mind, was going to take her far one day. She'd be a dangerous adversary. As it was, she was challenging. "If I said I enjoyed being able to move pieces around on a chessboard, would that make sense?"

"If you were the queen, yes."

"Why not the king?"

"Too limited. The queen has greater reach, more maneuverable." Margie grinned. "More power."

Presley laughed. "Well then, you understand."

"Come on, Harper!" Margie called. "You can hit that ball."

Harper dug her feet into the dark earth in the batter's box and squared off against Carrie again. Carrie's pitch sailed past her.

Margie hooted. "Business is a good field for people who like to be in charge and in control, and who enjoy power."

"I hadn't thought of it that way, exactly, but you're right. And what about you?" Presley said, finding yet another Rivers sister who somehow managed to turn the conversation in directions she'd rather avoid. "What do you enjoy?"

"People," Margie answered instantly. "I like watching them, figuring out what makes them work."

"Are you planning to follow in the family tradition, then?"

"Maybe. I haven't decided yet. If I do, though, I'll be a psychiatrist."

"You'd make a good one. You're observant and perceptive."

"Thanks!" Margie's grin widened. "Are you going to date Flann?"

"Ah," Presley said, deciding they'd reached the boundary of personal revelation. "If I were, I don't think I would tell you. That would be a question better put to Flannery. However, I can easily say no."

"Okay, fair enough."

"How about you," Presley said. "Boyfriend? Girlfriend?"

Margie shook her head. "Nobody special. My group doesn't really pair off much, and I figure when I meet the person who wants to see inside me and I want them to, then I'll know. Boy or girl, I don't think it will matter."

How was it this girl could be so sure about something so confusing to so many? Presley found the thought of wanting anyone to see inside her not just foreign, but dangerous. Inside was where she hid her weaknesses—the things she wanted and was willing to sacrifice for. At least, once she might have been. Not any longer. "Your family is terrific."

"Yeah. I know." Margie studied her with that sharp, inquisitive stare. "You'd fit in, you know."

"Oh," Presley said, "I don't know about that. I'm more of a loner, I think."

"We all are sometimes. That's why Harper has a tree house and Flann rides her motorcycle and Carson runs."

Yes, but you all come home. I never do. Presley said, "Thank you for saying so."

As the sun slowly dropped, Margie pointed out the various players, all hospital employees, and they chatted about casual things until finally the players began to gather up their equipment and drift off toward their vehicles. Harper, Flannery, and Carrie walked over together.

"That was awesome," Carrie said, beaming.

"Great pitching," Harper said.

"Word is going to spread fast." Flannery grinned at Carrie. "They'll be gunning for you."

"Let them come," Carrie said.

Flannery laughed.

Harper looked up at Presley. "Doing okay?" The damp ends of her hair clung to her throat and neck, and a smudge of dirt streaked her left cheek. She looked sweaty and outrageously sexy.

"Doing great, thanks."

Flannery pulled off her red ball cap and ran her hand through her hair. The sandy waves were wet and darker than usual. Her eyes sparkled with enthusiasm and energy. "Everybody up for pizza?"

"Yeah," Carrie and Margie exclaimed together.

Harper was silent, still looking at Presley. Waiting. She should make an excuse, go home. Get away from Harper until her system settled and she was herself again.

"I'm hungry," Presley admitted.

Harper smiled. "Me too."

CHAPTER SEVENTEEN

The pizza place turned out to be the bar Flannery had pointed out to them in the village. The Hilltop was crowded even at five in the afternoon with men and women drinking at the bar, talking boisterously, while the televisions at either end played competing sports events. A few tables in an adjoining room comprised the eatery. The smells coming from the back where the kitchen must be instantly reminded Presley she hadn't had much lunch, and breakfast was a muffin a long time before that. They took seats around a big round table covered with a bright yellow oilcloth dotted with blue roses. She ended up sitting between Harper and Carrie. After everyone gave their preferences and vetoed certain other toppings, they chose three pizzas and ordered from a friendly waitress in jeans and a T-shirt who greeted the Rivers sisters by name.

Once the food was ordered, Flannery said, "Tammy's slammed. I'll get our drinks. What does everyone want from the bar?"

"Beer," Harper and Carrie said simultaneously.

"Coke," Margie said.

"I, ah, suppose wine would be out of the question," Presley said.

"Possible to get," Harper said, "but possibly lethal." She paused, a whisper of a smile flickering across her mouth. "Are you feeling adventurous?"

"Not that much," Presley said, instantly reminded of their conversation in the tree house. She'd never sought adventure, only conquest. Her pleasure had always been more in the outcome rather than the process of attaining her goal. She'd never have imagined adventure would take the form of a quiet community in the foothills of the Adirondacks or a woman who challenged everything she thought she knew about herself. "I'll have beer too."

Flannery rose and Carrie followed, saying, "I'll give you a hand."

Harper asked Presley, "Did this afternoon's revelry convince you to give softball a try?"

"I'm afraid not," Presley said, "although I did enjoy watching everyone play. When's the first game?"

"Midweek. We're hoping to keep the word about Carrie quiet until after the first game."

"Good luck on that," Margie said.

"Yeah, I think I saw a few spotters in the crowd today."

"It sounds like you take your softball seriously," Presley said offhandedly.

Harper and Margie both stared at her.

"What?"

"Well, of course we take it seriously," Harper said as if explaining something very simple to someone very dense. "The league champions get to ride in the first car in the Labor Day parade. It's very prestigious."

Carefully, Presley studied first Harper, then Margie. Both wore identical innocent expressions. "You are all truly frightening."

They both laughed.

"What's so funny?" Flannery set glasses down on the table and passed them around to the appropriate people.

"I was being briefed on the importance of winning the softball tournament," Presley said.

"Oh yeah. Our team has been first car three years in a row. Everyone wants to unseat us."

"First car?" Carrie asked, sounding confused.

Flannery dropped into a chair and explained to Carrie.

"Oh, we are so going to win, then," Carrie said.

We. Presley sipped her beer, wondering at how easily Carrie had embraced the community. Wondering too what that meant for the work they had to do—work it was so easy to forget, sitting here with the charismatic Rivers sisters.

An hour and half later, after finishing off most of the pizzas and two rounds of drinks, everyone allowed they were ready to leave.

"I'll take you and Carrie home," Harper said.

Flannery looked like she was about to protest, then cupped Margie's neck and said, "Come on, kid. I'm your ride."

"See you at the game," Margie said to Presley.

"Oh…" Presley scrambled for an excuse, but the look on Margie's face left her no alternative. "Yes. I'll be there if I can."

Margie beamed. "Awesome."

"It's really not necessary for you to chauffeur us around," Presley said as Harper drove her and Carrie home for the second night in a row.

"It's not like it's out of my way. I don't mind."

"I appreciate it, but I'm sure you're busy, and as I recall, weekends are always the worst—"

"Shh," Harper said. "We don't talk about—" Her cell phone rang and she shook her head. "As I was saying, never say it out loud."

She pushed a button on the dash next to a small speaker. "Dr. Rivers."

"Doc," a male voice said, "it's Don Reynolds. I'm sure sorry to bother you this time of night, but I'm worried about Jimmy. He's been complaining all week about not feeling right, and when he stopped eating, we kept him home from school. But today seems even worse. Now he's got the runs on top of everything else."

"Does he have a fever?"

"Not that I can tell."

"Is he complaining of a bellyache or anything else like that?"

"He's not much of a complainer, but he just…Doc, he just doesn't look right. I'm worried."

"I'll stop by in an hour or so and take a look at him."

"I sure would appreciate it."

"No problem, Don."

Harper ended the call and turned down the driveway to Presley's.

"Why not just send them to the emergency room?" Presley asked.

"Because it's probably not an emergency, and tying up the ER staff is a waste of their time and an inconvenience for the family. I'm twenty minutes away. It'll take me another twenty, maybe, to take a look at the boy and let them know what needs to be done. It's the best allocation of resources."

Carrie asked, "If you don't think it's an emergency, couldn't he wait until the morning and go to the office?"

"Tomorrow's Sunday."

"What about urgent care?" Carrie said.

"We could send him there. But chances are he'd see someone he doesn't know and who wouldn't recognize some of the things that I would because I know him. And besides that," she slowed in front of the porch, "we like to take care of our own."

Presley said, "You've been doing a good job taking care of those of us who aren't even yours. Thank you for the ride."

"Yeah, thanks," Carrie said. "I had a great time today. I can't wait for the game."

"You were terrific," Harper said.

"Thanks. I'm also out of shape. I'm going to turn in early and pretend I'm reading in bed."

"Night," Harper called as Carrie got out.

Presley lingered. "I hope your night isn't too hectic."

"It's early yet. I've got a change of clothes with me. Would you mind if I changed here? Then I can head right over to the Reynoldses'."

"Of course not. Do you want to shower? We've got an extra bathroom you're welcome to use," Presley said.

"I don't want to put you out."

Presley clasped Harper's forearm. The muscles under her fingers tensed. "You've been looking after us since we got here. Let me return the favor."

"If you wouldn't mind." Harper leaned toward her, the air in the cab suddenly growing heavy and still.

"Of course not." Presley scented grass and earthy strength. Her fingers drifted down to Harper's hand. For an instant their fingers touched. She drew her hand away. "Come inside."

Harper reached behind the seat, her shoulder brushing Presley's. Her body was hot, her face inches away. Presley pushed open the door and climbed out, taking a deep breath. Blood pounded in her belly, urgent and wild. Thank goodness Carrie was inside. She wasn't afraid to be alone with Harper, she was afraid of herself.

"All set," Harper said.

Walking quickly toward the sanctuary of the house, Presley took Harper upstairs and showed her the bathroom. "I'll let Carrie know you're here. Make yourself at home."

"Thanks."

After warning Carrie Harper was using the shower, Presley headed into the kitchen, opened a bottle of wine that Lila had gotten her from the list she'd provided, and took it outside to the back porch. The sun had just gone down. Rooster was in the tree. She sipped her wine and thought about building a chicken coop. She didn't think about Harper naked upstairs in the shower very much at all.

"I appreciate the hospitality," Harper said, walking out onto the porch. The kitchen light behind her illuminated her face, but her eyes were in shadow. Her eyes were so often shadowed. She wore a navy short-sleeved button-up shirt outside dark pants and loafers without socks. Her hair was wet and slicked back.

Presley rose with her half-empty glass of wine. "You're more than welcome."

"Tired?"

"I wasn't the one running around in the sun all afternoon."

"You want to come with me? You can start your practical internship early."

Harper touched her hand, a fleeting touch. Not a caress. Just an automatic, unthinking touch. One she probably didn't even notice.

Presley swallowed. "Do you think the family will be bothered by a stranger?"

"I know this family. I went to school with Don's wife, Emmy. They're easygoing, and Jimmy is a good kid. He's eleven."

"It's hard to believe someone you went to school with has an eleven-year-old child."

"People tend to start younger around here."

The light went out in the kitchen. Carrie must have turned it off, not realizing they were outside. Moonlight surrounded them. "You haven't, and as I recall, you're planning on…what was it, four or five offspring?"

"I figure I'll catch up when I meet the right woman."

"And who's going to be doing the reproduction? You or the right woman?"

Harper laughed softly. "I want kids, but I don't have a strong drive to actually make them. Part of being the right woman for me is wanting to have children, but if she doesn't want to do it, we'll adopt them."

"Why do I have the feeling that the right woman is going to resemble your mother to a large degree?"

"That doesn't sound right somehow."

Presley shook her head. "I'm not being critical. Your mother is incredibly strong, that's obvious. She's raised amazing children, and I'm guessing a lot of that she did on her own when your father was away."

"That's true," Harper said. "I love my father, but I hope to figure out a way to spend a little more time at home, especially while my kids are young."

"You know, Harper," Presley said, "if you joined a multi-physician practice group and had people to cross-cover for you, you'd have a lot more time to yourself and your family in the future."

Even in the dim light, the tightening of Harper's jaw was clear. "I had a couple offers like that when I was finishing my residency. It's not for me."

"Solo practice is hard on you, hard on your wife, and will be difficult on your children."

Harper shrugged, as if dismissing the possible problem. "Maybe that's why I'm not married yet." She slid her hands into her pockets and stared past Presley to the tree where Rooster's dark shape stood out against the silvery shadows. "Maybe there are no women like that anymore."

"Now you're getting morose."

"You're right." Harper grinned wryly. "And I don't have time for that. Are you coming?"

"Yes," Presley said, admitting she wanted to. She wanted to know Harper, and nights like this were a huge part of who she was. These moments, when she went out to take care of people, giving them part of herself, were the moments no one else saw, and if Harper even thought to talk about them, how much would be lost in the translation? How much would Harper see only as ordinary, as opposed to extraordinary? This was a chance to glimpse the real Harper, the true Harper. "Yes, I would like that very much."

Presley left a note for Carrie in the kitchen on the way out.

"So, what's your take on kids?" Harper rolled the windows down as she pulled the truck out onto the two-lane. Presley's scent drifted to her on the breeze, vanilla and spice. She'd never taken anyone with her on callouts before. Margie was the right age, but that was for her father to do. She would take her own children someday, but right now, she enjoyed taking Presley.

"Generically?" Presley asked.

Harper laughed. "No, I meant for yourself. Seeing as how a relationship isn't required for that part much anymore."

"I…Children are a huge responsibility, and I'm not sure I'd ever have the time for them."

"Sometimes being short on time makes every minute more important."

"Did your parents make that work?"

"Absolutely." Harper slowed for a deer bounding across the road. "When my father first started his practice, before I was born, he took my mother with him on calls sometimes."

"Did he," Presley murmured. "I imagine that was special."

"I think it was. When we kids came, he went alone until I was old enough."

"Who looks after patients when you're away?"

"My dad or Flann. I'm not away all that much. A medical meeting now and then. Every once in a while I'll go down to New York for a show or an exhibit."

"By yourself?" Presley regretted it as soon as she asked. Harper's personal business was none of her business, and she didn't especially want to know about who shared her free hours. Then again, maybe it would be better if she did.

"Sometimes Carson will go with me. Flann, if it's a baseball game." Harper glanced over at her. "Sometimes I'll take a date."

"Someone special?" Presley asked lightly.

"No. You?"

"No, no one. No one special."

"I told you who I'm waiting for. What are you waiting for?"

Presley's immediate instinct was to say nothing. She had no aspirations for marriage or family. As she started to form the words, she caught herself. Was that really true? When she thought of her family, she was certain that wasn't what she wanted. Her parents were well-matched. They enjoyed entertaining, enjoyed seeing and being seen, but she couldn't remember witnessing a hint of passion or even intimate companionship. They shared a love of power and success and money. She enjoyed those things too, but more as personal satisfaction, not what she wanted to cement a relationship with. "I don't know. I'm not sure I'm waiting for, looking for, anything. Some people just aren't meant for serious relationships."

"Not sure I believe that." Harper turned down a narrow dirt road, the headlights illuminating trees and the occasional bright eyes of animals by the side of the road. "Sometimes I think people who say they prefer to be alone are just afraid to be with someone else."

Presley fisted her hands. "That's a rather arrogant thing to say."

"Is it?" Harper stopped in front of a big, white, two-story rambling farmhouse like so many of the others they passed everywhere, with a larger barn, a cluster of outbuildings, a truck in the yard, and other signs of a working farm. "You're probably right. Even so, I think it would be a loss to someone if you decided you really would prefer to be alone."

Heat stirred in Presley's depths. "And I think your Ms. Right will be very lucky."

CHAPTER EIGHTEEN

A light burned over the front door, outlining the Reynolds house against the inky sky. The farmhouse was smaller than the White place, a long porch with a metal roof and a white railing with a few missing spindles running along the entire front. Symmetrical windows on either side of the door were echoed by matching ones on the second floor. A soft light glowed in one upstairs window. Before Presley and Harper reached the worn wooden steps, a man came through the screen door, the hinges creaking loudly in the still air. He didn't bother to hold it, and it slammed behind him. He wore brown canvas work pants and a faded red T-shirt stretched tight across his broad shoulders and small paunch. He looked to be about forty, but in the dim light, his age was difficult to tell. Like so many of the men Presley had seen around town, his wide jaw was whiskered and his face lined and weathered. His thick dark hair, cut close, still held the circular indentations of a farm cap. His forearms were ropy with muscle, and his hands large. He pushed his hands into his pants pockets, his movements jerky and uneasy.

"I'm real glad you could make it, Doc," he said as Presley and Harper reached the porch. His deep voice was as scratchy as a day-old beard.

"No problem, Don."

Harper held out one hand in greeting. In the other she carried a large black leather satchel, something Presley had not seen in almost a decade of visiting hospitals and doctors' offices. *Harper L. Rivers, M.D.* was embossed on the side in inch-high gold letters. The leather was worn at the corners and scraped in places on the sides where she imagined Harper had pushed it into the compartment behind the seat of her truck and set it on the floor in dozens of houses such as this. Harper looked completely natural, completely right, carrying that bag into this worn and faintly tired-looking house. Presley was the one who felt out of place.

Was it possible she had stepped back fifty years when she'd gotten off the airplane? That seemed like a long time ago now. And if that was true, did she really want to go back?

Presley shook the whimsy aside as Harper motioned to her and said, "Don, this is Presley Worth. She's from the hospital."

"Ma'am."

"Good to meet you, Mr. Reynolds," Presley said.

Don Reynolds focused on Harper again and pulled open the screen door. "He's upstairs in bed. Emmy is with him."

"What about Darla? Is she sick?" Harper asked as they followed Don Reynolds into his house.

"Not as near as we can tell. She's eating fine and doesn't have a fever. Emmy took her temperature."

"That's good. What about the two of you? Noticed anything out of the ordinary lately? Been any place new—eaten out at an unfamiliar spot?"

He laughed harshly. "Not hardly. Haven't been off the farm to speak of all spring and with money tight…"

"Jimmy's school friends? Any of them sick that you know of?"

"We didn't ask him." Don Reynolds's voice held a hopeful note, as if Jimmy sharing an illness with other kids must mean it couldn't be very serious.

"Well, we'll take a look at him and see," Harper said.

The foyer was more a hall barely big enough for a coatrack on the wall and a small table where a pile of mail sat unopened. Rooms on either side looked well lived in, with big sofas and end tables holding empty drink glasses and a scatter of magazines. A wooden staircase, not as wide or elaborate as that in the White place, led to the second floor.

They trooped upstairs and down the narrow hall to a room where an open door emitted a slanting square of pale yellow light onto the bare wood floor. Presley hung back a little, letting Harper enter first with Don Reynolds. She stopped just inside the door. The room was small with a single window and a dresser connected to a desk piled with the things boys played with: a baseball glove, a motorized truck of some kind, a stack of books. The wall held a few posters from movies Presley didn't recognize.

A woman in a white T-shirt, blue jeans, and purple rubber flip-flops sat on a straight-backed chair by the side of the single bed. Her dark wavy hair was caught back in a yellow scrunchie. She looked eighteen, but Presley knew if she'd gone to school with Harper she was at least ten years older. A gold wedding band glinted on her left hand, the same hand that was currently stroking the hair of a pale-looking boy with frightened eyes. Harper had said he was eleven, but his thin body and wan expression made him look eight.

"Hi, Emmy." Harper introduced Presley as she had before, and the boy's mother nodded, though Presley didn't think she actually paid any attention to anything other than her son.

"Glad you're here, Harper," Emmy said in a monotone.

Presley remembered the eerie wail of the mother in the ER, and sweat broke out on her arms. Such misery. Was this Harper's life?

"Can I sit where you are, Emmy?" Harper said. "You can sit on the bed on the other side with him if you like."

Wordlessly, Emmy Reynolds went around the end of the narrow bed and gently sat next to her son, her hand going back to his hair. Don Reynolds leaned against a spot next to the window, his hands back in his pockets again as if he didn't know what to do with them.

Harper turned the chair until it faced the bed and sat, leaning forward with her elbows on her knees. She'd put her bag on the floor next to her but hadn't moved to open it yet. "I'm Dr. Rivers. How you doing, Jimmy?"

"Okay." The boy's voice was weak and whispery. He glanced at his mother anxiously.

"It's okay, baby, the doctor is here to make you better."

Harper's calm expression never changed. "Your dad tells me you haven't been eating much the last few days. Not hungry?"

"I don't know. I guess not."

"Does your stomach hurt?"

The boy shook his head.

"What about the rest of you? Does anything else hurt?"

"My head a little bit," he said shyly. "It just feels funny."

"Funny like dizzy?"

The boy shrugged. "I guess."

"Okay, then. I'll just take a look at you and listen to your heart and your lungs and your belly."

The boy's brows drew down. "Why are you gonna listen to my belly?"

Harper smiled and reached down with one hand to unclasp her

bag, the motion automatic and practiced. Still gazing at Jimmy, she came up with a stethoscope that she put in her ears. "You know the sound it makes when you're hungry, right? Well, I'm going to listen to see if maybe you're hungry and didn't notice."

He grinned. "Okay."

Harper pulled down the sheets to just below his navel and moved her stethoscope over his chest and abdomen, right side, left side, all the way down to the top of his Spider-Man pj's. When she was done, she swung the stethoscope around her neck and put her hand on his belly. "I'm going to press and you tell me if it hurts. If it does, I'll stop right away, okay?"

He nodded. Her touch appeared sure and gentle as she examined his upper abdomen and then lower down. At one point he told her it felt funny.

"Funny, like hurt?" Harper asked.

He shook his head. "Just funny. Like…sore, a little."

"Okay." She shone a light in his eyes and his throat and felt his neck. When done, she put her stethoscope back in the bag and smiled at him. "You were terrific. I'm going to talk to your mom and dad outside for a few minutes, okay?"

"Sure," he said and closed his eyes.

Presley stepped aside until Don and Emmy Reynolds filed out into the hall with Harper behind them. She slipped out, and Harper slowly closed the door. Presley's heart kicked in her chest and she realized her palms were damp. She couldn't even imagine how the boy's parents must feel. Harper hadn't given any indication that anything was wrong, but in that moment, when everything hinged on what Harper was about to say, the hall felt suffocating. Harper had become the center of these people's world. Presley tried to imagine what that responsibility must feel like, the burden it must be to carry, and the cost it must extract in emotional coin.

"Jimmy has some enlargement of his spleen," Harper said immediately, her tone calm and matter-of-fact. "That's an organ in his belly like the glands we have in our neck that get swollen when we have a cold. I'm not finding anything else that might be causing his problems. There are a lot of things that could cause his symptoms, and I think we need to put him in the hospital to do some tests."

"Hospital?" Emmy grabbed her husband's arm with one hand and reached for Harper with the other. "God, Harper. Is it bad?"

Harper took her hand. Don Reynolds slid his arm around his

wife's shoulders almost as if he needed to lean on her to keep standing as much as to comfort her.

"I can't tell, Emmy," Harper said. "It might be something as simple as a virus or it could be something else. Whatever it is, I want to find out quickly so we can start to take care of things. Can you get someone to come stay with Darla so you can take him over to the hospital?"

"Tonight?" Don Reynolds's voice cracked. "You want to take him to the hospital tonight?"

"I think that would be best. He hasn't been eating, and he's probably dehydrated. He'll feel better when we give him some intravenous fluid, and I can get the tests I want started right away."

Don looked at Emmy, his expression stunned. "I...I can call my mother. She'll come over."

"Good," Harper said.

"Don, honey," Emmy said soothingly, "why don't you go call your mom. I'll talk to Jimmy."

"Okay, sure. I can do that. Sure."

Emmy watched her husband trudge away before asking Harper, "Can I stay with him in the hospital?"

"Absolutely. Once we get him settled, we'll have the nurses bring a cot into his room for you."

Tears glistened on Emmy's lashes, and she brushed at them impatiently. She stared down the hall as if checking to see they were still alone. "Harper, I want the truth."

Harper brushed Emmy's shoulder. "I'm telling you the truth, Emmy. I don't know what's wrong."

"But you suspect something, don't you."

Harper smiled, still calm and unruffled. "It's my job to be suspicious. That's why I want him in the hospital. My guessing right now is not going to help him or you."

"We don't have insurance. Last year's crops were so bad, we had to let it go."

"There are ways to handle that. And now is not the time to worry about it. What matters is Jimmy."

"I want you to tell me first, soon as you know. Don..." Her voice shook. "Don is the best husband I could ever want, but he's not strong about some things. He won't...if it's bad, he won't do good."

"You first, I promise."

"All right, I'll go talk to Jimmy alone if you don't mind. If I need you, I'll call."

"Sure. You go ahead. Pack enough clothes for a few days."

Emmy stopped and gave Harper a hard look, but finally disappeared.

When the door closed, Harper sighed tiredly and rubbed her face. Presley wished she could help her—help all of them somehow—and had never felt quite so useless in her life.

"We'll be ready to go in just a few minutes," Emmy said when she came out. "As soon as Don's mother gets here."

"All right, I'll meet you at the hospital," Harper said.

Emmy Reynolds nodded distractedly. "I'm going to get Darla ready to go to Sally's."

Harper and Presley let themselves out. When they reached the truck, Harper said, "I'll take you home."

"No," Presley said. "I'm in the opposite direction from the hospital. The family will need you to be there when they get there, and I'm sure you have things that you need to do before they arrive."

"I could be there a while."

Presley opened her door and climbed into the truck. "Then we should get going."

Harper got behind the wheel, grateful that Presley understood without her needing to tell her what was happening. Cases like this were some of the hardest she ever had to deal with. Emmy was scared, Don was terrified, and she feared she wouldn't have good news for them. She started the truck and headed for the Rivers.

"Can you tell me what you suspect?" Presley asked.

Harper sighed. "Both his spleen and liver are enlarged. A boy his age, with his symptoms, we have to worry that he's got leukemia or lymphoma. Either one is dangerous. It might be something simpler, but…"

"But you don't think so."

"No," Harper said, "I don't think so."

"Are these things treatable?"

"Yes, and a lot more successfully than ten or twenty years ago, depending on exactly what he has. No matter what the type, though, if he has leukemia, he's in for a rough ride. So are his parents."

"God, that's horrible."

"Yes, it is." Harper glanced over at Presley. "I'm sorry, this is going to take a few hours. Your night will be shot."

"Don't be silly. Just do what you have to do. I'll be fine." Presley clasped Harper's wrist. "If I were home, I'd probably be working. I can do that while I wait just as well at the hospital."

"You work too much."

"Says the doctor who makes house calls on Saturday night."

"I can see why my father liked company. It helps." Harper turned her hand over to grasp Presley's. Presley's fingers on her forearm were comforting, a connection she welcomed as she thought about the night ahead and the pain she was likely to bring to Don and Emmy. Pain not of her doing, but pain she would have to deliver all the same. And she worried about Jimmy, a boy who shouldn't have to deal with anything more serious than improving his baseball swing and what he would do on summer vacation. She held Presley's hand a moment longer and let go.

"I'm glad it helps," Presley said softly. "And I'm glad I'm here."

Chapter Nineteen

I'll be in my office," Presley told Harper as they stopped in front of the ER entrance. "I'm sure you'll be tied up awhile, so don't worry about calling."

"I will when I've finished," Harper said. "But if you want to leave—"

"I won't, but if I do, my car is here. So don't worry about me. I'll be fine."

The big red-and-white sign overhead painted Harper's face in stark relief. Gone was the quiet, careful woman who favored a secluded hideaway up among the branches of a great oak. Her jaw was set in granite and a hard light burned in her eyes. The warrior had emerged, and seeing her this way was enough to make Presley believe she was undefeatable. The family would believe that too, she had no doubt. "If I can do anything—"

"You have." Harper stared up at the blazing sign and the building looming beyond. "I love this place, but there's a lot of pain inside these walls." She glanced at Presley. "Sometimes it's lonely."

Presley's throat tightened. Had she ever been this brave? Had she ever admitted, even to herself, all the things she longed for? "Not tonight."

Harper touched her hand. "No. Not tonight."

"Go, do what you need to do. I'll be here."

"Thanks," Harper said.

They parted company just inside. In her office, Presley settled behind her desk and pulled up the projections Preston's team had provided along with the hospital financials she'd collected earlier. She keyed in data and ran various scenarios, looking for loss points and duplications, wide margins between billables and receivables, searching for the places where the cash flow might be converted from negative to positive. Unfortunately, one of those areas was the number of staff—an overabundance or poor allocation of staff was a drain on resources.

She appreciated the importance of a low staff-to-patient ratio, but in some areas where patient outcome was not as critically impacted by a higher ratio, some of the nursing and technical staff could be reassigned or even eliminated. The same, she was certain, was going to show up in many areas of direct services. The physicians themselves were not salaried, being private practitioners with admitting privileges who consulted at the hospital and admitted patients when necessary. Those patients then funneled revenue into the system via their insurance or, in rare instances, direct pay. Unfortunately, as she scanned the accounts for the last five years, it was obvious the percentage of insured and/or direct pays was declining and the percentage with some kind of state or federal assistance rising. Patients on government subsidy had a very poor ratio of billables to receivables. And worst of all were the self-pays, which almost always meant no pay.

She leaned back, thinking about Jimmy Reynolds. His mother had said they had no insurance. They were a prime example of the working poor who couldn't afford insurance, despite being above the poverty line. Who would pay for his care? Should it be the hospital's burden, when it meant that too many Jimmy Reynoldses would result in no hospital at all? Should the community shoulder the burden, through taxes paid to the state that were used to provide medical assistance for families like Jimmy's? Or, as the current administration proposed, was the answer in federally guaranteed health care? Would health care for all result, as it had in so many other countries, in a two-tier system where those who could afford private insurance would always have it, and with it, greater access to the system—the best doctors, the hospitals of their choice, and the most expedient care? Presley couldn't change the system, she could only figure out ways to work within—or more often around—it. And no matter how she aligned and realigned the numbers, the Rivers needed a new source of revenue and a way to stop the current losses, or as Preston had rightly predicted, it would die.

A few days ago, that conclusion would have been not only inevitable, but totally acceptable. Now part of her wondered if there might be a different solution somewhere. At the very least, they could look at the reimbursement structure and perhaps find a way to cut the losses in that area during the transition. Carrie had already begun working on that. In the meantime, she would proceed with the current plan to convert ACH to a more lucrative institution. Ideally, SunView's goal was to repurpose the physical plant with the least amount of construction. Usually, with staff already in place as it was here, that meant either a rehab center with long-term care potential or a retirement community with nursing care facilities.

She'd need to put together a local construction team to look at the hospital blueprints and draw up plans for conversion. SunView had done this all over the country, and once preliminaries went back to the design department, she'd have something to work with within a month. On that kind of accelerated schedule, she had a bit of time before she'd need to close the ER to admissions and redirect the staff to discharge or transfer in-house patients. But in one month she had to be sure.

An hour and a half later when she'd done as much as she could, she shut down the computer. Harper hadn't called. She didn't want to leave without finding out how Jimmy was doing, and she didn't want to leave without seeing Harper. She already knew the family, so stopping in the ER wasn't going to be intrusive. She packed her laptop and walked through the empty halls of the administrative wing into the clinical area. Unlike her office building at home where she was often the only one working late at night, the hospital was somnolent, but not asleep. Maintenance engineers pushed big machines with giant rotating brushes back and forth, polishing the worn tiled floors. Transport personnel pushed patients on litters and in wheelchairs toward X-ray and the elevators. Doctors and nurses talked in low voices as they passed. The lights in most of the hallways had been turned down, leaving the corners in shadow. Her footsteps seemed an intrusion on the solemn quiet.

The bright lights of the ER entrance signaled a return to activity. A middle-aged woman in sweatpants and a wrinkled checked shirt sat in the waiting area adjacent to the treatment area with a teenage boy who was holding his left arm against his chest, a grimace on his face. Just as Presley went to press the red button on the wall to open the automatic ER doors, they swung toward her. She stepped aside as a husky blond in a scrub shirt and jeans strode out.

"Jason Smith?" he called.

The boy and his mother stood up. Presley walked into the ER behind the trio as the man said, "Hi. I'm Will Eddy, a PA. You flipped your ATV, huh?"

"Yeah," the boy said. "I think maybe I broke my arm."

"Lucky he didn't break his fool neck," the woman muttered, stroking the boy's hair as they walked.

The PA led the mother and son down the hall toward the treatment areas. "We'll get an X-ray of your arm and see what's going on."

Presley checked the whiteboard. Three patients' names were printed in precise black letters. Jimmy Reynolds was listed in room nine. No one was in sight, so she waited by the long counter opposite the board until someone turned up and she could ask about Jimmy. A minute passed and Harper came around the corner carrying a clipboard. She checked her watch when she saw Presley.

"Sorry, the time got away from me," Harper said.

"That's all right. I've been working. How are things going?"

"His labs should be done by now. I was just about to pull them up on the computer." Harper gestured to a row of black-vinyl-topped stools on the far side of the counter where several monitors and bins of loose papers stood in a line. "Have a look."

Presley followed Harper around the counter and sat next to her. Harper typed in her name and a password, then some other identifying data for Jimmy, and lab work appeared on the screen. Presley looked over the numbers, and she didn't need to be a doctor to see the string of asterisks marking the abnormal values. WBC: 65,000. Blasts: 80%. She caught her breath.

"We'll need a bone marrow biopsy in the morning," Harper muttered, "but it looks like AML."

"AML?"

"Acute myeloblastic leukemia. He's in crisis." Her voice was flat and hard.

"Meaning what?"

Harper pushed back and rolled her shoulders. "Meaning he needs chemo right away, and maybe a stem cell transplant. That will be the hematologist's call."

"Can you handle that here?" Presley thought of St. Joseph's and Banner Good Sam and the other huge medical centers in Phoenix. The shiny glass-and-steel complexes, so different than this centuries-old stone-and-timber edifice, were cold and impersonal, but their very imposing size inspired confidence. But was newer always better?

"It depends on what the heme guy says," Harper replied. "Chemotherapy is chemotherapy, and if Jimmy stays here, he'll be closer to home. His parents have a seven-year-old at home, crops in the field, and animals to tend. They'll want to be with him as much as they can, but they can't leave everything behind, either."

"Where's the hematologist?"

"About thirty minutes away in Saratoga. They've got a satellite office near here and admit patients now and then. They'll also see consults."

"Can you get one of them here tonight?"

"For this, you bet."

"I'm going to wait."

Harper said, "It might be morning before we get this sorted."

"Are you going to be able to get any sleep?"

"Probably not."

"Then we'll have an early breakfast."

Harper studied her for a long moment. "I'm cooking, then."

"We'll discuss it."

"Deal." Harper rose. "There's a staff lounge down the hall if you get tired of working. Bad TV and decent coffee, usually."

"Thanks, I'll find it."

"I'm going to go tell his parents."

Presley grasped her arm. "Harper?"

Harper stopped, a question in her eyes.

"It's good that it's you. They trust you."

Harper blew out a breath. "Yeah."

❖

Presley contemplated going back to her office, but for once, the appeal of dry facts and figures eluded her. Her stomach was jittery with agitation, but she headed for the cafeteria for a cup of coffee anyhow. Compared to the rest of the first floor, the cafeteria was a beehive of activity. Not many tables were occupied, but cafeteria workers were slotting big aluminum trays of food into the wells in the long steam tables. The coffeemaker was perking away. Hospital personnel were straggling in, in pairs and small groups. Presley paused at the head of the food line, contemplating whether she was actually hungry or not. The pizza she'd shared had been hours ago, but she finally decided coffee was all her stomach could handle.

"Passing on late-night supper?"

Presley spun around. "Flannery. What in the world—" She caught herself, taking in Flannery's scrubs. The last time she'd seen her had been after the practice, in a ratty T-shirt and gym shorts. "Saturday night. An accident?"

Flann shook her head. "For once, something better. A delivery."

Presley could feel her brows climb. "You're here delivering a baby?"

"Right now, I'm just babysitting. Valerie Simpson, the OB, was up at Lake George with her husband and twins when one of her patients decided to deliver early. She called and asked me if I could cover for her until she could get here."

Presley immediately thought of the liability issues. OB was one of the specialties with the highest malpractice insurance rates and the largest number of suits brought against practitioners, primarily because anything involving either the mother or the child for years to come could potentially result in a suit. Flannery was no doubt capable, but she wasn't a board-certified OB/GYN physician. There had been a time, not that many years before, when a general surgeon like Flannery would routinely provide care in many of the areas that were now relegated to subspecialists. General surgeons used to set fractures, deliver babies, treat trauma, and operate on every part of the body. Now some surgical specialty existed for almost everything—the eyes, the ears, the chest, the abdomen, the vascular system, the soft tissues, the female reproductive organs, the male urinary system, and of course, the world of the fetus before and after birth. "Does this happen often?"

"Not too often—I've assisted on a few tough deliveries when I've been handy. Every once in a while I'll scrub in on a hysterectomy if Valerie needs help."

"I'm beginning to see why you and Harper like this kind of practice. The things you do are almost unheard of in other places."

Flannery's gaze was direct and unwavering. "That's a shame, don't you think?"

"For doctors like the two of you, yes, it probably is. There are those, though, who would argue that you can't possibly be good at all of those things, and specialization is the best way to provide the most effective care."

Flannery didn't appear offended. She made a face as if to say, *so what*. "I know my limits. So does Harper. That counts for more than anything." She grinned, and the devil was back in her eyes. "I know what I'm good at too, so that helps."

Presley laughed. "It's in the genes, that surgical arrogance, isn't it?"

"Might be in my blue jeans."

"God, I walked into that one, didn't I?"

"Pretty much." Flannery picked up her tray and tilted her chin toward the hot table behind her. "You sure you don't want something to eat? It's free."

"Really? Every night?"

"Yes, for the night staff and whoever else might be here working."

"That's got to be pricey." Presley followed as Flannery walked toward a table.

"That's it for you, isn't it, the bottom line?" Flannery sat down, her comment not delivered critically, but simply matter-of-factly.

Presley took no offense. Why should she? "Yes, it has to be. That's my job. Don't you think being profitable is important?"

"It's one thing that's important." Flannery picked up half of a huge triple-decker sandwich and took a healthy bite. She chewed for a few moments and sipped some coffee. "It's not everything, though. Sometimes sacrificing a little of the bottom line for quality is worth the trade-off."

"One hopes not to sacrifice either."

"Let me ask you something. SunView—big hospitals, little hospitals, everything in between?"

"More or less. Fewer of the smaller ones all the time."

"If you were sick or someone you loved was sick, where would you want them to go?"

"It would depend on what was wrong. I would want them to go where they could get the best care."

"Okay, fair enough." Flannery went back to her sandwich for a minute. "Define the best care."

Presley pushed away the cup of coffee she didn't want anymore. "I would think that would be obvious. The most up-to-date, accurate, effective care possible."

"So you wouldn't care if a robot delivered the treatment, as long as it was effective."

Presley sighed. "I know where you're going with this. Yes, the personal factor matters. Of course I would rather have a doctor like you or Harper, someone who knows me, who understands what's important to me, who cares about me and my life beyond the illness, but—"

"You noticed? Harper must be doing a good job."

Presley stiffened, a chill rippling down her spine. "I'm sorry?"

"Harper—she's taking you around to show you the human side of things. Smart of her."

"And I suppose that's all part of some grand plan?" Presley said, feeling the coolness in her voice. "To sway me somehow?"

"I didn't say that," Flannery said, her tone conciliatory. "You can't have a plan until you know where all the pieces fit on the board, and you're pretty good at keeping that to yourself."

"And what's your role in all of this?"

Flannery's eyes danced. "I was hoping to seduce you and then get the inside scoop, but I don't see that happening now."

Presley could not contain her laughter. "My God, your ego is lethal."

Flannery lifted a huge piece of berry pie off her tray and placed it on the table between them. She picked up a spoon and handed it to Presley. "Share some pie?"

"I'm not even going to ask why you decided not to seduce me."

"Can't," Flannery said, cutting off a piece of pie and forking it into her mouth. "It's an unwritten rule."

"I'm sorry?"

"No poaching, not when it's serious."

"I'm not following the metaphor."

The laughter in Flannery's eyes winked out. "Harper. She's interested, you got that, right?"

Slowly, Presley sat back in her seat. "This is a conversation we're not going to have."

"All right, as long as we're not having it, let me just mention one thing. She's not like me. She doesn't go in for variety. When she notices a woman, it's because the woman means something to her."

"Is that a warning?"

"No. Harper's a big girl, she can take care of herself." Flannery picked up the spoon Presley had put down on the table and broke off another piece of pie. She held it out to Presley. "But you don't know her well enough to know any of that, so I just wanted to give you a heads-up. Try it, it's really good pie."

Presley took the spoon and contemplated flinging its contents. *When Harper notices a woman, it's because she's serious.* She didn't want Harper to be serious about her. Did she? "Have you had very many pies thrown at you?"

Flannery grinned. "Quite a few, actually."

"I'm not surprised."

"I'll back off now so you can eat that instead of throwing it."

"Thank you." Presley tried it. "Excellent pie."

"Told you. What are you doing here so late, by the way?"

"Harper got a call while she was taking me and Carrie home, and I went out with her. She had to admit the boy and I came along."

Flannery frowned. "Who?"

"Jimmy Reynolds. Harper thinks he has leukemia."

"Son of a bitch," Flannery said. "If that's what Harper thinks, then he does. She doesn't make mistakes about things like that." Flannery rubbed her face. "That's going to be hard on her."

"Yes, children must be so difficult—"

"Especially after Katie."

"What do you mean?"

"Katie, she came between Carson and Margie. She died of leukemia."

"Oh God," Presley whispered. "I'm so sorry for all of you."

"Do me a favor," Flannery said.

"All right," Presley said, not needing to hear what Flannery wanted. Flannery was thinking of Harper, and so was she.

"If she doesn't get out of here tonight, call me. I'll come and drag her home. She's gonna wear herself out trying to cure this kid."

"Do you always look after her?"

"It's mutual. That's what siblings do."

"Yes. Of course." The cold settled around Presley's heart. She had no idea what siblings did, only what competitors did. "Actually, we're going to have breakfast, so I'll be sure she gets some rest after."

"Are you now?" Flannery studied her before sliding the pie a little closer. "Good. Have another bite."

CHAPTER TWENTY

A little after four a.m., Harper checked the staff lounge adjacent to the nurses' station for Presley. She expected her to have left, even though she'd said she wanted to stay. The nights got long and lonely in the hospital after midnight. A single counter light burned in the kitchenette tucked into one corner. The television suspended on the wall by a thick metal bracket was silent, a rare and blessed event. Usually the set played day and night, tuned to a network talk show or, more often, a soap. Presley was stretched out on the sofa, her shoes lined up neatly on the floor beside it, her iPad resting on her chest. Her eyes were closed, her face relaxed, her breathing even. She was deeply asleep. Harper leaned against the door and looked at her.

Despite the fact that they'd both been in the same clothes going on a day, Presley looked a hell of a lot better than her, as if she could open her eyes and stride to the front of the boardroom in perfect command. Her pale green shirt and black trousers were apparently made of some miracle material that never wrinkled or lost their crisp, fresh appearance. Her hair appeared lustrous and tangle free. Presley was the embodiment of style and power, a combination Harper had never given much thought to before and now found seductively appealing. But what made her want to run her fingers through those perfect blond waves and wake Presley with a soft, claiming kiss had only a little to do with Presley's attractiveness. She wanted to see that surprised look of wonder again—the one Presley had displayed when she first took in the tree house, as if she'd made a marvelous discovery. The pleasure she'd revealed when she'd slowly walked around, fingers trailing over the wood, the furniture, the old books on the shelves, as if everything was remarkable and new to her.

Harper had wondered then what kind of world Presley had

come from that something as simple as that tree house could be so enthralling. Presley's enchantment enchanted Harper, and from that moment on, she wanted to be the one to put that look of simple joy back on Presley's face. She wanted to share with Presley what mattered most to her and learn what mattered to Presley, in the places Presley hid away from others. She had no doubt those soft, vulnerable places were there. She'd seen them in Presley's eyes in the tree house, heard them in her voice when she'd talked to Margie, witnessed them when Presley stayed through the night to find out about a boy she'd just met. Stayed for Harper too. That thought was one she didn't quite know what to do with. Presley turned her head and opened her eyes as if Harper had made some sound or movement that awakened her. But she hadn't.

"How did you know I was here?" Harper asked.

Presley smiled. "I felt you."

"Did you."

Presley's eyes were languorous and inviting. "Yes. You were watching me."

"I was." Harper's throat was dry. "Do you mind?"

"No. I like it." Presley's gaze roamed over her. "I didn't know I would."

"You must get looked at a lot. You're very beautiful."

"I like that you think so. Another surprise." Presley's lips parted ever so slightly. "You do that a lot. Surprise me."

"I like that." Harper clenched inside, imagining the softness of Presley's mouth on her body. She wanted the press of Presley's flesh beneath her hands.

Presley touched the sofa by her hip. "Come sit down. You must be exhausted."

"I don't think that's a good idea."

"No?"

Harper shook her head. "Just now I won't be able not to touch you, and this is hardly a private place."

Presley sat up and pushed her hair back with both hands. As if by divine design, every strand seemed to fall into place perfectly. "Do you have another suggestion?"

"Yes. My place." Harper swallowed, tried to ignore the pounding in her belly. "I promised you breakfast."

"Yes, you did." Presley rose and slipped into her shoes.

"How do you do that?" Harper asked.

"How do I do what?"

"Look so perfectly put together when all the rest of us mortals would look like yesterday's dinner."

"Just lucky, I guess." Presley laughed and color flooded her face.

Harper was very glad she'd stayed in the doorway. She liked seeing the heat in Presley's face, liked that she'd been the cause. "Where's your car?"

"In the back lot. Not far from where you parked."

"Follow me, then?" Harper asked Presley as they walked out into the night.

"I will."

Dawn was still an hour away and the night was cool beneath a starlit sky. The half-moon gave just enough light to see by.

"Wait," Harper said.

Presley stopped. "What?"

Harper slid her fingertips into Presley's hair and drew her close. "I have to do this."

She kissed her slowly, savoring the softness of her lips. She stopped before she couldn't, her breath trapped in her chest and desire a sharp pain in her belly. "You're beautiful in the moonlight."

"And you are dangerous," Presley said in a husky voice, "in any light."

"No," Harper murmured, "not me. Flann is the charmer. I don't have her way with women."

Presley pressed her palm to the center of Harper's chest and kissed her, a firm but fleeting kiss. "There you are quite wrong, Dr. Rivers."

"I have a terrible urge to put my hands on you," Harper confessed.

Presley drew a shaky breath. Harper was trembling. *I have a terrible urge to put my hands on you.*

Presley couldn't think why she should stop her. Harper just made her want so damn much. She summoned the last of her willpower. "And I would like it very much if you would go get into your truck and show me how to get to your house."

"Is that what you want?"

"I want a lot of things, but right now I think the safest place for us is in our separate vehicles."

"All right. My place isn't far."

Presley sighed in relief when Harper turned away, doing what she had not been able to do—break the connection between them. Somehow Harper managed to do what no one and nothing else in her life had ever accomplished—broken her control. She didn't want to want her.

She didn't want to touch her, and she couldn't seem to stop either one. Hopefully by the time she'd driven a few miles, she'd have regained control of her reason and put her runaway hormones back where they belonged—behind locked doors until she was in charge again. Perhaps by the time she reached Harper's, the kiss would no longer tingle on her lips. She could only hope, because she didn't seem to have the ability to do anything else.

❖

Harper watched Presley's headlights in her rearview mirror as she traveled the empty roads home. The kiss left her agitated and high at the same time. She ought to back off, the timing was all wrong. Hell, Flann was probably right. Everything was all wrong, but Presley *had* kissed her back. And she wanted more.

The short drive wasn't long enough to dispel the simmering in her gut, but the cool air had cleared her head a little by the time she reached the house. She stopped in front of the barn, and Presley pulled in behind her and got out.

"I'll just be a minute," Harper said when she climbed out of the truck. "You can wait for me on the back porch or come with me if you want. I need to do a few things in the barn."

Presley walked toward her. "Is there anything I can help with?"

"Company would be nice." On impulse, Harper held out her hand. When Presley's hand slipped into hers, a sense of rightness filled her. "I just need to feed the animals since I never got back here last night."

The cats, one yellow male and a tortoiseshell female, were curled up together on a window shelf in the back of the barn, the same place they'd slept since they were kittens. They raised their heads when she opened two cans of food and jumped down as soon as she put the bowls on the floor.

"I have kittens," Presley said.

"Oh yeah? How many?"

"Four. I haven't seen the mother."

"She might have left them."

"No. Really?"

"It's possible." Harper petted the tortie. "Their mother hung around until they were about five weeks old, and then one day she just didn't come back. They stayed, though."

"I'd better check on them later. They might need food."

Harper laughed. "It depends on what you want."

"I'm sorry?"

"All you have to do to keep barn cats is feed them."

"Well, of course I'll feed them."

"Then they'll be yours forever."

Clouds passed through Presley's expressive eyes. "But what will happen when I'm not there anymore?"

"Then I imagine they'll miss you," Harper said softly.

Presley took Harper's hand again. "Who else?"

"What do you mean?" Harper murmured.

"Who else do you need to feed?"

Harper smiled. "The goats."

"Goats. What do you do with goats?"

"These particular goats are mostly pets, but they have excellent coats, and right before winter, we'll strip them and donate the fiber to a local fiber mill. They'll spin it into yarn."

"Do you—knit?" Presley tried to hide her disbelief but failed.

"Not hardly. That's why I donate it." As they talked, Harper led Presley outside and around the back of the barn to another pasture. She opened the fence. "Be careful of the top line there, it's electrified."

Inside, she called to the goats, who bounded out of their shed and came toward her at a trot, several of them bleating in recognition. She checked their water, added more hay to the rack, and scratched their ears.

"Now it's our turn for food." Harper locked the pasture gate, and Presley took her hand again. They reached the house just as the sun came up.

"I can't believe it's morning." Presley paused on the top step and took a deep breath. "God, the air smells good."

"Tired?" Harper held open the screen door on the back porch. She rarely locked the house and hadn't the day before when she'd left. The kitchen still smelled faintly of cornbread and bacon from the meal she'd cooked for Flann.

"I'm used to late hours and erratic schedules," Presley said. "I'm more hungry than tired, and maybe a little grimy too."

"Me too." Harper grinned. "What would you like? Coffee or how about a shower?"

Presley stilled. The idea of a shower, one she didn't take alone, was suddenly all she could think about. All she could see was Harper, steam rising around her, her hair plastered to her neck as water coursed over her shoulders, streaming between her breasts and down the length of her abdomen. The thought of sliding her palms where the water had just been, over the curves of Harper's breasts and the hard, smooth plane of her abdomen, made her hands ache. Going to her knees and pressing her mouth to the heat between Harper's thighs drove the hunger to a fever pitch.

"Coffee."

Harper's eyes searched hers. "That's not what I thought you were going to say."

"Were you reading my mind?" Presley laughed ruefully. "I certainly hope not."

"I caught a glimpse of what you were thinking." Harper rested both hands on Presley's hips. "I hope I saw right."

"What do you think you saw?"

"Us, naked, under the water, touching."

Presley's legs trembled and want clutched at her throat. "It's crazy. We'd be crazy to even once—"

Harper pulled her closer. "How much crazier is it going to get if we don't?"

Presley shivered. Heat poured from Harper's body. "I don't know. I'm not thinking very clearly."

"I'm not thinking at all." Harper kissed Presley's throat. "You know what? That feels really good—just feeling you." She kissed her again, palms sliding down the length of Presley's back. "Feels right. You taste amazing."

"Shouldn't we talk about—"

"I don't think we should talk about anything at all. Not right now." Harper raised her head and her eyes were endless. "Tell me no now, if you mean it."

"I wouldn't," Presley whispered.

"Then come with me."

The next instant they were upstairs—at least Presley had no memory of anything other than suddenly being in a large stone-tiled bathroom with a glass-walled double shower, and warm water already streaming from the showerhead. Maybe she was still imagining... She blinked, but everything remained exactly the same. Only now Harper was opening her shirt. Somewhere a voice warned her she should stop, think, but the sound faded with every passing second. When the backs of Harper's fingers brushed over the top of her breast, she heard only the steady beat of water on glass and her own heart pounding in her throat. She needed to feel her. Grasping Harper's shirt, she tugged open the buttons and pushed the sleeves down Harper's arms, realizing only after she did it she'd trapped Harper's arms by her sides.

"I'm sorry, I—"

"Don't stop there," Harper gasped.

"No." Presley dropped to her knees, opened Harper's pants, and pulled down the zipper. She kissed the hollow at the base of Harper's belly. "I can't."

"Presley," Harper said, her voice so deep and husky Presley wouldn't have recognized it under any other circumstances. "You should be very careful there. I'm very much on the edge."

"So am I." Presley looked up and couldn't hide her smile. Dominating someone as strong as Harper was an aphrodisiac so exciting a single touch would make her explode. She pulled Harper's shirt the rest of the way off. "And I want you."

Harper's lids flickered closed. Her fingers wove into Presley's hair. "Then I'm all yours."

All yours. A figure of speech, one she liked. Presley pulled Harper's pants and underclothes down over her hips and Harper stepped out of her shoes and the rest. Presley kissed low down on her belly again and rubbed her cheek against the soft skin. Muscles twitched beneath her mouth. "Hold on to something."

"I am." Harper's hand tightened on the back of her neck, drawing her mouth closer.

Presley pressed a kiss to the delta between Harper's thighs. Harper went rigid as stone beneath her palms. She kissed her again, deeper, and Harper groaned. The sound went through her like the surgeon's knife, swift and clean and bright. She slid her arms around Harper's hips and held her close, held her up, as she stroked and kissed and licked and drove her up…up and up and over. Harper trembled and groaned Presley's name, rocking against her.

Presley slid one hand to her own trousers, opened them, and pushed them down. She was ready to come but she wanted Harper's skin against her when she did. As soon as Harper stilled she rose, dragged Harper under the water, and kissed her. The water was cool compared to the heat of Harper's mouth, the burning invitation of Harper's skin.

"Ah God, I'm so ready for you." Gasping, Presley pressed her face to Harper's neck. "Please."

Harper backed her against the cool tiles and slid one hand between her thighs. "I'm here."

Presley threw her head back as Harper filled her, the pressure and pleasure catapulting her to the edge. She gripped Harper's shoulders, digging her fingers in as the spasms radiated from deep within her, ripples in a pond, spreading and spreading. "Oh God. I'm coming."

"Yes," Harper breathed.

Presley needed to see Harper's face, but the pleasure was so intense, for an instant she was blind. She shuddered, and when she could focus again, Harper was there, filling her, taking her, like no one ever before.

CHAPTER TWENTY-ONE

Harper didn't know how long she'd been in the shower. The water beating against her back was beginning to cool, but her blood still burned. Every sense was saturated with Presley—her taste, her scent, the silky glide of her skin. The soft catch in her breath when she started to come. She buried her face in Presley's neck and ran her hands over Presley's back to her ass. Realizing she was leaning on her, she mumbled, "Am I too heavy yet?"

"No. You're good. Better than good." Presley rested with her head back against the tiles, her eyes half-open, one hand clenched in Harper's hair, the other lax against the shower wall. "I can't move anyway, and I like the way you feel against me."

Harper liked it too. More than she'd ever imagined. "We're going to lose the hot water in a couple of minutes."

"I don't care."

Harper chuckled. "You will."

"Uh-huh."

With a sigh, Harper braced her arm against the wall and pushed away, severing their connection. Instantly, she wanted her again. She enjoyed sex, although she didn't think about it much and never set out on a date with sex as a goal. This was more than sex—this need to touch Presley, to explore her, to undo her, was a craving that fascinated and, in a way, terrified her. What happened to the craving if it went unfulfilled? Did one die of hunger or go mad from yearning? She felt nearly mad now, and Presley was only a few inches away.

"What are you thinking?" Presley asked languorously.

"I'm not thinking anything." Harper wasn't sure even her thoughts were her own at the moment. Her mind was an electrical storm of raw nerve endings.

"Yes, you are. Your eyes just went dark, the way they do when you're thinking serious thoughts."

Harper settled her hands on either side of Presley's shoulders, keeping her caged, not wanting to let her away too quickly. "How do you know that?"

Presley's smile was secretive and seductive. "I've been watching you."

"I know. You do that a lot."

"Do you mind?"

"Not when you're watching *me*."

Presley's brow raised just a little bit. "Who else do you think I've been watching?"

"Flann." Harper had never once in her life been jealous of her sister. Not when Flann hit better than her in Little League softball, even though she was the oldest and bigger and should've been stronger. Not when the girls in high school, even the seniors a year or two ahead of them, chased after Flann and never her. Not even in college when they took the same courses and once in a while Flann would beat her on a test. They were almost always evenly matched, physically and intellectually, but Flann always had an edge. Always the sharper sword, the faster wit. The pirate to her navigator. Not this time, though. This time there was no room for Flann.

"I don't look at her like I look at you." Presley curled her fingers through Harper's hair and tightened her fist at the back of her neck. She kissed Harper hard on the mouth, then lightly on the jaw and lighter still on her throat. "Not once. And I never will."

"I don't have any right—"

"You're right, you don't." Presley bit Harper's shoulder lightly and Harper growled. "But it's true all the same. And my choice."

"Thank you. I already get crazy enough when I look at you."

Presley licked the water running down Harper's neck. "Do you?"

"You couldn't tell?" Harper caught Presley's chin between her fingers and kissed her, deep and long. "We have to get out of the water."

Presley stroked Harper's chest. "Afraid of the cold?"

"No. I want you again, in bed, under me."

Presley's breath hissed in and she raked her nails down Harper's back. "Are you asking or telling?"

"Do I have to ask?"

"No. Because I want you again too."

❖

Flann pulled in to the White place a little after six thirty in the morning. She'd driven by Harper's and seen the two cars in the driveway. Her first thought had been *Go, Harper!* but almost immediately a fist of unease had settled in the pit of her stomach. Presley Worth was the first woman to come along who had the ability to shred Harper's heart. Considering all the circumstances, that possibility was likely. Flann couldn't just stand by and watch. She left her Jeep and walked around to the back door, hoping Carrie wouldn't take her for a prowler and call 911.

Carrie sat on the back steps with a mug in her hand and something that smelled fabulous on a plate balanced on her knees. She looked up expectantly and then her welcoming smile turned to one of concern. "Has something happened to Presley?"

"No," Flann said quickly, "everyone's fine. I take it you haven't heard from her."

"Not this morning. She left a message last night that she was at the hospital, but I haven't heard from her since then, and she didn't come home—" She broke off and her cheeks flushed, making her look as innocent as a teenager. "Oh. Crap. Could you forget I said that?"

"That's okay. You're not giving anything away. I already knew that."

"And I suppose you know where she spent the night?" Carrie asked slowly.

"I do. That will be up to Presley to tell you, though."

Carrie rolled her eyes. "As if there were a lot of possibilities."

"Right. We can both pretend surprise, then." Flann pointed to the plate. "Is there more of whatever that is somewhere?"

"It's bread. With cheese or something so delicious in it I'm in danger of eating the entire thing."

"Can I help you dispose of it?"

"I'll get you some. Have you been up all night?"

"No. Only most of it."

Carrie shook her head. "You're all crazy, you know that, right?"

"All of us who?"

"All the Rivers doctors."

"Possibly. Probably. Bread?"

"Coffee?" Carrie rose and the rooster who'd been pecking in the yard waddled toward the stairs, his head cocked.

"You've got a friend."

"Presley's been spoiling him. Now he expects breakfast."

"That's what happens when you feed a vagabond."

Carrie grinned over her shoulder. "What happens when you feed wandering doctors?"

"That's a secret."

Laughing, Carrie disappeared inside. Flann followed and said through the screen, "Do you want me to do anything?"

"Do you want breakfast?"

"Some of that bread with a whole lot of butter will be fine for now. And the coffee. Especially the coffee."

"Goes without saying," Carrie called back. "Sit down, I'll be out in just a second."

Flann settled on the top step with her back against the porch post. The sun was up, the sky was clear, and birds were singing. She couldn't think of any place she'd rather be or anything else she'd rather be doing. Carrie came out and handed her a cup of coffee and a plate with a thick slab of bread that smelled fresh from the oven. Carrie sat opposite her and tossed another piece of crust to the rooster.

"I think he gets bored during the day."

"He needs some hens," Flann observed.

"I was thinking the same thing. How do you go about doing that?"

"Plenty of farmers around here have some. There are probably even chicks left at the local feed store."

"Are they hard to take care of?"

"Not as soon as they get big enough to run away from predators. And you've got the rooster. Instinctually, he'll protect them."

Carrie sighed. "I'd love to get some, but I don't think we're going to be here long enough."

"A quick turnaround, huh?"

Carrie grew still. "That will be up to Presley."

"But you and Presley are a team, right?"

"Wrong," Carrie said quietly. "Presley is my boss."

"Just in name only, I bet."

Carrie shook her head. "No. She really is my boss, and she's very good at what she does."

"And what she does is take places like the Rivers and turn them into something else."

"Sometimes. It depends on the circumstances." Carrie's tone had cooled. "And I don't have anything else to tell you."

"Fair enough. This is jalapeño cheddar, by the way." Flann finished the bread, which was about the best bread she'd ever tasted next to her mother's. "My sister is not a player."

"I know a player when I see one." Carrie stood up abruptly. The chill in her voice had turned to ice. "And I know which of the Rivers sisters that would be."

Flann looked up at her, grinning. "No argument from me. And I'm not trying to piss you off."

Carrie crossed her arms over her chest. "Let's get something straight, Flannery. Presley is my boss, and she's also my friend. What she does in her personal life is her business, and none of mine or yours. I'm sure your sister is quite capable of looking after herself."

Flann stayed sitting, letting Carrie have the upper hand and the dominant position. She liked her fire and she liked her loyalty. "Under most circumstances, I'd agree with you on all counts. But if the two of you really are only here for a short time, that means the Rivers is probably not going to stay the way it is now. Harper will fight it, and that means trouble for your friend and my sister."

Carrie sighed. "That's something neither of us is going to be able to change."

"Maybe. Maybe you're right."

"And what about you? How do you feel about what's happening?"

"Me? I go with the flow. I'll land on my feet one way or the other."

"If you don't invest much, you can't lose much, right?"

Flannery rose and dusted off the back of her jeans. She stacked the cup on the empty plate. "You've clearly got my number."

"I never asked for it," Carrie said dryly.

"Would you like it?"

"No."

Flann grinned, automatically hiding her disappointment. She didn't always win, and she rarely minded when she was refused. This time she did. That was reason enough to back off. "Thank you for the coffee and the food."

"You're welcome." Carrie took the dishes. "Thanks for letting me know that Presley's okay."

"Yeah. Let's hope."

❖

Presley straddled Harper's hips, both hands braced on her shoulders. The window was open. Somewhere a rooster crowed. Early morning sunlight made Harper's dark hair glint against the snow-white pillow. They were naked in the center of her big bed, and the cool air whispered over Presley's flushed skin like a kiss. She was wet against Harper's abdomen, the faint friction keeping her on a razor's edge. The threads of her control were stretched tight but she held on, loving the tension strumming through her muscles. When Harper cupped her breasts and teased her nipples with her thumbs, Presley threw back her head and moaned.

"I love the way you look right now," Harper said. "I love you moving on top of me."

"I'm going to come on top of you any second." Her breath came out in ragged pants. She was oh so close now. Her vision swam. Harper's hands tightened on her breasts, the pressure on her nipples sending a jolt to her clitoris. Electricity rippled down her spine. "God. Soon."

The room disappeared and Presley clung to Harper's body, found her eyes and held to the solid strength of her, rocking harder, faster. Her head dropped, her hair curtained her face, the pleasure so intense she bit her lip to hold back a cry. Harper gripped her hips, pulled her back and forth, rubbing their flesh together. Higher, faster, closer. Breaking, falling, flying.

Presley's spine snapped back and she shattered with a cry.

Harper's arms came around her, and in one swift movement, Presley was beneath her, still coming when Harper entered her, forcing her back to the peak. She came again. Lost her breath, lost her mind.

"Don't move," she whispered when Harper would have withdrawn. She wrapped her arms around Harper's shoulders. "I love to feel you inside me."

"I want to make you come again." Harper kissed Presley's throat. "I love the way you come."

Presley laughed shakily. "I need a few minutes…or maybe a few hours. I'm not used to—" She broke off, for some reason not wanting the past to intrude on this moment. This moment, the last hour, maybe the last day, weren't part of her normal life. She'd stepped beyond the known, and soon, in an hour or a few more, she'd have to return to the life she knew. These moments with Harper would remain apart, as separate as everything about this place—these people, this life, this painful beauty. She had been right all along—she was a time traveler, and as long as she was, she had to keep her secrets.

"Neither am I...used to this," Harper said, unafraid it seemed, to expose her secrets. "And I—"

"I was wrong." Presley kissed Harper, silencing her before either of them could reveal any more. "I'm ready for you again now."

CHAPTER TWENTY-TWO

Presley woke to the sensation of pleasure. Every muscle was relaxed, her body humming in the aftermath of being incredibly well used and thoroughly satisfied. She stretched with a sigh, and her fingertips grazed Harper's hip. Harper lay curled beside her, one arm encircling her waist. Pleasure gave way to panic.

What in God's name had she done? She knew the answer. She'd lost her mind. She'd followed her instincts and fallen into bed with a woman who couldn't be more wrong for her on any level she could possibly define. Professionally, at least, the worst she could be accused of was bad judgment, but for her that was the worst indictment possible. Success in the take-no-prisoners world of corporate supremacy demanded she always be on top of every situation and ten steps ahead of her competition. Some would see her involvement with Presley as a smart strategic move—bringing every weapon to bear against one of her strongest foes. But she knew better. She was in greater danger of being swayed by Harper than she was of influencing her. A weakness she must keep to herself.

Already she'd exposed too much—physically and emotionally— allowing Harper in a near-suicidal gesture to draw her into the Rivers's world of community and family, to put faces to the numbers she must see dispassionately, to create a sense of responsibility and empathy that could only cloud her judgment. Harper was dangerous. She made Presley do things—worse, made her want to do things—that she knew were ill-advised. How many more Jimmy Reynoldses would she see before she too disregarded the bottom line and started making exceptions that would end in disaster?

She saw these dangers clearly, had seen them from the first moment Harper caught her attention, yet here she was, naked, body and soul, and the thing utmost in her mind was more. More of what Harper made her feel. Singularly special. Infinitely desirable. Uniquely essential.

When she was with Harper, when Harper's hands were on her, inside her, she knew what she had never known before—that she mattered not for what she had done or could do, but for what Harper saw inside her. She mattered for those parts of herself she'd held back for so long, knowing they were not wanted. She should not be here, but she wanted nothing else, at least for a little while longer. She turned on her side and kissed Harper.

"That's a nice way to wake up." Harper pulled Presley tighter until their bodies touched. She played her fingers down Presley's stomach, feathering lower, over and over, until Presley's thighs tensed and her belly hummed.

"We can't," Presley said.

Harper partially opened one eye. "Why not?"

"I don't have the strength. I need food. You must too."

"Food before sex. Hmm." Harper grinned. "Obviously not a country girl."

Presley delicately bit Harper's lower lip. "City girls have other virtues."

Harper rolled over on top of her, pinning her arms to the bed, a hand around each wrist. She slid one thigh between Presley's and kissed her. "Virtues? I certainly hope not."

Presley felt herself melting again, a wanting so sharp the pleasure was nearly pain. She lifted her hips and when Harper pressed down against her, she moaned. "You'll have trouble explaining the dead body in your bed."

"Nah. I'll hide you in the barn. No one will ever know." Harper shifted lower on the bed and settled her shoulders between Presley's thighs.

Presley watched her, a pulse beating in her center, anticipating, needing. She tilted her hips. "Then let me die happy."

"I won't let you die." Harper kissed her.

"Oh," Presley sighed. "I don't care as long as you do that."

Harper kissed her again, her lips a soft circle of power and pleasure.

Presley whimpered and closed her eyes. "So good."

"Mmm. Yes." Harper raised up, kissed Presley's belly, and rolled over her and out of bed.

Presley's eyes flew open. "What do you think you're doing?"

Naked, Harper strode across the room to a big chestnut armoire by the window. She opened it, pulled out a pair of faded jeans, and yanked them up her long, lean legs. "I promised to fix you breakfast, remember? I keep my promises."

"Now?" Presley heard the edge in her voice and didn't care if she sounded petulant or demanding or both. She wanted. Needed. God, she had to come.

Harper's gaze swept over her and her eyes darkened. "You're not going anywhere right away, are you?"

"I'm not going anywhere at all until you get back over here and finish."

"Is that right?" Harper's voice held a dangerous edge, one Presley liked very much.

Presley slowly stroked the inside of her thigh, letting her fingers brush as near as she dared to where she wanted Harper's mouth. She was afraid if she got too close she might explode. "That's right. Unless you want me to do it myse—"

Harper strode to the bed, gripped Presley's hips, and swung her around until her legs drooped over the side. She knelt on the floor, lifted Presley's thighs to her shoulders, and took Presley into her mouth in one swift motion.

"Damn you." Presley arched off the bed, gripping the sheet with one hand and Harper's head with the other. She was close to fracturing into a thousand brilliant shards. Harper's mouth was hot and wet, fierce, demanding. "I'm going to…oh!"

Presley came hard, faster than she wanted, unable to stop a cry. Shaken, she could only struggle for breath.

Harper leaned back, shirtless, her neck flushed and her eyes triumphant. "Are you good for now?"

"For now," Presley gasped. "Go away…for now."

Laughing, Harper rose and gently eased Presley's legs back onto the bed. "I'll get to work on that breakfast."

Presley watched her pull on a T-shirt, captivated by the way the muscles in her shoulders and chest shimmered beneath her smooth skin. She loved the arch of her rib cage, the indentation of her navel, the hollow above her hipbone. Unbelievably, desire stirred. "You are dangerously sexy."

Harper regarded her solemnly. "If I am, it's because you do things to me. Make me a little crazy."

"I'm glad I'm not alone, then."

The dark brooding look was back in Harper's eyes again. She leaned over the bed, stroked Presley's hair away from her face with one hand, and kissed her so softly Presley felt tears come to her eyes. "You're not alone."

Presley caught her hand. "Do I need to say last night was amazing?"

"No," Harper said softly. "For me too."

Presley shivered, hid it with a smile. "I need a shower."

Harper straightened. "Go ahead. My pants won't fit you, but I've got some cut-off sweats and a T-shirt that will. Not your usual style, but it'll do for now."

"It'll do just fine," Presley said, ridiculously pleased by the idea of wearing Harper's clothes.

She waited until Harper put the clothes on the bottom of the bed and left the room before rising. She didn't trust herself anywhere near her for a few minutes. How was it possible she could still want her so fiercely? And how was she possibly going to hide that from her?

❖

The phone rang while Harper was rummaging in the refrigerator for food. She grabbed her cell off the table, swiped answer, and automatically tapped speaker. "Dr. Rivers," she said as she pulled eggs and spinach from the fridge.

"I'm making breakfast," her mother said. "Why don't you come on over. Flann is here and says you've been up all night."

"I…" Harper listened and couldn't hear the shower running upstairs any longer. She turned off the speaker and lowered her voice. "Thanks, but I can't."

Her mother was silent for what felt like half a lifetime. "You're welcome to bring company."

Harper groaned. "Mama, please."

Ida laughed. "Harper, darlin', I know you're an adult. You think I don't know what adults get up to on a Saturday night? In fact, your father and I—"

"Come on, give me a break here."

"I promise Flannery will not embarrass you."

"Yes, I will," Flann yelled from the background.

"Flannery O'Connor Rivers. Hush, now," Ida said sternly. "The invitation stands. You do what you think best, but I expect to see you to dinner later today."

"Yes, ma'am. I'll be there." Harper hung up, smiling, and walked upstairs. Presley was pulling on one of her old T-shirts as she walked into the bedroom. "My mother invited us to breakfast."

Presley stopped, sheer horror freezing her blood. "Your mother? Oh my God. How does your mother know I'm here?"

"She didn't exactly invite us, just me and my guest."

"Then she doesn't know it was me?"

"No," Harper said slowly. "Would that be a problem?"

"Harper, think of the situation." Presley put her hands on her hips. She hadn't wanted to have this conversation now, not yet. She'd wanted to sit with Harper in the big kitchen in the sunlight for a few more minutes and pretend that none of this had to end. She should know by now that the things she wished for were almost always the things she could never have. "I'm not the woman to take home to your family on Sunday morning, for God's sake."

"Are you ashamed or embarrassed that you slept with me?"

"What? No, of course not. But—"

"But what? Which one is it? Embarrassed or ashamed?"

"Neither, damn it." To give herself time to formulate some kind of rational response, Presley gathered up her underwear and the pants and shirt she'd shed in her haste to get Harper's hands on her the night before. "But it wasn't very wise."

"Why not?"

Presley clutched the bundle of clothes to keep from tearing her hair out. "You know why not. You know why I'm here. I have to make some hard decisions that are going to make a lot of people unhappy. It won't do your reputation or mine any good for people to think—" She broke off in exasperation. "Damn it."

"To think what, Presley? Our personal life is our own business."

"We do not have a personal life. Not together. We just slept together."

The muscles along Harper's jaw might have been made of stone, they moved so little as she said in a low ominous tone, "We just slept together. Just a little sex—seven or was it eight times? Is that what you think it was?"

"I wasn't counting," Presley said archly. "I wasn't aware you were."

"Don't try turning this around. I'm not some flunky in the boardroom. Just sex—is that what you think it was?"

"What else could it be?" Presley gestured to the ridiculously beautiful scene outside the bedroom window. Blue skies, fluffy clouds, birds singing, for goodness' sake. "You live in this fairy-tale world, but you can't possibly believe in fairy tales. You know why I'm here. The hospital is dead, Harper. It's been dying for years. Everything is going to change, some people are going to be very unhappy, and the last thing either of us needs is rumor about collusion or special favors."

"You've already decided, haven't you," Harper said. "All this vague talk about analyzing usage and patient referral patterns and all the rest of the doublespeak was just smoke and mirrors to placate the simple country folk."

"The simple country folk who thought they could seduce me or charm me or appeal to my sense of personal responsibility in order to change my mind?" Presley shot back. Damn her for refusing to see reason. Why did this have to be so hard?

Harper cursed under her breath. "You're wrong about me and you're wrong about the Rivers."

"You can't see it," Presley said softly, "because you're built to fight death."

"I don't give up, if that's what you mean," Harper said slowly. "Not everything changes. Not me. Not who I am, what I care about, what I feel."

"I'm sorry. Really, I am." Presley meant it. She was sorry she would likely destroy a part of Harper's world, sorry their goals were so opposed, sorry she couldn't go back a few months, a few years, and change the future of the Rivers.

"For what? For not being able to see beyond the cold, empty numbers you fill your life with? Sorry for touching me, for letting me touch you? Sorry for feeling something—anything?" Harper shook her head. "No, I don't need you to feel sorry for me about anything at all."

Presley's chin lifted, and she kept her voice steady despite the pain. She had lots of practice at that. "I think it would be better if I go."

Harper stepped aside. "You've already left."

CHAPTER TWENTY-THREE

Harper didn't look up from the book she'd been staring at for the last hour when she felt the tree house sway and someone enter.

"I saw your truck." Flann, wearing her usual weekend uniform of T-shirt, blue jeans, and sneakers, dropped onto the sofa next to Harper and put her feet on the crate that served as a coffee table. "You missed a good breakfast."

Harper lifted the book without looking at Flann. "Reading here."

Flannery craned her neck. "The Case of the Missing Girlfriend."

"I should have put up the no-visitors sign," Harper said.

"I came to see why you're brooding. Night didn't turn out the way you thought?"

With a sigh, Harper closed the book, *The Secret of the Old Clock*, and set it aside. "What exactly did you tell Mama this morning?"

"Not a thing. Except that I'd seen you at the hospital and figured you'd been up all night. Were you?"

"Almost."

"I heard about Jimmy Reynolds."

"How?"

"I ran into Presley in the cafeteria last night. She said you thought he had leukemia."

"AML—confirmed. Frank Cisco did the bone marrow biopsy a few hours ago."

"Hell. That sucks."

"Yeah. I just came from seeing him. He got his first dose of chemo already."

"How are Emmy and Don?"

"Don broke down, but Emmy is a rock. Jimmy takes after her that way."

"Let me know if you need anything," Flann said.

"Thanks. For now we wait and see how he responds after a round or two."

Flann nodded. "So getting back to last night. Was your missing breakfast a good sign or bad?"

Harper scrubbed her face with her palms, put her head back, and laced her fingers behind her neck. Her back ached faintly—pleasantly sore from propping her body up over Presley, from Presley's fingers digging into her when she came. "Goddamn it."

"That doesn't tell me much."

Harper stared at the ceiling, tracing the grain in the wood, fascinated as she always was by the thoughts of where the wood had been before it became part of this sanctuary. Part of a barn, most likely, felled on some farm a couple hundred years ago. The wood had survived long after the lives of those who had hewn it had ended, would continue on long after her too, unless someone came along and knocked the tree house down and used the wood for kindling or left it in the underbrush to rot. "The night—or what was left of it after I got Jimmy squared away—was fine. The morning was the problem."

Flann laughed wryly. "Aren't they always? Of course, knowing you, you'd want to talk, and that always leads to trouble."

"What do you do? Sneak away in the dead of night?"

"Of course not. I don't sneak away until dawn. Most women like a repeat first thing in the morning after a night of great sex."

Harper clenched her jaw. Presley had wanted her again in the morning too. She wished she could think of the night with Presley as just great sex, but she couldn't. The sex had been wonderful, to be sure, but it was the hitch in her heart every time she thought about Presley that kept her tethered to the memory, that kept alive the longing to touch her again, to hear her sounds of pleasure again, to lose herself in the beauty of her coming and the annihilation of coming with her. "Fuck."

"That good, huh?"

"Have you ever been with a woman who makes you forget everything except her?"

Flann's face closed the way it always did when something cut too close to the bone. "No. And I hope you haven't either."

"Do you think that's something you can control?"

"I think it's something you can avoid with a little bit of thought." Flann raked a hand through her thick sandy hair. "Jesus, Harper. Didn't we talk about this? You had to know it was a bad idea."

A bad idea. Presley had said something very much the same. Harper's temper frayed. "You can't really be naïve enough to think you can dictate something like that."

"Of course you can! Keep things light. Keep things casual. Don't give yourself away." Flann swept her arm to take in the room nestled in the high branches. "Jesus, you brought her up to the tree house already."

Harper looked around the space. It was only a tree house, not exactly a confessional. But then she wondered what it said about her and had to admit it said everything. She'd made it with her own hands, building on the rudimentary structure she and Flann had knocked up as preteens. She'd filled it with things that mattered to her and came back to it when she was troubled or lonely or weary. She brought Presley here because she didn't know a better way to show her the parts of herself that mattered the most. "I had to."

"Why?" Flann asked, looking honestly puzzled.

"Because she got to me and no one else ever has."

Flann made an exasperated sound. "Maybe you wanted her to or just think she did. Maybe it's not Presley at all, but just what you want her to be. There are plenty of other women who could give you what you want."

Harper rested her head against the back of the sofa and studied Flann. "Do you really believe that? That one woman would do just as well as another?"

"Why not? Sure, it's nice to have a similar outlook on the big things, but I could name a dozen women who would love to have your babies."

Harper couldn't help but laugh, but the laughter left an ache in her throat. "You think that's all it's about? Having someone in bed at night, someone to have your kids, or raise your kids? What about in here…" She closed her fist over her heart, and as she expected, Flann made a face.

"You're a romantic, Harper. You read too many books as a kid. Most of the time what you see is what you get. Be grateful when you find a woman who won't ask more than that. And for God's sake, don't choose someone who's already a sure bet to break your heart."

"Is that what you want? To just make do?"

"Don't make this about me. It's not about me."

"Maybe not, but I still want to know."

Flann looked away, a sure sign she was going to avoid the whole truth. She wouldn't lie, but she would keep her secrets. "I'd be happy with a woman who was into good sex and occasional company and wouldn't want me to be someone I'm not."

"Like a friend with benefits?"

Flann lifted a shoulder, still staring out the tree house window toward the river. "I suppose that's a good enough name for it. Just so I don't have to constantly be worried about someone wanting more."

"It's the wanting more that makes it special."

Flann glared at her. "What exactly happened this morning?"

"Presley reminded me that sex was just sex, sort of like what you've been saying. She probably should've gone to bed with you and not me."

Flann barked out a short, sarcastic laugh. "Oh yeah, right, then you and I would've been pistols at dawn. Why can't you just be happy you got her into bed?"

"It's not enough, and you'd know it, if you weren't too afraid—"

Flann jumped up and paced to the opposite side of the room, putting as much distance between herself and Harper as possible. She kept her back to Harper as she looked out the window. "I'm not afraid."

"Fuck, you're not. I just don't know why. Look at Mama and Dad—"

"Yeah, look at them." Flann swung around. "Sure, they've got a great relationship. How many women do you think there are like Mama? Willing to raise a family practically by herself while Dad does what he wants."

"Not just for himself," Harper said. "You think he's sacrificed all these years taking care of other people just for himself?"

"What has he given up? He's got a home, a woman who waits for him, kids who are crazy about him, while he's out taking care of other people who think he's God. Tell me, what's he given up?"

Harper sprang to her feet. "You've got to be kidding me. That's what you think? That it's all been easy for him?"

"You can't see it because you're just like him. Maybe you should look for a woman just like Mama—and good luck with that."

"Where is this coming from?" Harper said quietly.

Flann's fury seemed to abate as quickly as it had come and she sank back against the rough-hewn plank wall. She pushed her hands into the pocket of her jeans and stared at the floor. "I don't know. I guess I've been mad at him for a while."

"For a while? Like ten years or something? Why?"

Flann raised her head. "He wasn't here when Katie died."

"He didn't know she was going to go so quickly. It was septic shock. You know that."

"He wasn't here then. He wasn't at the hospital the night Davey was born. He wasn't here for more things than I can count."

"And you think that didn't hurt him? Come on, Flann. What is it you're really afraid of?"

"That I'll be just like him," Flann said flatly. "And I won't be able to be there when it matters."

"So you've decided you just won't try."

"I've decided that I want a different life."

"You'll change your mind when you meet her."

Flann's eyes darkened. "There is no her."

"You can believe that all you want, but you're wrong."

"Well, if you're any example, I prefer to be wrong for the rest of my life."

"It's worth it."

"What is?"

"The pain—the amazing sense of being filled with everything that's right is worth the pain. What I felt with her—"

"Oh come on. Give me a break. Get your head out of the clouds. You had a great roll in the hay. All that says is she's good in bed, and all that means is she's had enough practice—"

Harper tackled her around the waist, and they went down in a pile of arms and legs. The tree shook and leaves fell like rain as they rolled and tumbled and fought to be on top.

Flann was quick and wiry and they'd had a lot of practice wrestling as kids. It took Flann five minutes to flip Harper onto her back and straddle her middle, but eventually she pinned Harper's arms to the floor.

Harper was panting and sweating, but so was Flann. Flann's face was inches above hers.

"Say it," Flann said.

"No."

"Say it." Flann bounced on Harper's middle until Harper thought she was going to puke. "Say it."

"Uncle," Harper gasped.

"I can't believe you went for me like that."

"Get off," Harper grunted.

Flannery bounced one more time. "Man, she has got you by the gonads."

Harper grinned, but the sadness still filled her. "Yeah, I guess I'm well and truly fucked."

Flann sat back on her haunches, taking her weight off Harper's torso so she could breathe again. "I'm sorry."

"For which part?" Harper sucked in air. She needed to run more.

"I'm sorry things with Presley didn't work out. I'm sorry for talking bullshit about Dad. I'm not sorry for whipping your ass."

"You're wrong, you know," Harper said. "You'll be there when it matters, Flann. You always are."

Presley grabbed the items she'd bought the day before out of Harper's truck, drove home as fast as she dared, and went directly to her room to take off Harper's clothes. The intimacy of Harper's touch, even imagined, was too sharp when what she needed was distance. She folded them carefully and set them on the dresser. She'd have to find a delicate way of returning them, but that quandary could wait. After pulling on a pair of capri workout pants, a lightweight V-neck tee, and running shoes, she went downstairs to sweat out some of her self-recrimination. She actually loathed running, so the activity would serve a dual purpose—with every aching step she'd be reminded of the cost of impetuosity and would wear off the lingering pulse of desire that still beat deep inside. As she passed through the foyer to the front door, Carrie called out a good morning from the living room.

Presley stopped and poked her head through the doorway. Carrie looked cheery and relaxed curled up in the corner of the couch in threadbare red plaid pj pants and a pale blue Henley, her laptop open and balanced on her knees. Presley mustered up a smile. "Hi. How was your night?"

"All things considered, amazingly good. The absence of noise— well, at least the noise I'm used to—still weirds me out a little bit. But now I'm starting to hear other things—croaking and chirping and some sort of groaning that I think might be cows."

"Hopefully it's cows. I don't want to think about it being anything else." Presley couldn't help but laugh. "I know what you mean about the sounds, though, and not just the noises. It's like a different version of everything we know here. Sometimes I feel like I've tumbled into an alternate universe."

"Or just a very old version of our own." Carrie stretched her bare feet out onto the big steamer trunk repurposed as a coffee table. Her toenails, Presley noted absently, were bright pink. "I kind of like it. That old-time feeling."

"Yes, I suppose it has its charms." Presley could easily see Harper in a horse and buggy, her big leather satchel by her feet, a horsehair blanket over her lap, riding through a cold fall morning on her way to a call, the trees a sunburst of colors surrounding her, the crystal-blue sky icing gray at the edges with the promise of winter to come. She could see, too, Harper returning after a long night of tending to families spread far and wide over the countryside, stomping her boots on the porch, getting rid of the snow before she trudged inside to where a fire burned in the hearth. To where Presley waited, curled up in a chair with a book. Presley shook her head, dispelling the whimsical hallucination. "Something about this place does things to you. Dangerous things. I wouldn't get too used to it."

Carrie gave Presley a curious, concerned look. "Is there something wrong?"

"Is there anything right?"

"Maybe you should sit down." Carrie patted the sofa. "There's fresh coffee. And Lila baked bread."

Presley caught herself just before she took Carrie up on her invitation. Carrie worked for her, and it wouldn't do for her to know how conflicted she was about what they were doing here. Conflicted wasn't exactly the right word. Ambivalent? No, not that either. She knew well enough what needed to be done. She was angry, furious, that the job had been foisted onto her for no other reason than Preston's ploy for political advantage. Now she was going to disrupt the lives of a lot of good people so Preston could have room to maneuver while she was gone. How venal was that? How meaningless and petty compared to what Harper and Flannery and Edward Rivers did every day. She thought of Jimmy Reynolds, probably struggling right this moment to survive while his parents agonized. And what was her goal? To beat her brother at a game they'd been playing since birth in a hopeless attempt to win their parents' approval? She didn't have to play Preston's game, but she did need to do her job. She had a responsibility to the shareholders, no matter what she might feel personally about the outcome for the people here.

"Tomorrow morning I want you to set up appointments with the three top-rated construction firms in the county. I want to see them this week to discuss bids, and I'll need blueprints of the physical plant and the surveys when I meet with them."

"All right," Carrie said slowly. "I'll have some other figures for you—"

"Fine. Bring me what you have after lunch tomorrow. I want to get the endgame in place. I don't want to spend any more time here than I need to."

"Of course," Carrie said.

From her tone, Presley knew Carrie was bothered by something, but she didn't have the emotional strength or patience to find out what it was. The best thing for both of them was to get the job done and get home.

"I'll be back in an hour or so."

"Have a good run," Carrie said uncertainly.

"I intend to." Presley banged through the front door and clambered down the steps to the drive. She jogged toward the road, surrounded by green waving stalks of corn that seemed taller overnight. She damned the beauty even as her heart leapt. Everything about the place drew her in, until she couldn't escape the sweetness or the sorrow. She picked up her pace, determined not to be touched by either.

CHAPTER TWENTY-FOUR

Presley arrived at the hospital early every day for two weeks, well before anyone else arrived, and left after everyone else had gone home. She saw Carrie and no one else, carefully avoiding the clinical areas of the hospital. Harper hadn't contacted her to accompany her on rounds or house calls, not that she'd expected her to. All well and good, and a reminder, one she shouldn't have needed, that mixing personal and professional business was a very bad idea. Besides, she appreciated having more time to work and less time to be distracted by Harper and her patients, things she should've known better than to involve herself with to begin with.

The long hours paid off, and by mid-month, she'd digested most of the significant data, all of which had confirmed what she'd originally suspected. The patient base at the Rivers—she winced and caught herself—at ACH was poor and underinsured. Although the hospital census had remained relatively high throughout the last decade, revenues had declined, costs had risen, and no new sources of income had appeared to bridge the gap. Numbers never lied, no matter how much she wished they did.

"Carrie," she said from the doorway of her office, "would you contact Dr. Rivers and ask him to meet with me before the end of the day."

"Of course," Carrie said.

Carrie had been keeping the same hours as Presley, although Presley hadn't asked her to. She'd left early a few days for softball games, extending an invitation for Presley to join her. After the first few times Presley refused, Carrie stopped asking. Presley was grateful for Carrie's perceptiveness.

"Oh," Carrie said, "I've set up a second appointment for you on

Monday with the contractor you liked. All the necessary schematics are on your computer already."

"Thanks."

"Just Edward Rivers?" Carrie asked.

"Yes. I don't need to see anyone else."

Carrie's expression was neutral, but her eyes spoke volumes. She wasn't happy, and ordinarily Presley would've asked her for her opinion, but right now, the last thing she needed was someone else distracting her from doing what had to be done.

"And book me a flight to Phoenix on Tuesday. Schedule a meeting with finance and Preston."

"Which order?"

Presley considered. "Finance."

"How long will you be gone?" Carrie asked.

"A few days. Book a return flight for Thursday, and we can always change it if need be."

"All right." Carrie hesitated. "By the way, I sent some other information you might find interesting."

Presley paused. Carrie was too good an admin to ignore and, besides that, they were friends. "What other kind of information?"

"Population density in the county, patient-physician ratios, and the network—or I should say, lack of network—of urgent care facilities."

"Are you trying to tell me something?" Presley tempered the bite in her voice that she was almost too tired to hide. Carrie was not to blame for her sleepless nights or her sore heart.

"I know in other locations SunView has tied new acquisitions into local networks. There doesn't seem to be one here, but if there were, it would be a pipeline of patients to the hospital."

"Yes, but as you say, there is no network."

"I just thought you should have all the information."

"Thanks, I'll look at it but, Carrie…"

Carrie looked at her expectantly.

"Don't get too…attached. Short term, remember?"

"Right. I know."

Presley shut her office door behind her, sank into her chair, and closed her eyes. She hadn't been sleeping well. Too damn quiet at night. She worked when she got home until her eyelids were closing, but that didn't seem to help. When she finally fell asleep, she dreamed—restless dreams filled with frustration. Missed planes, doors that wouldn't open, phones she couldn't use. She awoke feeling frustrated, helpless, and—even more aggravatingly—aroused. Not the kind of arousal easily dismissed or sated by a few extra moments of attention, quickly forgotten. She couldn't find her rhythm here, in this place where time flowed differently, and hoped that if she went back to Phoenix, she would find her balance again. Besides, she needed to make an appearance to remind everyone that she wasn't going away, particularly Preston. A quick trip to update everyone on this project was a good excuse.

Work. That was what she needed to be thinking about. She reviewed what she intended to tell Edward Rivers. In the midst of her mental planning, she wondered how Jimmy Reynolds was doing. The thought, popping into her mind out of nowhere, was just another sign of how she'd carelessly let herself be caught up in things outside her domain. Harper was taking care of him, and that was all she needed to know.

Harper. How many times a day had she thought of her? Too many to count. She groaned under her breath. She had no one to blame but herself that she could still feel Harper's hands on her, still taste her, still catch the scent of her skin on an errant breeze. Still want her.

She reminded herself daily that Harper was not the first woman she'd awakened with, not even the first one she'd wanted again, albeit briefly. Why then was Harper the first one she couldn't forget? The first one she ached for.

"Enough," she muttered, opening her eyes and pulling up her email, determined to put Harper out of her mind.

When Carrie rang her, it was after one thirty and she'd missed lunch again. She didn't have much of an appetite. If Lila hadn't left food, morning and night, that smelled too delicious for her to ignore, she probably would've lost twenty pounds by now instead of eight. "Yes?"

"The doctors are here."

"I'm sorry?"

"Drs. Edward, Harper, and Flannery Rivers are here to see you."

"I asked for Dr. Edward Rivers."

"Yes, I have that ready for you," Carrie ad-libbed. "I'll be right there."

Carrie let herself into Presley's office and closed the door behind her.

"What's going on?" Presley asked.

"Edward Rivers says that since Flannery is chief of surgery and Harper the assistant chief of staff, they should be here for anything pertaining to the hospital."

"And if I don't agree, I'll appear to be uncooperative at best, or hiding things at worst," Presley said stiffly. "Why not. Send in the Rivers contingent, by all means."

She rose and pulled on her suit jacket, steeling herself to face Harper for the first time since she'd walked out of Harper's bedroom. Edward entered first, with Harper and Flannery side by side behind him. Flannery, as usual, was in scrubs. Harper wore casual black pants, a gray shirt, and loafers. Her dark hair needed a trim, although Presley liked the roguish contrast to her otherwise conventional style. An inappropriate desire to ruffle the ends of hair drifting over her collar flickered through her mind, and she quickly quashed it.

"Doctors," Presley said, looking away from Harper with effort. Shadows deepened her eyes to nearly black, and for an instant, Presley's throat tightened with longing. She lifted her chin, smiled. "Thank you for making time in your busy schedules. I'll try not to take up too much of your time."

"That's quite all right," Edward said. "This is too important to rush."

"Please sit down." Presley gestured to the small conference table that faced a screen on one wall. She smiled in the direction of Harper and Flannery. "And the other Drs. Rivers too, of course."

"Thanks," Harper said, sitting across from Flann while her father sat at the head facing the screen. Harper had hoped the next time she saw Presley, the meeting would seem no different than any other professional encounter. She'd been fooling herself. She did that a lot where Presley was concerned. Just looking at Presley stirred her up. Presley appeared a little tired, a little thinner, but as totally cool and in control as ever. She stood facing them from the far end of the table, her hair held back with a burnished copper clasp, her pale green shirt the perfect complement to her beige suit jacket and pants. She was a beautiful woman. Harper knew just how beautiful. She didn't have to close her eyes to see her again, naked and pliant and unrestrained— the image came to her at the most inconvenient times, igniting a rush of desire followed quickly by disappointment. The best times were when she woke in the morning and, for just an instant before her mind registered reality, she thrilled to the possibility of reaching out and touching her. But that was not going to happen. She forced herself to concentrate on Presley and see only the businesswoman and no one else.

"Let me bring you all up to date," Presley said, taking a small remote from her pocket and clicking on her computer.

A slide appeared onscreen. A pie chart with a variety of colors and numbers. More charts and graphs followed. For the next fifteen minutes, Presley concisely and lethally explained to them why the hospital was failing and why the board had, for all intents and purposes, sold it out from under them. When she was done, she clicked off the projector and the screen went blank behind her. She leaned forward, the fingertips of each hand pressing lightly against the table. She made eye contact with each in turn and focused on Harper's father at the end.

"I'm sorry that it's come to this, but the hospital is not viable. SunView has rehabilitated any number of institutions such as this, and in this case, I'm afraid it's clear. Within the next six to ten weeks, we will close the hospital. You'll need to inform the physicians to make arrangements to transfer inpatients who cannot be discharged in that period of time and to begin setting up new lines of referral for those who will need to be admitted in the near future for anything more than a day or two."

Edward said, "Are there no alternatives?"

"I'm afraid not."

"May we have a few weeks to explore alternate possibilities before advising the staff?"

Presley's inclination was to decline. She understood the doctors' need to resist; she'd seen it before. No one wanted to hear they were about to not only lose their own jobs but would have to advise hundreds of others of the same thing. However, delaying the inevitable rarely made a difference. "I don't—"

Harper spoke up. "You've had the opportunity to look at all the facts and figures. We're just hearing this now."

"But surely you knew this was coming." Presley had told Harper as much weeks before.

"The three of us know more about the medical systems in this area than you could possibly have learned since you've arrived," Harper said. "Let us talk about it. We might be able to present you with an alternative."

"Dr. Rivers," Presley said with as much patience as she could muster, "I don't presume to tell you how to treat patients. It's my job to look at all of these issues from every side before reaching a decision. Believe me, we've done that. As things stand—"

"Yes," Harper said, "as things stand *now*. But perhaps we could make some changes that would make a difference."

Presley shook her head. "You can't put more money in the pockets of your patients. You can't force insurance companies to pay more for your services. You might be able to influence your fellow practitioners to some degree, but the system remains the system."

Flannery said, "There must be somewhere we can find a new revenue source."

"There isn't," Presley said. "You may not believe this, but I've looked. There are basically three sources of revenue for an institution like this—government funding, insurance reimbursement, and patient self-pay. You have precious little of any of those."

"What if we could get more government subsidy," Harper said.

"How?" Presley said.

"I'm not sure yet. Give us a little time—"

"Ten days," Presley said, knowing they would be more willing to do what needed to be done when they failed to find an alternate solution. She could give them ten days. "Then we will make an announcement to the staff that the hospital is closing."

"We'll do our best to see that doesn't happen," Edward said flatly.

She nodded and the three Rivers doctors rose. Edward and Flannery started toward the door, but Harper hesitated. "Thank you."

Presley nodded, the tightness in her throat making it hard for her to speak for a moment. When Harper turned to leave, she said, "Harper."

Harper paused, letting the door close, leaving them alone.

"How's Jimmy?" Presley asked. *How are you? Do you know I wish we'd met somewhere else? Sometime else?*

"Holding his own. He's not responding as quickly as we hoped, but he's stable."

"Good. That's good, then."

Harper studied her for a long moment, then nodded silently and left.

Presley waited a few minutes until she was sure they were gone before packing her laptop. It was only midafternoon, hours before she usually left the hospital, but she couldn't stand the confines of the office any longer.

"I'm going to spend the rest of the day working at home," she told Carrie.

"There's a game tonight," Carrie said cautiously. "Why don't you come? You've been spending eighteen hours a day on this. Take a break."

"No. But thanks."

It was bad enough she couldn't get Harper out of her head. The last thing she wanted was to see her again. Phoenix couldn't happen soon enough.

CHAPTER TWENTY-FIVE

A crack like a rifle shot punctured the warm afternoon air. A white projectile rocketed straight toward Harper and jerked her to attention. She extended her glove and dove to her right. The missile impacted earth, altered its trajectory, and caromed upward, its speed barely diminished by the ricochet. The ball sailed over her glove and hit squarely on the left side of her jaw. Pain lanced through her head, and for an instant, the world disappeared.

"Lie still," a faraway voice ordered.

Harper opened her eyes, blinked, and watched strands of cotton candy drift and tumble overhead. Calliope music tinkled faintly and she was a kid again, back on the fairground, holding on to the huge plaster horses as they glided up and down the poles, screaming with joy as the platform went round and round, so fast it felt as if she would fly off if she let go. Her father stood beside her, his arm gripping the pole above her head, his body a shield ensuring she would not fall.

She lay on her back, trying to understand how she had fallen off this time.

Flannery's face came into view, the set of her mouth uncharacteristically serious.

"I'm fine," Harper said. The words seem garbled. She swallowed, tasted blood. The sky stopped spinning and the clouds slowed their movement to a lazy glide across her field of vision. She checked her upper and lower teeth with the tip of her tongue. All intact, none broken. A sore spot on the inside of her left cheek seeped blood. She must've bitten it. She tried the words again. "I'm fine."

"Somebody get me some ice," Flann yelled, one hand pressing Harper's shoulder to the ground. "Just lie there for a minute, hotshot."

"Help me over to the bench." She sounded a little more understandable now, but every little bit of movement triggered a bolt of pain from in front of her ear straight into her brain. She touched her jaw and Flann caught her wrist.

"What part of be still isn't getting through to you?"

"Just want to see if it's broken."

"Why don't you let me do that?"

Harper closed her eyes and got ready for more pain. Flann's fingers traced gently along the bone and Harper was reminded again what a good surgeon she was. How quick and deft her hands were when she worked. "Ouch."

"Ouch for real, or ouch 'cause you're being a pussy?"

"Ouch like I need some ice, but I don't think it's broken."

"Ought to be X-rayed."

"Hell, no."

"How are your teeth?"

"All there, none loose. Bite's okay."

"I suppose we can ice it tonight and see about an X-ray in the morning, then." Flann slid an arm behind Harper's shoulders and helped her sit up. "You dizzy?"

"Not anymore."

"How many?" Flann held out three fingers.

"Five."

"Stop fucking around."

Harper tried to grin but her mouth didn't really seem to be working right. "Three. I told you I'm fine."

Carrie dropped to her knees beside them. "Oh my God, that was really a shot. How are you feeling?"

"Like an ass. Come on, get me off the field. I'm okay." All Harper's teammates and most of the opposing team were standing around her in a circle. "Come on, we're winning. Let's not lose the momentum."

"Right." Flann tightened her grip behind Harper's shoulders and pulled her to her feet. Harper had to lean on her, but she tried to make it as subtle as possible. "You sure we don't need the hospital tonight?"

"No, but I might need a ride home."

"I'll take you to the big house."

"What for?"

"So Mama can look after you for a while. Otherwise you're just gonna lie on your sofa feeling sorry for yourself."

"True. But we're not leaving until you finish kicking their asses."

Flann got her settled on a bench with a bag of ice. "Hold that. I'll be back after I'm done ass kicking."

When the team finished creaming the opposition, Carrie joined Harper. "How you doing?"

"Looks worse than it is."

"That's good to know, because it really looks terrible. You've got a lump the size of—well, a softball on your jaw. Do you think it's broken?"

"I doubt it. Maybe a hairline crack, but nothing that won't heal on its own."

"That was a freakin' missile she hit," Carrie said. "I put it high and outside, but she teed off on it. Sorry."

"Not your fault."

Flann strode up. "Wouldn't have hit you if you'd had your head in the game. You shouldn't be playing if you can't concentrate."

"Kiss my ass," Harper said, and was pleased the words came out clearly.

"You're lucky daydreaming about a woman didn't end you up in the ER," Flann said.

"Who says I was—"

"Tell me you weren't thinking about a certain blonde with a killer body and a mind like a buzz saw."

Carrie jumped up. "Okay, I'm out of here for this conversation."

"No need," Harper said carefully. "The conversation's ended."

Flann looked at Carrie. "You going with everyone to the Hilltop for pizza?"

"I was planning on it."

"I'll see you there after I drop this one off."

Carrie smiled. "Okay."

Flann was mercifully quiet for the first half of the drive home. Harper rode with her head back, her eyes closed, and the ice slowly melting as she held it to her face.

"You asleep?" Flann finally said.

"No."

"What do you think about what Presley said earlier?"

"I'm not surprised. Are you?" Harper had been thinking about Presley all afternoon. About what she'd said, the way she'd looked, and the sadness in her eyes. She'd been remembering, too, the way she'd looked naked, straddling her, wild and triumphant.

"What?" Flann asked.

"What?"

"You kind of groaned. Are you feeling worse?"

"No, I'm fine," Harper said, tortured by the memories she didn't want to give up.

"Got any bright ideas about what we might be able to do to change things? 'Cause Presley is pretty set on what needs to be done."

"Maybe," Harper said. "I'll talk to you and Dad about it when I get things a little more worked out in my head."

"Don't take too long. Presley isn't likely to give us an extension."

"She's not the enemy." Harper wanted to defend Presley even as she struggled to find a way to stop her from doing what she planned.

"Nope," Flann said lightly, swinging into the drive at the big house. "She's just the enemy's hatchet man."

Flann stopped in front of the house, jumped out before Harper could argue, and came around to help Harper out of the car.

"I'm okay," Harper griped, shaking off the arm Flann wrapped around her waist. "I don't need a damn wheelchair."

"I wasn't getting you one."

Harper's mother came out onto the back porch. "What are you two squabbling about now?" She folded her arms and narrowed her eyes as Harper drew closer. "Bat or ball?"

"Ball."

Her eyebrows rose. "That's what the glove at the end of your arm is supposed to be for, Harper."

"It took a funny jump."

"And that's what your eyes are for," she went on, holding open the screen door. She glanced at Flann. "How exactly did you let this happen?"

"Me? It's not my fault she was sleeping at shortstop."

"You know the rules. If one of you has been up all night and is too tired to play, the other one makes the call to pull you out."

"Wasn't her fault," Harper said, slumping into a chair at the table. "I just took my eye off the ball for a second."

"I see."

Flann kissed their mother quickly on the cheek and backed toward the door. "I'm going for pizza. See you later."

The door banged shut and she was gone. Ida opened the icebox compartment and pulled out a tray of ice cubes. She ran it under cold water, popped out the cubes, refilled the tray, and put it back in the freezer. After filling a plastic bag with the cubes, she handed it to Harper and took the melted bag from her. "Something happen today? Problem with one of the patients?"

Harper stretched out in the chair, her legs extended under the table, the bag of ice back against her jaw. "Presley called Dad, Flann, and me into her office today. SunView plans on closing the Rivers."

"Closing it," Ida said slowly. "That would be hard on everyone around these parts."

"Yeah, it would."

"Is there anything you can do?"

"We need more money."

"Don't we all." Ida shook her head and slammed a plastic dish basin into the sink. She yanked on the faucet and hot water gushed into the tub. She rinsed glasses and laid them in to soak. "Didn't the board see this coming?"

"I don't know. If they did, I don't think they let Dad in on it."

"They didn't, not until very recently."

"I've maybe got an idea, but it's probably harebrained."

Her mother stood behind her and gently kneaded her shoulders. "Maybe a harebrained idea is what it's going to take."

"Maybe." Harper closed her eyes. Her mother's hands were strong and tender on her tight muscles, and just as soothing as they'd been when she was a kid and her mother would tend to her bruises and scrapes.

"What really happened tonight?" Ida asked.

"I wasn't paying attention."

"Why not?"

Harper thought of a million excuses as she let herself relax into her mother's hands. "I was thinking about Presley."

"What she told you today about the hospital?"

Slowly, Harper shook her head. "No. About...personal stuff."

"That overnight visit, you mean."

Harper felt her face glow bright red. "Yes. Well, not just that."

"Harper, sweetie," her mother said gently, "you don't have to be embarrassed about having feelings or what you got up to with her."

"That's just it," Harper said, "I do have feelings. Feelings that won't go away."

"And she doesn't?"

"She says not."

"Do you believe her?"

"That's what she says."

"You know as well as I that sometimes what we say is not what we feel. Sometimes what we feel scares us. Ask yourself, what scares her?"

Harper opened her eyes and looked into her mother's face. "One of the first things I noticed about her was how confident she seemed, how in control. I want to say nothing scares her, but I don't think that's true. I imagine not being in control scares her a lot."

Ida nodded. "That makes sense. Although I don't see you as one to take away anyone's control, at least not under ordinary circumstances."

"This is a very embarrassing conversation."

Ida smiled and continued to massage her shoulders. "I noticed she didn't talk much about family."

"Her parents are business tycoons, like her. She's got a brother, a twin, but she doesn't mention him much."

"That's unusual, don't you think?"

"Yes, but it never occurred to me any of that would have anything to do with what was happening between us."

Ida shook her head. "For my oldest, you still have a lot to learn. Family is what makes us who we are, Harper. What we get and what we don't get from them. Family teaches us what to expect, or what not to expect, in life. And what to be afraid of."

"Maybe I don't think about that because family has always been everything to me."

Her mother kissed her forehead. "Well, you give it some thought. You're smarter than you look right at this moment."

Harper tried to grin. "Mama?"

Her mother laid out a dish towel on the counter. "Yes, baby?"

"Do you resent Dad for not being here a lot when we were all little?"

"Resent him?" Her mother pulled a glass from the dishwater and ran it under tap water. "No, I don't resent him. Was it hard? Sometimes, terribly." She dried the glass and carefully set it down. "But I've always loved your father, and being a doctor's who he is." She picked up another glass. "You have to love the person for who they are, even when it hurts."

❖

Presley jerked awake on the front porch at the sound of tires crunching on the gravel. The sun hung low in the sky as Carrie parked and came up the path with her softball gear slung over her shoulder. She deposited her equipment by the door, dropped into the other rocking chair next to Presley's, and slowly started to rock.

"How did the game go?" Presley asked, striving for normalcy when she felt anything but normal. She'd not only left work early but actually taken a nap, although unintentionally.

"We won, three to two. It was a tough game."

"Did you pitch?"

"The last half."

"I'm glad you won."

"Me too, especially after losing Harper in the seve—"

"What do you mean," Presley said sharply. "Losing Harper? Did she have an emergency?"

She immediately thought of Jimmy, although of course Harper had hundreds of patients and any of them could have called. Still, Jimmy was the patient she knew, and the patient who would challenge Harper on every level.

"Oh, no. Not a patient. She got hit with the ball and had to come out of the game."

Presley's pulse rate rocketed, and her stomach slowly twisted into a knot. "Was she hurt?"

"Flann isn't sure. She might've cracked her jaw."

Presley sat up straight, stopping the rocking motion of her chair with both feet flat on the floor. "Where is she? The Rivers?"

"What? The hospital? No. Flann took her to their parents'. I don't know if she's still there or not."

"Then how does Flann know she's not injured seriously?"

"Well, Flann looked at her jaw—"

"Oh, and she has X-ray eyes now? What is wrong with these people? Haven't they ever heard of modern diagnostic measures?"

Carrie stared at her. "Harper's fine, Presley. She's probably going to have a huge bruise on her jaw, but she's all right."

Presley forced her breathing to settle. What was wrong with her? Harper had plenty of people to take care of her. But she couldn't help wishing she'd been there. "Of course she is. I know that. I was just—curious."

"Uh-huh."

Presley took in the small smile and the sound of self-satisfaction in Carrie's voice. Her ire swelled. "It's nothing to me if Harper Rivers ends up with a black-and-blue mark."

"Of course not."

"Good, then that's settled," Presley said. She should've gone to the game. She'd fallen asleep sitting here thinking about the game, imagining Harper at bat, her shoulders and forearms bunching as she swung. Imagined Harper out in the field, her jaw tight with concentration as she fielded the ball. Harper was very good. Harper was outrageously sexy. Harper made her skin tingle. Damn her. "I can't believe she let a ball get to her."

"I got the feeling," Carrie said, treading carefully, "that she wasn't really mentally in the game. I think this afternoon's meeting threw her off."

"I'm sorry about that." Presley sighed. Harper wasn't the only one thrown by the meeting. "But it had to be done."

"What would happen if you presented Preston with a totally different scenario. One in which the Rivers doesn't die?"

"It's not just about Preston. I can't take risks with the shareholders' money. And…"

"And?"

Presley sighed. "I need to deliver this project on time and without major obstacles if I'm going to have any hope of taking over from my father. I need to lock in the support of key people, and I can do that by demonstrating I can get the job done quickly and efficiently. This job, any job. *And* by showing I can be ruthless when I need to be when profits are at stake."

"What do you think would happen to Preston's position if you turned this place around and it made a profit again?"

"That would take a miracle," Presley said, "and I'm fresh out of those."

CHAPTER TWENTY-SIX

Presley closed the file, shut her laptop, and swung her desk chair around to face the window. The bright sunny day did little to lighten her mood. The numbers didn't look any different now than they had on Friday. The weekend had dragged, and she'd finally driven to the hospital to look at some of the data Carrie had pulled together for her, hoping the change of scenery would distract her from thinking about Harper. It hadn't.

A heavy sensation tugged at her with every breath. Summer bloomed with inexorable beauty, as if mocking her burgeoning unhappiness. Usually when she was lost in the numbers, she didn't think about anything else—but not today. Today thoughts of Harper pulled at her, and she'd catch herself wondering if Harper's jaw was giving her trouble, or simply missing her and wishing they could escape for a few hours to the tree house, where the world was reduced to a lazy river flowing by, the flutter of young green leaves, and an impossibly blue sky. She imagined lying on the worn sofa flanked by handmade bookshelves with her head on Harper's shoulder, listening to the birds, a world apart. A world of their own.

She shook her head. When had she become so foolish? That was Harper's world, not hers. They shared something, though—they shared the Rivers, and she was about to destroy that. How could Harper—either of them—ever have imagined they could be anything other than adversaries? Still, she'd tried again today to find some other path. Carrie might have been on to something with the urgent care network, or as things stood currently, the lack of any centralization of the scattered facilities, but without an immediate infusion of funds, she couldn't justify the time and money it would take to build a strong referral base. Nor could she justify the risk to the shareholders. If she went back to SunView and proposed they put more money into the Rivers when she'd come here for a quick turnaround and a nice profit to show in the quarterly shareholders' report, she'd lose the support of half of management. And not just on this issue, but on the matter of succession.

Still, the potential in Carrie's figures nagged at her. Potential was what made the game so exciting. Turning potential into profit was what she was good at.

Maybe all she needed was a little distance, a little perspective, and a fresh look at the big picture. She locked her office and walked to the cafeteria for coffee and a late lunch. Somehow the day had gotten away from her, for which she was grateful. If she worked a few more hours here she could avoid coming in the next day. Avoid running into Harper.

As she carried her coffee to her favorite table by the window, she spied Emmy Reynolds coming through the line, seeming to ponder the food as if she didn't recognize any of it. When she'd stood for at least a minute in front of one of the hot food selections, apparently not hearing the question put to her by the food service employee, Presley set down her tray and walked over to her.

"Mrs. Reynolds?"

Emmy Reynolds stared at Presley through blank, exhausted eyes. Her hair appeared clean but tangled. She wore no makeup. Circles ringed her puffy lower lids.

Presley touched her arm. "I'm sure you don't remember me. I'm Presley Worth. I was with Harper the night your son Jimmy was admitted to the hospital."

Emmy started and life returned to her eyes. "Oh yes. I'm sorry. I do remember you now."

"How is Jimmy doing?"

"He was doing really well, everyone said," Emmy blurted. "Then just this morning he developed a fever. It might be nothing"—she rushed on, picking at a loose thread on her sweater, tugging it and twirling it around her index finger—"but they're having trouble getting it down and Harper said Jimmy might need…if he doesn't improve…" Her voice choked off and tears filled her eyes.

"Why don't you sit down and let me bring you something to eat. Is your husband here with you?"

"Don? Oh, no. He's home with Darla, our youngest." She looked away. "One of us tries to be here all the time, but it's hard with the farm, and we can't leave Darla for too long. Scary for her." Her gaze came back to Presley. "If we weren't so close to the hospital, I don't know what we'd do."

Presley thought of the hour drive to the nearest medical center and remembered the worn farmhouse surrounded by fields and machinery and animals, of the life that needed tending and a boy who needed his parents by his side. "Go sit down now—I'll bring you something to eat."

Emmy did as Presley suggested and Presley brought her a plate of food, a glass of milk, and some juice. "I'm betting coffee has been your main staple for the last few weeks. So I brought you something else."

Emmy laughed faintly and a tiny bit of color came back to her cheeks. She picked up the milk. "You're right and thank you."

"Is there anything I can do?"

"No, thank you. Carson has been helping with the paperwork for the financial assistance we need for the medical bills, and Harper is taking care of everything else. There are lots of doctors looking after Jimmy, but Harper is the one we count on. She hasn't left Jimmy all day. She'll make sure everything that needs to be done is done."

"Yes, I'm certain she will," Presley said, as sure as Emmy.

Emmy ate a few bites of meatloaf and set down her fork. "They're saying the hospital might close."

Presley wasn't surprised the rumor mill was churning. "That's not something you need to worry about now."

"You're in charge of all that, right?"

"Yes, I am." Presley had never had to face the individuals impacted by SunView's policies in such a personal way. They had PR people who handled that at community meetings and the like. A wave of disquiet passed through her.

"I hope you can find a way so that doesn't happen. We need this place."

"Yes, I understand that." Presley pushed back her chair. "I'll let you finish in peace. I hope Jimmy is feeling better soon."

"Thank you," Emmy said softly.

❖

When Rooster crowed at barely dawn, Presley rolled over and immediately thought of Harper. Was she still at the hospital? Was

Jimmy better? How was Harper dealing with a boy so like the sister she had lost to the same disease? Harper. The ache of missing her left her hollow.

She got up, showered, and tried to settle into her morning routine. She failed. She couldn't keep pretending none of this mattered—this place, these people, this woman.

When she pulled into the hospital staff lot, Harper's truck was in the same spot it had been in when Presley had left fourteen hours before. Of course, Harper could be making early rounds and just happened to park in the same place, but something told her the explanation wasn't so simple. As she hurried into the hospital, she debated what to do. In the end the decision was easy.

She turned in the opposite direction from her office and toward the pediatric intensive care unit. The unit was small, only four rooms. Two were occupied. Jimmy Reynolds was in bed number four. Presley didn't go in, but the low lights inside were enough to see by. A man slept with his head on the bed. Don Reynolds. Only Jimmy's head and shoulders were visible. He looked like a doll beneath the sheets, so small and fragile surrounded by monitors and equipment. The scene was heartbreaking and horrifying, and one she would never be able to erase. How many scenes just like this had Harper witnessed? Her throat closed. Where was she?

A woman in scrubs came up to her. "Can I help you?"

"Yes, I'm sorry. I'm Presley Worth. I'm—"

The woman smiled fleetingly. "Yes, Ms. Worth. I know who you are. I'm the charge nurse. Were you looking for someone?"

"Is Harper here?"

The nurse shook her head, a faintly wry expression on her face. "Believe it or not, she finally left. I told her she was too damn tired to drive, so hopefully she's taking a nap in one of the on-call rooms."

"The on-call rooms? Where—"

"Around the corner and down the hall. One's marked surgery and the other medicine. Usually no one's in there."

"How's Jimmy?"

The nurse sighed. "The fever's better, but his white count is just about zero. Any kind of infection now…" She glanced into Jimmy's room, her expression compassionate. "He's got nothing left to fight with."

Dread tightened around Presley's heart. She couldn't imagine how Don and Emmy must feel. Anger followed close behind the terror. How could this happen? What kind of justice was there in the world where an innocent child… She cut off the fruitless rumination. There were no answers to questions like that. All that could be done was to fight.

"Thank you." Presley quickly walked away.

A minute later, she stood in front of the door marked medical on-call room, pondering whether to knock. If Harper was sleeping, she shouldn't bother her. If she was awake, she had no cause to disturb her either. She had no reason to be there at all beyond her need to see Harper, to somehow help. On the other side of the door, a phone rang and then a voice murmured for a few seconds.

When silence fell once more, Presley tapped on the door.

"Who is it?" Harper's voice was rough and hoarse.

"Harper, it's Presley. I'm sorry—"

The door opened and Harper stared out at her. She wore a rumpled shirt, and her stethoscope no longer hung around her neck. Her eyes were bloodshot, her face slack. She looked like she'd lost a dozen pounds. The left side of her jaw was swollen and discolored.

"God," Presley whispered, gently touching the bruise. "That looks awful."

"Hi." Harper's smile was lopsided and just as devastating as ever.

Presley laughed shakily. "Hi. Sorry. You're trying to sleep, aren't you?"

"Don't think I can."

"Let me drive you home."

Harper shook her head. "I need to be here in case Jimmy—"

"You can't take care of him if you're falling apart. The nurse said he's stable right now."

"You checked? How did you know he was in trouble?"

Presley's face flamed. "I saw his mother yesterday and she told me he was having a rough time. And then I saw your truck and I thought—anyhow…" She took Harper's hand. "Please let me take you home. Let me take care of you for a change."

Harper's shoulders sagged. "You know what? That would be good."

Presley linked her arm through Harper's on the way out to her car, almost afraid if she let go, Harper would drift away. As Presley drove, Harper dropped her head back against the seat and closed her eyes.

Weariness washed off her in waves. Presley reached over and took her hand, needing the contact. Harper's fingers threaded through hers.

Presley turned carefully into Harper's drive, trying not to wake her, and slowed by the back porch. "We're here."

Harper opened her eyes. "Thank you."

"You need to be in bed."

Harper smiled faintly. "I need breakfast, I think." Her lids slowly closed.

Presley eased out of the car, came around to open the passenger door, and gently shook Harper's shoulder. "Harper? Come on. Let's get you inside."

Harper followed without resistance. Presley circled her waist and together they walked in the back door, through the house, and upstairs. The bedroom looked as it had before, neat and orderly and very much Harper. She'd made her bed. Of course she had. When Harper made no move to get into bed, Presley pulled down the sheets. When she turned, Harper was watching her with an expression Presley remembered all too well. Harper had looked at her that way in bed, when she'd been inside her. As if Presley were everything and all that mattered.

"I've imagined you back here in my bed," Harper said quietly. "A thousand times."

Presley swallowed around the lump in her throat. "Come on. You need some sleep."

"If I said I needed you—"

Presley pressed her fingers to Harper's mouth. "Shh. Not now."

Carefully, Presley unbuttoned Harper's shirt, helped her shrug it off, and tugged at the white tank underneath. She opened Harper's trousers and dragged down the zipper. "Get these off and climb into bed."

Harper braced one hand on Presley's shoulder, pushed her pants down, and kicked them off along with her shoes. She stood naked, unself-conscious. Harper was beautiful, her throat and arms tanned golden all over, her chest and breasts and belly a creamy beige.

Presley cast desperately about for something to take her focus off Harper's body. She trembled to touch her. "Should I get you something for your jaw?"

"You could kiss it and make it better."

"You're half-dead on your feet, but"—Presley leaned forward, careful not to brush against Harper's nudity, and kissed the bruise on her cheek—"there. Now, bed."

Harper dropped onto the bed. Presley pulled the sheet over her and smoothed back her hair. Harper's eyes were already closing.

"Get some sleep. Sweet dreams."

Harper's eyes opened, startlingly clear. "I hope I dream of you."

Presley's heart clutched painfully. Leaving her was the hardest thing she'd ever done.

CHAPTER TWENTY-SEVEN

Presley's cell rang a little before six that evening. The readout said *private caller*, and half expecting a wrong number, she answered absently. "Presley Worth."

"Presley, it's Harper."

Presley rose from the top step where she'd been sitting with a glass of wine, as if standing would somehow give her more control over the excitement surging through her. "You're awake, although I have no idea how or why. Feeling better?"

"Enormously. I owe you—"

"No, you don't." Presley leaned against the porch rail, warmed by the sound of Harper's voice. Rooster stopped scratching in the dirt where she'd thrown some fruit scraps and eyed her with his small black bead of an eye, as if sensing something important had just happened. Could he tell her blood was racing? "What can I do for you?"

Harper laughed and Presley flushed. Even over the phone Harper's voice woke something hungry inside her, a delicious hunger she hadn't known before.

"Ah—" Presley hadn't been so tongue-tied since the first time a girl in high school had asked her for a date. Come to think of it, not even then. "I'm sorry. You were saying?"

"I was wondering if we could meet in the morning. There's something I'd like to discuss."

"I can't."

"Later in the day, then—"

"Harper, I'm flying to Phoenix tomorrow."

"Phoenix…" Harper was silent. "Are you leaving?"

"Not just yet," Presley said, sadness softening her voice.

"Tonight? Can I stop by? I know it's unorthodox and probably an inconvenience—"

Presley half laughed, half sighed. "Harper, really. I think at this point we can dispense with the formality. If you want to talk, by all means come by. Have you eaten?"

"Not yet."

"Then come over now. Lila left cornbread and stew that smells delicious. I was just about to eat."

"That's hardly necessary, considering I'm barging in on your evening."

"It's fine. Please."

"All right. I'll be there in about fifteen minutes."

Presley disconnected. Fifteen minutes. She looked at the shapeless jeans and plain gray T-shirt she'd thrown on to feed the barn kittens and clean up their corner of the barn. Well, that would never do. She sprinted inside, left her wineglass on the kitchen table, and hurried to the stairs. Carrie was just coming down dressed in her softball gear.

"Coming to the game after all?" Carrie asked.

"Harper's coming over. Impromptu meeting."

Carrie's eyes narrowed. "Here? Must be important. Do you need me?"

"No. You go ahead."

"I guess Harper won't be at the game." Carrie sighed. "There goes my night."

Presley stopped in the middle of the stairs and stared. "Harper?" she said carefully, fighting the strangest urge to growl. "I didn't realize you—"

"Teasing, Presley. Teasing." Carrie laughed. "I don't have designs on her, and if I had given it a thought—well, I suppose when I first saw her, the thought crossed my mind, I'm sure it crosses every eligible woman's mind for a few seconds—I certainly wouldn't be thinking it now. Not when she's got your scent all over her."

"I'm sorry?"

"Just a figure of speech, but she's a marked woman. She just doesn't know it yet. And neither, apparently, do you."

"You do realize you're not making any sense."

Carrie continued downstairs. "I'm making perfect sense, and you'd understand what I'm talking about if you'd stop trying to talk yourself out of it."

Presley held up a hand. "I don't have time for cryptic conversation. Have a good game. Be careful."

"I will." Carrie paused at the bottom of the stairs. "Hey, Presley?"

"Yes?"

"You've never had any trouble leaving your mark at SunView. Maybe you should try that here."

Presley nodded as if she understood and hurried to her room. In her bedroom, she quickly pulled on black pants and a short-sleeved cobalt-blue shirt, slipped into loafers, and gave her hair a quick brush. After a glance in the mirror, she threw on enough makeup to make her look like she'd been sleeping far better than she had been. She was downstairs in the kitchen when Harper's truck came down the drive. A few minutes later footsteps on the back porch announced her presence. Presley tried valiantly to ignore the rapid pounding of her heart, but it was hard when the knock came on the screen door and she saw her there, backlit by the setting sun. Something that had been swirling around inside her, uneasy and unsettled, floated into place. For the first time in days, her world brightened.

"Hi," Presley said, unable to hide the eagerness in her tone. And why should she? She was glad to see her and pretending otherwise was akin to lying. She wouldn't do that—not after what they had shared. "Come in."

Harper wore dark jeans and a red polo shirt. Some of the fatigue had disappeared from her face, and even with faint smudges beneath her eyes, she was sexier than most women who'd just walked out of a high-end spa. The purple welt on the left side of her jaw wasn't sexy, though. Presley winced inwardly and imagined how much that must have hurt when it was fresh. She stifled the urge to stroke the spot. "Sleep all right?"

"Yes." Harper grinned and set a folder on the counter. "Would have been better if you'd stayed."

Presley's face warmed. "Somehow I doubt that."

"Memory problems? I seem to remember the night went pretty well the last time we shared a bed."

"Are you channeling your charmer of a sister now?" Presley said, trying to sound stern, secretly pleased Harper hadn't forgotten that night.

Harper's eyes took on an interesting shade of blue-gray, rather like the storm clouds that blew in on a hot afternoon. "What has Flann been up to? Because if she's been charming you—"

"She hasn't," Presley said, stirred by the heat in Harper's gaze. When had any woman ever looked at her like that? As if she were desirable—more than desirable, essential. She tried to steady her breathing so her voice wouldn't shake. "I'm just not used to you flirting quite so—"

"No? I'll have to remedy that." Harper took a step, gripped her arms, and tugged her close.

The kiss came out of nowhere—a bolt of lightning that set Presley's nerves on fire. She gasped and clutched Harper's shoulders. Harper's eyes flashed and Presley parted her lips when Harper demanded entrance. The kiss went on and on, stealing her breath, making her thighs weak. She leaned into Harper, her breasts crushed to Harper's chest. Wanting simmered deep inside, and she moaned.

Harper drew back a fraction, still holding her. "How am I doing?"

"What?" Presley asked numbly. She slipped her fingers beneath Harper's collar and caressed her neck. "I've lost track of what—"

"Good," Harper murmured against her mouth. "I want you to stop thinking of anything except me when I kiss you."

"That's the trouble." Presley nibbled at Harper's lower lip, teased along the inner edge with her tongue. She tasted so good, felt so right. God, she wanted her. She tried to make her mind work. "I *don't* think when you're around. And you're not making sense."

"Yes, I am," Harper said, "finally. And you should be flirted with, regularly. By me."

Presley kissed Harper's throat, pressed her mouth to the bounding pulse. "Yes. I think I'd like that."

Harper slipped her hand under the back of Presley's shirt and stroked the hollow just above her ass. "Are we alone?"

"Yes." Presley swayed, pushed her pelvis into Harper's. "No."

"We're not alone?" Harper flicked the top of Presley's shirt aside and kissed her chest. "I passed Carrie coming in. Who else is here?"

"No one." Presley closed her eyes. Harper's mouth was all she knew—everywhere, inside her, turning her flesh to fire. She was losing her mind. Pressing both palms to Harper's chest she leaned back. "You said you wanted to talk."

"Did," Harper muttered, fingertips tracing Presley's spine lightly. "Do. Later. Let's go to bed."

She wanted to. Oh, how she wanted to. And then where would they be—another morning when she'd have to leave, and everything still unsettled between them. "I have to go to Phoenix in the morning."

"You said that already." Harper stilled, her mouth against Presley's throat. "Why?"

"I present the finding on the Rive…ACH." Presley's heart broke a little feeling Harper pull away. Somehow she'd ended up with her back against the counter and Harper's weight pinning her there. She couldn't escape. She should want to, but she didn't.

"Before you go anywhere," Harper said, "there's something I need to say."

"I know," Presley said. "You said on the phone—"

"Not business. Personal." Harper cupped her chin, captured her gaze. "We have something special between us—something I don't want to lose."

Presley tensed. No, no, no. This was not a good idea. The words caught in her throat. Part of her, a very large part of her, waited, wanting Harper to say it again.

"I wasn't thinking very far ahead—" Harper grimaced wryly. "I wasn't thinking at all, really, when we tumbled into bed together, but I knew I wanted to. Wanted you, more than I ever wanted any woman before—"

"God, Harper, this is crazy."

Harper went on as if she hadn't heard. "Not just because you're quite possibly, no, absolutely, the most beautiful and desirable woman I've ever seen—"

"Harper—"

"I wanted you, I think, from the first second I saw you in the hall outside the emergency room. You looked so damn cool and composed and above it all. I like that about you. Nothing is ever going to get you rattled."

"You rattle me," Presley whispered, running her fingers through Harper's hair. "You have from the first."

"Good." Harper's eye's glinted. "I know you're not unshakeable, but I know nothing is going to make you break and run either. This morning you were there when I needed you. I need that, knowing I can lean when I need to, and it will be all right."

Presley trembled and fought the urge to run out the back door. "Oh God, Harper, I'm not who you think—"

Harper swept her thumb over Presley's lips. "You know what? I think you might not be who you think you are."

Presley frowned. Harper still held her close, and she'd forgotten to try to get free. "I know exactly who I am. I've always known exactly who I am and what I wanted. I know that's hard to believe, because it's so different than what you want—"

"Is it? I've always wanted to do the work that gave me pleasure and made me feel like I was doing something worthwhile. I wanted to make my parents proud. I wanted to take care of the people I loved. That's not that much different than you."

Presley shook her head. "That's a million light-years away from me. I do what I do because it gives me satisfaction, yes. I also do it because it's expected of me, and it's the only thing that the people I care about respect. I want that respect and the love—" She bit her lip. "Not love perhaps, but what passes for love anyway. Success is the key to getting those things in my world. As to taking care of the people I love? I wouldn't know where to begin, and I doubt they would either."

"You know. You've been taking care of me. Emmy told me how you took care of her."

"Emmy? How…"

"This afternoon when I checked in on Jimmy."

"Did you sleep at all?"

Harper kissed her chin. "Yes, and don't change the subject."

"I'm not—"

"You're trying." Harper kissed her again, leaning into her—her body hot and hard and possessive.

"I wish you wouldn't do that," Presley murmured.

"Why?"

"I can't think."

"Good. I don't want you to go to Phoenix."

"I have to."

"Why?"

"Because…" Presley ordered her brain to focus. "Because I have to finish this. I'm sorry."

"What happens to us when it's done?" Harper asked, finally stepping back and letting her breathe.

I'll come back, but will you still want me, after what I have to do? Presley shook her head, her soul bleeding. "I don't know."

"Read the proposal," Harper said, gesturing to the folder.

"I will, but I can't promise—"

"I don't want you to promise." Harper stepped back. "Not about that."

"I thought you wanted to talk," Presley said quickly as Harper headed for the door. She was seconds from begging her not to leave. She clenched her jaw, afraid if the need came pouring out, she'd drown.

"You can discuss what's going to happen to the Rivers with my father when you come back." Harper pushed the door open, her expression so intense Presley shuddered. "Come find me if you want to talk about us."

CHAPTER TWENTY-EIGHT

I saw your truck in the drive," Flann said as she poked her head through the hatch in the tree house. "Are you hiding out or is company allowed?"

Harper turned her head and regarded her sister. She'd been lying on the sofa staring at the ceiling, she wasn't sure how long. She might've slept a little but she wasn't positive about that either. The hollow ache in her stomach reminded her she hadn't had breakfast, and from the angle of the sun coming through the window, it must be going on nine a.m. Presley was probably in the air already, well on her way to Phoenix.

"Come in if you want to," Harper said.

Flann climbed up and sat on the crate in front of Harper. "I heard you had a tough one with Jimmy again last night."

"Yeah—he spiked a temp again. But if nothing changes, I think we might have turned the corner this morning." She'd just left Presley's when she'd gotten the call that Jimmy was looking worse. She'd driven straight to the hospital and spent the rest of the night conferring with the hematologists and infectious disease specialists about the best antibiotic regimen. "We're about out of options if the drugs don't work this time."

"Bone marrow transplant?" Flann asked.

"We've been holding off making the call, hoping the chemo would've cleared his marrow and he'd start regenerating. Then last night, it looked like he was gonna go the other way."

"You've been there most of the weekend, haven't you?"

"The last few nights." Harper rubbed her face. "Why is it nights are always the hardest? No wonder all those myths always have the

Grim Reaper showing up in the middle of the night to collect souls. Are we just more vulnerable then?"

Flann sighed. "Jesus, Harp—don't go all metaphysical on me." She paused, her expression distant and dark, a rare glimpse beneath her mask of casual indifference. "Maybe it's just that we're all afraid of the dark—too many ghosts."

"Maybe," Harper said quietly.

"What else happened?"

"What do you mean?"

"If you're winning with Jimmy, or at least holding the line, there's got to be some other reason you look like your dog died."

"Me, my dogs, and all the other animals are just fine."

"Woman problems, then. What's happened now?"

"Nothing. Let it go."

"Last night at the game, Carrie mentioned Presley was headed to Phoenix today."

Harper contemplated throttling her. "Did you come down here just to annoy me?"

"I'll go and let you sulk as soon as you tell me what put the burr in your saddle."

"Presley."

"Well, yeah. I got that part."

"Every time I think I'm getting closer, she gets further away." Harper's skin still burned from the memory of Presley pressed against her. Every time she wasn't totally absorbed in making a medical decision, her entire being was consumed with wanting Presley—and her absence left her starving. She shuddered. God damn it.

Flann snorted. "That's appropriately vague, and considering the subject, probably accurate. Try small sentences with simple words. What. Happened?"

Harper sighed. "Presley seems to think we don't have anything in common."

"Probably because you don't."

Harper shot up straight on the sofa. "That's bullshit. We're part of the same world, we're just coming at it from slightly different directions. She understands what I do. And even though I don't always like it, I understand what she does."

"Same world, maybe—different continents. Come on, Harp. You're on opposite sides on this. The two of you couldn't be further apart."

"No, that's just the thing. We should be, but we're not." Harper recalled opening the on-call room door and finding Presley outside in the hall, how grateful she'd been to let someone she trusted take charge for just a little while. She didn't have to hide how scared she was, how the fear of losing Jimmy Reynolds was eating her alive. Presley knew. "She—gets me. Gets what I do, what I need."

"Uh-oh. That sounds bad."

"It wouldn't be, if she'd just let herself believe it."

"Maybe she doesn't feel the same way," Flann said with a gentleness she rarely showed to anyone other than her patients.

Harper braced her elbows on her knees and put her face in her hands. Maybe Presley really didn't feel what she felt, the connection, the understanding, the desire. Maybe it was one-sided and she'd been deluding herself the whole time. "I guess that's possible. I guess when you want something so bad, it blinds you to what's real."

"Crap," Flann muttered. "Look, what exactly did you tell her? Did you use the L-word?"

Harper almost laughed. "What are we, in high school now? No, I didn't tell her I loved her."

"But? I hear a great big fat but at the end of that sentence."

"But I do. I don't even have to think about it. It just is." Harper rubbed the spot in the center of her chest that hurt every time she took a breath. It wasn't a physical ache, this longing in her soul for the sight and sound of the one person who filled the empty spaces inside, but every bit as real...and agonizing. "She fits. She fills me."

"Yeah, and she's smoking hot too."

"You keep it up, and I might throw you out the hatch headfirst."

"Are you sure it's not just that? That, you know, you're thinking with your hormones? You wouldn't be the first."

Harper shook her head. "You might be a sucker for a hot body, but I'm not. I don't work that way. Sure, she's gorgeous and I want her, but there's always been more than that."

"This is sounding worse and worse."

"It isn't, at least it wouldn't be if I knew that she cared. That I wasn't alone in all of this."

Flann shrugged. "Okay, fine. Then you need a plan. What exactly did she say?"

"That she won't talk about anything between us until things at the hospital are settled."

"That makes sense. Things will get rough if she closes the place.

A lot of people will have hard feelings. That's gonna make any kind of relationship twice as hard. Maybe you should just wait—"

"Wait? For what?" Harper jumped to her feet and paced in the small space, circling the oak. "Until life is easy? Until there are no obstacles, no challenges? There will always be those things. I know what she does, and I understand the decision that she's made. I might not agree with it, but I understand it."

"Harper," Flann said sharply, rising too, pacing in the rest of the space so they barely had enough room to pass one another. "Think about it. If she closes the Rivers, how are you ever going to resolve that between you? The Rivers is everything to you. Always has been."

Harper abruptly stopped. "You're right. It has been. Past tense. I understand now that the Rivers isn't everything and can never make me completely happy. Maybe you're right, maybe Dad should've tried to balance things better—"

"Bullshit," Flann said. "I was wrong to criticize him. He wasn't alone in making the decisions. Mom is no pushover. If she'd wanted something different, she would've seen to it."

"Maybe." Harper recalled the conversation she'd had in the kitchen with her mother. "And maybe she just understood that that's what he needed."

"What do you need, Harper? Do you know?"

"I always thought I did. I wanted a life like Mom and Dad's. I wanted to be as good a doctor as Dad. I wanted to be important to people in the community, to be part of their lives. I didn't realize that even if I had all of those things, I would never be happy if I was still alone."

"And Presley is the one?"

"I want her. I need her in my life."

Flann sighed. "Well, sitting around up here isn't going to get that done."

Harper grinned. "Finally, we agree."

❖

As Presley's plane circled Detroit, she closed her laptop and stowed it in her computer bag under the seat. She flipped open the file folder on her lap and reread the few pages. Harper had been busy. As it stood, Harper's proposal to affiliate ACH with the Albany Medical School and RPI's combined BS-MD program to train medical students and residents in community-oriented specialties like family medicine and geriatrics was intriguing, but it wasn't enough. Harper was correct in concluding that such an association would bring in federal funding for every student and resident they trained, but it would be too little too late. They'd need more staff to run the program, for one thing. Student housing, more insurance. She rubbed her eyes. In all likelihood the initial investment to get the programs up and running would offset any new sources of revenue, at least for a few years. For long-range planning, the idea had promise, but it was not the salvation the Rivers needed.

She couldn't see any way to make it work. She'd give anything if things were different, but they weren't. That was the easy answer and the easy out for her. She'd tried, but the Rivers was beyond saving. Only each time she came to the same conclusion, the less happy she was about it. She kept seeing Emmy Reynolds's terrified eyes and Harper's bone-deep fatigue, and knew neither woman would ever quit. Emmy and Harper were warriors, and the community was filled with them—ordinary people fighting every day for the ones they loved. Harper would keep fighting to save the Rivers until the padlock went on the gates, and she'd come to Presley for help. Presley was failing her, and the failure was a bitter ache in her heart.

The plane taxied to the gate and Presley thought of the next few hours when she'd finally be home. She had her own fight in Phoenix. That was her battleground, and it was time for her to marshal her forces and take the fight to Preston. She wondered why the idea of winning what she'd wanted all her life left her feeling so empty.

CHAPTER TWENTY-NINE

Presley stopped at her condo on her way through the city to SunView's headquarters. The two-bedroom apartment in one of the most sought after high-rises was clean and orderly—she had a service come in weekly whether she was in town or not—but the air smelled artificially pure with the faintest undertone of chemicals she'd never noticed before. Floor-to-ceiling windows overlooked the city skyline, affording her a million-dollar view that held none of the pulse of life she was used to seeing out the leaded-glass panes of her hospital office window. No birds nesting, no branches fluttering, no flowers in bloom. There were planters along some of the avenues and elaborate window boxes on the fronts of many upscale boutiques, but the cityscape was one of concrete and glass rather than living plants and beings, unless you counted the people, and then the city teemed with life—the identities and faces of passersby anonymous and unnamed. The doorman in her building was one of the few people she saw outside the office whose name she knew. Within a few weeks back in Argyle, she'd learned the names of everyone on Harper's softball team, the nurses in the ER and many of the clinical areas, and the clerks at the gas station and mini-mart.

When she'd left Phoenix she couldn't wait to return. Now she was here and felt like a visitor. Maybe the airplane really was a time machine and she'd just been hurled into a different world. She wasn't sure she belonged here any longer, where success was measured in currency rather than inner satisfaction and where family meant status and obligation rather than support and loyalty and love.

Presley sighed. She might be straddling two worlds and fit in neither, but she was here now and she had a lot to finish. Resolutely, she put thoughts of Harper and the past—or future—aside. She showered off the fatigue and grime of travel, aware of the absence of the rattling pipes that usually accompanied her morning shower, dressed quickly in a skirt and jacket, stepped into medium heels, and relocated her papers and laptop into a briefcase that was coordinated with the outfit. As an afterthought, she slipped Harper's proposal in along with the preliminary reallocation report she'd printed out to review with Preston and the other managers.

On her way to the elevator, she called down to have her car brought around to the entrance. The expansive marble lobby was empty and sterile feeling. Rooster would find nothing to eat here. She nodded to the doorman and hastened outside for a breath of air. The heat was a wall that slapped at her, and she hurriedly upped the AC in her Mercedes. At SunView, she parked in her reserved spot on the first level close to the elevators and keyed herself in with her ID card. She didn't know the people in the elevator, and when she reached the executive level and walked through the central hall to her corner office, she passed only a handful of people who even knew she'd been gone. This had been her universe, her province, and now she was a stranger here too. Had she really been so rootless and never noticed?

Her desk was neat and orderly, just as she'd left it. She sat down, let the receptionist who handled calls when Carrie was away know she was in, and confirmed she had a meeting with Preston in an hour. She was about to call Jeff Cohen, her inside man, to catch up on the latest power moves among upper management, but stopped before she'd picked up her phone. She didn't really care. The politics and personal agendas seemed shallow and petty to her now. But then, what made her any different than Preston? Her goals were the same as his—to one day head the company, to walk in her parents' footsteps, to finally have them notice her, value her. Didn't all children want to please their parents? She thought of Harper and Flann and Carson and Margie—individuals all and yet each confident in the pursuit of her goals. She didn't doubt for a second, and neither did they, that they would be loved regardless of their choices, and not because they succeeded in something their parents valued. What did she value? What did she want?

She picked up her cell phone and quickly tapped in a number. The wait was interminable, but she knew it could only be a few seconds. She didn't really expect an answer.

"Harper Rivers."

"Harper," Presley said, caught as she always was by the smoky timbre of Harper's voice. She couldn't think for a second why she had called. Hearing Harper's voice suddenly seemed enough. Everything.

"Presley!" Harper's voice warmed, heavy with pleasure. "Where are you?"

"At my desk. In Phoenix."

"How was the trip?"

"No problem. How's Jimmy?" Presley pictured Harper at the nurses' station, leaning against the counter, sleeves rolled up, hair tousled, looking relaxed and confident. The image made her think of home.

"He's looking good this afternoon."

"Oh, that's good news."

"Are you okay?"

"Well, I—" Presley took in her surroundings again. "Yes. Fine. But I miss…a lot of things."

"Me most of all, I hope."

"Most assuredly," Presley said, delighting at the playful note in Harper's voice, "you most of all."

"Good. I like when you miss me."

The sexy tone was back, and Presley's heart jumped. "Then you should be happy."

"I will be when you're back," Harper said. "When will you be home?"

Home. She was already home, wasn't she? Why didn't it feel that way? The condo was more like a hotel room than home. Her parents' home hadn't been hers since she'd left to go to college, and even before that, it had been a little like living in a resort where her parents entertained between trips. This office was home, but the view when she looked out the window was of a land in which she had no place. "I'm not sure."

"You are coming back, aren't you?"

"Yes, of course."

Harper sighed. "I really miss you."

"I miss you too."

"I'm glad you called. You beat me to it. There's something I wanted to tell you."

"I've read the proposal—"

"No, not that." Muffled voices rose in the background and Harper murmured, "I'll be right there."

"I'm keeping you," Presley said. "I'm sorry. I know this is your busy time—"

"Yes, but look, I've only got a minute…I want you to know no matter what happens, the way I feel about you, it's not going to change, no matter what you do."

Presley's throat tightened. "How can you be sure?"

"Because that's not how love works."

Presley squeezed her cell phone, the blunt edges biting into her palm. "Harper. I'm not very good at this—"

"You're great at it. Come back, and I'll remind you."

"All right…" Presley laughed, the sky opening inside her. "Yes, I will."

"Hurry home," Harper said. "I've got to go. Call me."

Presley murmured good-bye, disconnected, and sat for a moment thinking of Harper, of family, of belonging. She had no reason to wait until her appointment with Preston. She gathered her papers and strode across the hall to his corner office opposite hers. She nodded to Marjorie, his personal assistant, and passed by without waiting for her to call in and announce her. She opened the inner door, walked through, and closed it. Her brother, tall, lean, tanned, and with the same sun-gold hair and blue eyes as hers, looked at her from behind his sleek glass-and-steel desk with the same cool appraisal that she often turned on others.

"I didn't expect you back so soon," Preston said.

"Really? There wasn't all that much to do up there."

"It's all wrapped up, then, is it?"

And there it was. She could be done with it all, have a quick kill, and get back to the business of winning her father's seat. Then she'd have everything she ever wanted. A month ago she wouldn't have hesitated, and she didn't now. She knew what she wanted.

She sat down in the chair in front of her brother's desk and crossed her legs. "I think it's time you and I came to terms."

"Are you sure you want to do this now?" Preston steepled his hands beneath his chin in a delaying gesture very reminiscent of her father. He wasn't her father, though. He wasn't quite as quick, quite as ruthless, or quite as able to generate the same loyalty. That wasn't her problem. She was quick and ruthless and she understood power.

Presley smiled in anticipation of the coming battle. "Quite sure. And long overdue."

❖

Harper woke at dawn to the sound of a car slowly crunching over the stones in her driveway. She checked out the window, saw Presley's car, and quickly pulled on sweats and a T-shirt. She found her sitting on the top step, her shirt rumpled and her dark trousers uncharacteristically creased.

Harper sat down beside her. "I guess you flew all night."

Presley leaned against her shoulder. "Yes. I'm afraid I look it too."

"You look beautiful." Harper wrapped an arm around her waist. "Been home yet?"

"In a way," Presley said, her voice thoughtful.

Harper entwined their fingers and kissed the top of Presley's hand. "Glad you came here. Nice way to wake up."

Presley smiled, half-whimsical, half-wistful, and her eyes sparked. "I rather thought you liked waking up with me next to you even better."

Harper's belly tightened and a wave of lust momentarily short-circuited her brain. When she could draw breath, she sucked in air and let it out slowly. "I wouldn't have minded if you'd come upstairs instead of stopping on the porch."

"Really?"

Harper leaned forward and braced her arm on the railing, caging Presley with her back against the post. She kissed her long enough to bring Presley's arms around her neck and a soft moan from her throat. When she pulled away, she whispered, "Really."

"I could use a shower."

"How about I wash your back."

"How about you wash all of me."

Harper tugged Presley up by the hand and pulled her close. Hunger clawed at her insides, and she kissed her again. Presley's taste fed her craving. "I could live on you forever."

"Let's see you try."

"Quick shower," Harper muttered and hauled Presley laughing through the house. She found clean towels while the water was warming and by the time she stepped into the bathroom, Presley was naked under the spray. She yanked off her T-shirt and sweats and got in with her, crowding her up against the wall and kissing her again. When she cupped Presley's ass, Presley pushed her away before she could get seriously involved.

"I want to be in bed when you make me come," Presley said.

Groaning, Harper had to lock her knees to stay upright. "I'll do anything you want. Anywhere, anytime."

"Good." Presley stroked two fingers along the edge of Harper's jaw, down the center of her throat, and between her breasts. "That sounds perfect."

Harper twitched. Presley's voice was cool, calm, with the kind of control Harper had seen the first day. She loved Presley's power, loved her fire, loved the command in her voice every bit as much as the softness of her mouth and the welcome of her body.

"I need you now." Harper slowly slid to her knees and pressed her cheek to Presley's middle. She closed her eyes. "Please. Don't make me wait."

Presley tugged her up with a fistful of hair and kissed her. Smiled. "I'm ready."

Harper twisted off the water, grabbed a towel, and wrapped Presley in it. She quickly dried off and, naked, led her into the bedroom. She yanked down the covers the rest of the way, took Presley's towel and tossed it toward the bathroom, and muttered, "Sheets are clean."

Presley laughed. "I couldn't care less as long as you're in there with me."

"I might never get out."

Presley grabbed Harper's hand and tumbled into the bed. They landed in a tangle of arms and legs, Harper on top. Presley moaned and wrapped her arms around Harper's shoulders. Her mouth was close to Harper's ear. "Inside me. Right now. I've been thinking about you there all night."

Harper pushed up on one arm and slid the other between Presley's legs, gliding into her in a long, smooth stroke. Presley cried out. Harper's breath stopped. She thrust, slow and deep. Presley tightened around her, hot and slick. Harper's heart thundered in her ears, the rush of blood through every cell as primal as the sea crashing to shore. The world condensed to the depths of Presley's eyes as she filled her, again and again.

"God," Presley gasped. Her neck arched and the tendons stood out on her neck. "I can't...Harper!"

Deep inside, Harper roared in triumph.

Presley's nails bit into her back. The sound of Presley's pleasure stripped Harper bare and she crashed with her. She groaned, muscles locked as every nerve ignited. She buried her face in the curve of Presley's shoulder and shuddered as the world disappeared.

"I thought I'd implode before I got here," Presley murmured lazily a few minutes later. She stroked Harper's hair, brushed her fingers over the sweat-dampened skin between her shoulder blades. "I love the way you make me come."

Harper feared she wouldn't be able to make words. She was fried, demolished. "Not…done."

"That's good." Presley kissed Harper's throat. "Harper?"

"Hmm?" Harper raised her head with Herculean effort. Presley was so beautiful she almost got lost in her again. The vulnerable look in Presley's eyes drew her in. "What, baby?"

"I love you."

Harper stilled. She'd heard the words before, but never like this. Never from the one woman she'd wanted to hear them from with all her heart. "I love you too. Totally out-of-my-mind in love with you."

"I want you so much," Presley whispered, "even though I know it's a crazy idea."

Harper tried to gather her wits. This was important. She needed to do this right. She pushed up on her elbows, kissed Presley, and gently framed her face. "Nothing crazy about us loving each other. It's the most absolute right thing in the world."

"I don't fit, you know that."

"My mother didn't fit here either when she married my father, but she's as much a part of this place, and this place of her, as anyone whose family has been here a hundred years. Do you love me enough for a lifetime?"

"What?" Presley asked faintly. Harper's eyes burned into hers. Her hands were hot against her face, her body a furnace.

"Do you love me enough for forever?"

"Yes," Presley answered instantly. "God, yes, I do."

Harper smiled and the sun burst in her eyes. "Then you fit."

"Don't you want to know about the Rivers?"

Harper kissed her again. "Yes, but not now, not here. This is ours. Business can wait."

"You might feel different—"

"No." Harper brushed a thumb over her mouth. "I won't. I told you that already. I know what you do and why. I understand."

"Your father, your family—"

"I love them, more than almost anything. But you, you're mine now, and I'm yours. Say yes."

Presley caught her breath. "Say yes to what?"

"Say you're mine."

"I'm yours." Presley knew it through every inch of her being. Tears trembled on her lashes. She'd never imagined the beauty of belonging like this and knew she would never want for anything as long as she had Harper. "Yes, I'm yours. I love you."

"Then say you'll marry me."

"I…" Presley kissed Harper, as demanding and possessive as Harper had been just moments before. "Yes, I will. Of course I will."

Harper threw back her head and laughed. "Yes. You will!"

Laughing too, Presley rolled her over and kissed her throat. Harper stilled as she kept kissing her, down the center of her chest and belly until she lay between her legs. She looked up and watched Harper watching her. "I've been thinking about this all night too."

"Take your time," Harper said, her voice husky.

"Oh, don't worry, I plan to." Presley kissed lightly between Harper's legs, a satisfied purr rising from her throat as Harper twitched. "I'm going to enjoy taking what's mine."

Chapter Thirty

Harper called the big house a little after six. Her mother answered. "Mama, we need a family meeting."

"What time?" Ida said.

"Breakfast?"

"Your father's about to leave for the hospital. Flann is probably on her way there too. Is it important?"

"Yes."

"Then I'll get them here. Half an hour."

"Thanks, Mama."

"Are you all right, Harper?"

"Yes, Mama. I'm perfect."

Silence sounded for a few seconds, and Ida said, "Will we need another chair at the table?"

"Yes."

"All right then. Don't be late."

Harper set her cell aside. Presley leaned against the counter in nothing but a half-buttoned, faded blue cotton shirt she'd taken from Harper's closet. She was drinking a cup of coffee, her hair a loose tangle that looked as if it had been finger-combed a dozen times, her face relaxed and her eyes ever so slightly hazy. Harper chuckled, a swell of contentment so potent overtaking her, her hands shook.

A crease formed between Presley's brows. "What's funny?"

"You look like you've just been fu—"

"Oh, aren't you smug."

"Uh-huh. I am feeling pretty pleased with myself."

Presley set the cup down, unbuttoned Harper's shirt, and let it drop on the floor. Harper suddenly couldn't move her lips, her mouth was so dry.

"Think about that today." Presley turned and walked toward the back door.

Harper lunged after her. "Jesus, Presley. You can't walk out there like that."

Presley grinned back over her shoulder. "Who's going to see me out here?"

"How about the farmer who's plowing the field next door?"

Presley jerked to a stop. "Where?"

"Just saying there might be someone—"

"I think I liked you better when you were all broody and quiet."

Harper grinned. "Where's your suitcase?"

"Backseat."

"I'll get it for you. In a minute." She grabbed Presley and kissed her. She took her time, tasting her, imprinting the shape of her mouth, the softness of her lips, the playful stroke of her tongue. She absorbed the fullness of her breasts, the hard points of her nipples, the soft curve of her belly and firm length of her thighs. She caressed Presley's ass, and Presley's head fell back with a soft moan. Harper's belly twisted. "I want you again right now."

"I want you to take me right now," Presley gasped. "Do we have time?"

"Ten minutes."

Presley pushed Harper's hand between her thighs. "Plenty of time."

❖

Harper pulled in behind Flannery's Jeep, turned off the engine, and took Presley's hand. "How are you doing?"

Presley shook her head slowly. "I've gone into boardrooms where I knew every single person was gunning for me without the slightest hesitation, without the least bit of nerves. The idea of walking into that kitchen fills me with terror."

Harper laughed and leaned over to kiss her. "You can handle them."

"Seriously, Harper." Presley rubbed the tops of Harper's fingers with her thumb. "This matters more to me than any merger, any acquisition, anything I've ever accomplished. This isn't just about the Rivers. This is about us."

"No, it isn't," Harper said. "We're solid, no matter what you say in there."

"I know what your family means to you." Presley took in the homestead with its stately manor house, the lush green fields, and the wide river beyond the trees. This place was Harper's touchstone, but the family gathered inside, waiting for them, was the heart from which she drew her strength. "I would never want to come between you and them."

"You won't. I promise." Harper squeezed her hand. "It would never come to this, but if I had to, I would choose you. Here, anywhere we needed to go to be together. I would choose you."

"I've gotten rather fond of the country, and of course, there's Rooster to be considered," Presley said around the love burning in her chest. The tears pushed forward again.

"Can't leave him," Harper said, brushing the droplets from Presley's lashes with a thumb.

"So we'll be staying."

Harper kissed her. "We'll be staying."

"Are you sure you don't want to hear what I have to say about the Rivers first?"

"It affects the family, we should hear it together."

"I love you." Presley drew a deep breath. "All right, let's go inside."

Harper jumped down and hurried around the front of the truck to take Presley's arm as she climbed out. She slid her fingers through Presley's as they walked around to the kitchen. Everyone was there, Edward at the head of the table, Flannery to his left, Carson to his right, Margie next to Carson, Ida at the far end of the table. Two empty chairs remained—one on either side of Ida.

"I love you," Harper murmured, let go of her hand, and took the empty chair on her mother's right next to Flann. Presley glanced at the single remaining chair next to Ida. Every eye was on her.

"Have you had coffee?" Ida said.

"I'm fine for now," Presley said.

"Then you should sit down." Ida smiled and the invitation reached her eyes.

"Thank you." Presley sat and folded her hands in front of her on the big hickory table. She thought she'd known what she was going to say—she had all the facts and figures lined up, had reviewed all the logic, analyzed the conclusions, formulated everything in terms a layperson could understand. Sitting here at this table, none of those things seemed to matter. She met each expectant gaze and focused on Harper. "I grew up believing success equaled happiness. In my family, success meant winning at business, mostly, but when I was younger it was anything…everything—sports, academics, social distinction. My brother and I competed fiercely."

Flannery said, "Sounds like me and Harper."

Presley smiled fleetingly. "No, nothing like you and Harper. We weren't competing to bring out the best in each other, but to gain our parents' approval. And it seemed that only one of us could ever have that at any given time."

No one said anything, but the calm, steady look in Harper's eyes gave her all the strength she needed.

"When I first came here, I thought I understood the situation at the Rivers. The hospital is a losing proposition and has been for quite some time. The patient base is geographically scattered, poor, and underinsured. Closing the institution makes fiscal sense."

Flann grumbled and Harper elbowed her. Presley kept going—this was her ground, and she ruled it without hesitation.

"The sooner I was done here, the sooner I could get back to Phoenix and concentrate on my next battle with my brother." She cleared her throat. "My father is retiring and gave us plenty of notice so we would be able to fight each other for his place. We've been doing that for the better part of the last year." She smiled at Harper and hoped Harper could see how much she loved her. "That's the only thing I ever wanted—I knew if I could prove that I was worthy, capable of taking his place, I'd have the respect and love I've been trying to get my whole life." She reached across the table and Harper took her hand. "I was wrong, and it took falling in love for me to understand that."

After a second, she released Harper's hand and faced Edward at the head of the table. Edward was watching her, his deep brown eyes calm and appraising. "I've reviewed Harper's proposal, and I assume you and Flannery and Carson have looked it over also. The idea is a good one, but not financially feasible as things stand."

A muscle in Edward's cheek twitched, but he said nothing. He was an observer, like Harper—slow to make a decision until he had all the facts.

Flann swore.

"Flannery," Ida said in a warning tone.

"Sorry, Mama."

"However," Presley said, still gazing at Edward, "if the Rivers acquired a fairly large infusion of capital to underwrite Harper's plan and set it in motion to take advantage of the coming fall semester and next round of residents, I think we could arrange for a federal subsidy to help bolster the hospital almost immediately. That would ease the burden going forward."

Flann said, "I think we've already determined there's nowhere to get the money."

"Flann," Harper snapped, "do you think you could shut up and let her finish?"

"Do you think you could make me?"

"Enough," Ida said quietly, "the both of you."

"Sorry, Mama," they said in unison.

Presley said, "SunView plans to sell the emergency room to a group of private investors. The proceeds will support the establishment of Harper's community medicine program. With the federal training subsidy and some hardball with the insurance carriers, I predict we will bring our bottom line into an acceptable range within five years."

"Sell the emergency room," Flann said. "How can you even do that?"

"Actually, it's fairly common. St. Vincent's Hospital in Manhattan, for example, just reopened the emergency room as a private facility, as have a number of medical centers elsewhere. Private-sector investors are eager to put their money into acute-care facilities where reimbursement is high and patient turnover rapid. Because the Rivers is physically associated with the emergency room, our direct admissions will benefit. As part of building the acute-care network, SunView will be purchasing a number of urgent care facilities, essentially creating a wide net from which to refer patients."

Flann frowned. "That's a big investment on SunView's part. How exactly did you sell this?"

"The plan will make money."

Carson said quietly, "If it all works, but there is considerable risk."

"Yes, but with risk comes the possibility of considerable profit."

Harper leaned forward. "How did you do it?"

Presley shrugged. "I told Preston he could have my father's seat with my support if he voted with me on this proposal."

"No," Harper said. "There must be another way."

"Harper," Presley said gently. "You're a wonderful doctor, but you don't know anything about business."

"I might not know anything about business, but I know what it means to give up a dream."

"It wasn't a dream, it was an illusion." Presley smiled. "Besides, as part of the package, Preston has guaranteed my autonomy—in writing. I'm going to control all of SunView's interests on the Eastern Seaboard. I'll have plenty to do to keep me busy."

Edward said, "How will we staff the emergency room?"

"The new corporation will hire the necessary physicians. We will need an independent chief of emergency medicine." She glanced at Flannery. "I understand that the emergency room is now part of the department of surgery, but that will have to change."

"Do I get a say in who you hire?"

"I'll certainly take your opinion under advisement."

"Good enough, then." Flann paused. "What about Carrie?"

"I'll need her if she wants to stay." She glanced at Harper. "We'll also need some of the local physicians to staff the urgent care centers. That will make the transition easier for their patients and help them into the system. We'll be bringing in other physicians as well."

Edward said, "This gives us a chance to keep the hospital and take care of the patients. We don't have a choice, but it's a good solution. We'll do our part."

"I'm sure of it." Presley leaned back, the tightness between her shoulder blades signaling just how nervous she'd been. "That's all I have. Does anyone have any questions?"

"Are you and Harper an item?" Margie asked.

Harper groaned. "Margie, for crying out loud."

Presley gave Margie's shoulders a quick squeeze. "We most certainly are."

Ida rose. "Everyone has work to do. I expect you all back here for dinner so we can celebrate properly."

Edward, Flannery, and Carson headed for the door. Harper slid her arm around Presley's waist and kissed her. "You're sure?"

"Totally," Presley murmured. "I have you. And I'll have plenty of work to do."

"I love you," Harper said.

Ida folded her arms across her middle. "I take it you two have finally sorted yourselves out?"

"We have," Harper said. "And we'll be getting married sometime soon."

"When were you planning on telling us that?" Ida said.

Harper laughed. "Dinner?"

"I suppose that's soon enough." Ida filled a coffee mug, handed it to Presley, and kissed her on the cheek. "Welcome to the family."

"Thank you." Presley took the mug and leaned her head on Harper's shoulder. "There's no place else I'd rather be."

About the Author

Radclyffe has written over forty-five romance and romantic intrigue novels, dozens of short stories, and, writing as L.L. Raand, has authored a paranormal romance series, The Midnight Hunters.

She is an eight-time Lambda Literary Award finalist in romance, mystery, and erotica—winning in both romance (*Distant Shores, Silent Thunder*) and erotica (*Erotic Interludes 2: Stolen Moments* edited with Stacia Seaman and *In Deep Waters 2: Cruising the Strip* written with Karin Kallmaker). A member of the Saints and Sinners Literary Hall of Fame, she is also an RWA/FF&P Prism Award winner for *Secrets in the Stone*, an RWA FTHRW Lories and RWA HODRW winner for *Firestorm*, an RWA Bean Pot winner for *Crossroads*, and an RWA Laurel Wreath winner for *Blood Hunt*. In 2014 she was awarded the Dr. James Duggins Outstanding Mid-Career Novelist Award by the Lambda Literary Foundation.

She is also the president of Bold Strokes Books, one of the world's largest independent LGBTQ publishing companies.

Find her at facebook.com/Radclyffe.BSB, follow her on Twitter @RadclyffeBSB, and visit her website at Radfic.com.

Books Available From Bold Strokes Books

Courtship by Carsen Taite. Love and Justice—a lethal mix or a perfect match? (978-1-62639-210-6)

Against Doctor's Orders by Radclyffe. Corporate financier Presley Worth wants to shut down Argyle Community Hospital, but Dr. Harper Rivers will fight her every step of the way, if she can also fight their growing attraction. (978-1-62639-211-3)

A Spark of Heavenly Fire by Kathleen Knowles. Kerry and Beth are building their life together, but unexpected circumstances could destroy their happiness. (978-1-62639-212-0)

Never Too Late by Julie Blair. When Dr. Jamie Hammond is forced to hire a new office manager, she's shocked to come face-to-face with Carla Grant and memories from her past. (978-1-62639-213-7)

Widow by Martha Miller. Judge Bertha Brannon must solve the murder of her lover, a policewoman she thought she'd grow old with. As more bodies pile up, the murdered start coming for her. (978-1-62639-214-4)

Twisted Echoes by Sheri Lewis Wohl. What's a woman to do when she realizes the voices in her head are real? (978-1-62639-215-1)

Criminal Gold by Ann Aptaker. Through a dangerous night in New York in 1949, Cantor Gold, dapper dyke-about-town, smuggler of fine art, is forced by a crime lord to be his instrument of vengeance. (978-1-62639-216-8)

Because of You by Julie Cannon. What would you do for the woman you were forced to leave behind? (978-1-62639-199-4)

The Job by Jove Belle. Sera always dreamed that she would one day reunite with Tor. She just didn't think it would involve terrorists, firearms, and hostages. (978-1-62639-200-7)

Making Time by C.J. Harte. Two women going in different directions meet after fifteen years and struggle to reconnect in spite of the past that separated them. (978-1-62639-201-4)

Once The Clouds Have Gone by KE Payne. Overwhelmed by the dark clouds of her past, Tag Grainger is lost until the intriguing and spirited Freddie Metcalfe unexpectedly forces her to reevaluate her life. (978-1-62639-202-1)

The Acquittal by Anne Laughlin. Chicago private investigator Josie Harper searches for the real killer of a woman whose lover has been acquitted of the crime. (978-1-62639-203-8)

An American Queer: The Amazon Trail by Lee Lynch. Lee Lynch's heartening and heart-rending history of gay life from the turbulence of the late 1900s to the triumphs of the early 2000s are recorded in this selection of her columns. (978-1-62639-204-5)

Stick McLaughlin by CF Frizzell. Corruption in 1918 cost Stick her lover, her freedom, and her identity, but a very special flapper and the family bond of her own gang could help win them back—even if it means outwitting the Boston Mob. (978-1-62639-205-2)

Rest Home Runaways by Clifford Henderson. Baby boomer Morgan Ronzio's troubled marriage is the least of her worries when she gets the call that her addled, eighty-six-year-old, half-blind dad has escaped the rest home. (978-1-62639-169-7)

Charm City by Mason Dixon. Raq Overstreet's loyalty to her drug kingpin boss is put to the test when she begins to fall for Bathsheba Morris, the undercover cop assigned to bring him down. (978-1-62639-198-7)

Edge of Awareness by C.A. Popovich. When Maria, a woman in the middle of her third divorce, meets Dana, an out lesbian, awareness of her feelings brings up reservations about the teachings of her church. (978-1-62639-188-8)